MW01504582

The Other Side of Destiny

The Other Side of Destiny

A Science Fiction Novel

Albert A. Di Fiore

VANTAGE PRESS
New York

This is a work of fiction. Any similarity between the names and characters in this book and any real persons, living or dead, is purely coincidental.

FIRST EDITION

All rights reserved, including the right of reproduction in whole or in part in any form.

Copyright © 2005 by Albert A. Di Fiore

Published by Vantage Press, Inc.
419 Park Ave. South, New York, NY 10016

Manufactured in the United States of America
ISBN: 0-533-15032-9

Library of Congress Catalog Card No.: 2004096454

0 9 8 7 6 5 4 3 2 1

Contents

The Other Side of Destiny

One
Trial in Progress

Bailiff: "Will Miss Choa Mio take the stand please."

Prosecutor: (with Mio's hand on the Bible) "Will you tell the truth, the whole truth, and nothing but the truth?"

Mio: "I will."

Prosecutor: "State your name please."

Mio: "My name is Choa Mio."

Prosecutor: "What is your occupation?"

Mio: "I teach language at Lakeland College. I am head of the Children's Orphan Foundation at Future Vision Cable Company in Ohio."

Prosecutor: "Is it true you belong to a group called the Thorme?"

Mio: "Yes."

Prosecutor: "What does this name stand for and what is its function Miss Mio?"

Mio: "The name is from a faraway place, translated to the French words déjà vu. Our function is to contact persons who think they are reincarnated."

Prosecutor: "Tell the jury, Miss Mio, where is this so-called place of faraway?" (For a few seconds Miss Mio was oblivious to the question, staring with a faraway look.) "Well, Miss Mio?" he snapped.

Miss Mio first looked at Al who was sitting at the table in front of the courtroom. The audience was packed to capacity. Then Miss Mio looked at the prosecutor and said in a soft voice, "It is called Thrae." The prosecutor snapped again, "You have to speak louder Miss Mio so the jury can hear you."

Miss Mio, in a much louder voice, "The place is Thrae."

The prosecutor in a lower voice, "Thrae huh, that really tells us quite a bit."

Prosecutor: In a louder voice, "Exactly where is this so-called Thrae; and I want a complete answer, so I do not have to ask so many questions about one place, Miss Mio."

Miss Mio again looked at Al. Al nodded his head at Choa Mio. She then looked at the prosecutor, clearing her throat. She said with a sharp clear voice, "Thrae is a planet from another solar system in this galaxy."

The people in the courtroom gasped and mumbled, hearing some people commenting, "What is she talking about?" "Must be a crackpot."

The prosecutor said, "Now let me get this straight. You are trying to tell me and the jury that you came from another planet, from another Solar System?"

Miss Choa Mio snapped back, "I did not say that!"

Prosecutor: "Exactly what did you say?"

Mio: "I said I was reincarnated from planet Thrae, in mind and soul, not in flesh."

"What makes you think you were reincarnated from this so-called planet Thrae?" asked the prosecutor.

"All my events coincide with my colleages' reincarnation from the same place," stated Miss Mio.

Prosecutor: "Whom, may I ask, are these so-called colleages of yours? Are they in the courtroom?"

"Yes they are," said Miss Mio, staring at Al with a tear in her eye.

Al was sitting at the plaintiff's table, thinking to himself, *What the Hell did I get my friends and I into? All I wanted to do was to see if there was life on another planet.*

(Flashback of Al's life when reincarnated to Earth from planet Thrae.) Planet Thrae is almost identical to planet Earth. Except for languages and different habits of living they had almost the same history. God made a few living planets to see if any of the different kind of people could live together. It was like God's experiment.

Al's memory started to drift away from the courtroom. He thought in a mesmeric way about life on planet Thrae and how the Thorme Club got started.

Al was born in Cleveland, Ohio, in nineteen hundred and thirty-one. He lived in the suburbs most of his sixty-eight years. He attended Berea High School, in Berea, Ohio.

All his life it seemed like he came from somewhere else, like another planet, in another time. Al thought he was reincarnated because many times when he would go places, it seemed like he had already been there, or he already did those things, like déjà vu. Everything he read throughout the years, it seemed like he already read it once before, like the big flood that caused the end of the World, all the wars, and especially World War Two. In World War Two the atomic bomb was deployed on Japan and ended the war. Of course, we have some asshole countries who think they can terrorize the world. They prey on other little countries first, and the United States has to intervene to stop the fighting. We had the Korea, Vietnam, and Gulf Wars, with some idiot named Saddam Hussein. But the countries we really have to keep an eye on are probably China and Russia.

Now in this nuclear and space age, the United States is competitive with Russia, and probably some other countries. Everything that's happening on Earth already happened on this other planet, which is named Thrae. Al never read about his planet anywhere on Earth.

Planet Thrae already had a World War Three, which was a nuclear war. It destroyed everyone and everything by fire. The chosen few were saved, because of a god who commanded the people to build a space city in outer space. Al was on this city in this other life, and watched the destruction of planet Thrae. This took place in the year 2010 planet Thrae time. They lived in space for twenty years before the planet was back to normal. Al was one of the leaders of this space-city called Orant.

When Al and his followers returned to planet Thrae after twenty years in space, they lived there for twenty years until Al reached age sixty-five. Al died in the year 2045, Thrae time. Planet Thrae is far more advanced than Earth, especially in space programs, computers, and other technical fields. Al and his people already visited other nearby planets and moons. They built stations on them with colonies. There were also twelve planets that they discovered.

Back on Earth, under the fictitious name of Joe Santini, Al already warned the people and the government that the Earth was going to be destroyed, due to the people's wickedness, wars, crime and all the non-believers in God. Al told them that everything that would happen on Earth had already taken place on planet Thrae. This meant that planet Earth would end by fire also. They told Al he was full of shit, and that he made up everything. Al had written many articles about this episode on the other planet. His experiences included his reincarnation, and his living in space in another place and time. The public considered the articles fictitious events that belonged in a science fiction magazine.

A very strange thing began to transpire. Al received correspondence from three other persons who had similar experiences to his. Al wrote back to these three people from different parts of the country so he could arrange a meeting with them to discuss the reasons why they were reincarnated to the Earth world. They set up a meeting at Yellowstone National Park for the last part of June 1984. The scheduled meeting was two months away, so they would have enough time to gather all necessary data to compare notes. Meanwhile, Al received two more letters, one from Mexico and the other from Alaska. He wrote back and told them about the meeting with the other three people to be held at Yellowstone National Park.

Since Al knew a little about spaceships and space in his other life on planet Thrae, he had no trouble getting a job at an aeronautics company near the city airport. He was hired as a rocket and space technician. The application and aptitude tests were very easy for him because of his knowledge in all aeronautics and space fields. In no time, he became head of his department for all the new apprentices. Al had not told anyone about being reincarnated, and did not want to jeopardize his position at NASA. They would think he was a nut and probably fire him. He never told anyone that he knew he was reincarnated from planet Thrae. The people he told and the articles he wrote were under a fictitious name, as you may recall, Joe Santini. He used a post office box for his correspondence.

Al had three weeks' vacation coming from NASA beginning the last week in May. He told his wife and the grandkids, who were living with them at the time, that they were going to Yellowstone National Park. They were thrilled and started planning for it. Of course, Al also told his wife that he was supposed to meet some people there for a meeting, and that he would not be long. He liked to enjoy himself too, and have fun with the grandkids.

The time had come. Al and his family chose to leave on a Monday. The Dodge Caravan was loaded. They left Mayfield Heights at nine A.M. to I-271, and then to I-480. It took them three days to reach their destination. They got themselves a motel room to rest up. The next day they took in some of the sights, including the Hot Springs and Old Faithful. It was very fascinating. On the third day of their stay, Grandma and the kids went sightseeing with a bus tour while Al met the five associates he had arranged to meet. They met at a resort at ten A.M. at Yellowstone National Park, with all their data, in order to compare notes and discuss what they would do in the future. As their meeting progressed, it became clear to them that there were many events they had all commonly shared in the past, that they had not recalled on their own. They all agreed on one thing, that this world was doomed to destruction, and the event was not far from happening. They discussed anything and everything that was imaginable. They came to one conclusion, that they should move to one location. The location they decided on was Chesterland, Ohio. Al had about twenty acres in this area, which was a quiet part of the country. The meeting came to an end. Everyone said their good-byes and left. Al and his family spent another week on vacation before heading back home.

Al and his newly found friends were to start a cable television business for all of the people around the area, including locations farther out. Since a few of them knew the technology in space communication, they would have no trouble setting up the station.

As far as money was concerned, they all had enough stashed away. They were also able to get backers to finance the project. It began in the spring of 1988.

The main purpose for this project was to build a large enough communication tower, not only for the television audience, but to see if they could get signals far enough into space to reach planet Thrae.

The next meeting would take place when all the constituents moved to Ohio, which took about a year. George would live in Chesterland, Joe in Gates Mills, Bart in Richmond Heights, and Tom and Mike would reside in Pepper Pike. Of course they brought their families too. After about a month, all the families were settled down with the children in their designated schools. With regards to religion each family was not of the same faith, but it did not make any difference, for they all believed in the same God. Among them there was a black person, and one Chinese (who later joined), and the rest were Caucasian.

The men had their first meeting in George's house in Chesterland. They discussed the site and drew up the plans. The project got started in the spring of 1990, and got under way without a hitch. They acquired all the permits necessary. It took a good six months to complete a large enough building, including a laboratory for experiments, and the newest technological gadgets that were needed. Of course, the tower was tall enough for any type of communications. For the year to follow they intended to build an observatory so they could study the universe. They needed all the information they could get their hands on.

The men had been pooling for Ohio lottery tickets and were lucky enough in 1991 to win sixteen million dollars. After taxes, they received five million, four hundred thousand dollars, which they put toward the company fund. Incidentally, their company was named Future Vision. It caught on pretty fast amongst new customers. They charged a reasonable fee for cable and gave everyone the best of service. As the company grew, they hired more and more employees. They made more money than ever. Now they could concentrate on their space projects, as well as educating the population of the possible tragedies that may happen to the world. Their staff had been compiling enough information to have at least one documentary a week for the ensuing five years. They showed events, like the beginning of mankind, the civilized world, and the rainforest on its good purpose for the world. For example, the rainforest distributes all of the ingredients in a continuous cycle throughout the world. However, with deforestation there will be slow destruction of the world with its people and living creatures. At this moment there are so many species that are extinct that the balance is uncontrolled for most other species that were dependent on the extinct species. In time they will also disappear.

They also had a documentary on space travel. This was very interesting for anyone who wanted to be knowledgable in that field.

After a few years of toil, with the building of The Future Vision Company and getting it to run smoothly, it was time for Al and his wife to go on a vacation. At the same time, the construction was being done on a new building attached to the observatory. Al said his good-byes to everyone and was wished a happy vacation. The grandkids were dropped off at relatives, and they left a couple of days later, heading toward Pennsylvania.

Al and his wife, Rose, were driving through Pennsylvania while on vacation in June 1997. As they were driving through the Allegheny tunnel, Al had the strangest feeling of a fascinating occurrence. They were driving through the tunnel and at a distance they could see at first a tiny speck of light growing bigger and bigger and brighter as they exited the tunnel. This stayed in Al's mind all day and evening, until they went to bed. Waiting to fall asleep, it started to come to him, very slowly, and soon he saw it clearly—how he died on planet Thrae. As he recalled, he finished his tour of duty as Captain Deton for the government on the space city of Orant in 2045, planet Thrae time. He then transferred back to planet Thrae for his discharge, so he could return home to his family, who lived in the city of Farna.

Deton and his wife, Taral, lived a happy and quiet life for a few years. They traveled all over planet Thrae, seeing the sights and occasionally visiting their three children and other members of their family.

It was the year 2050, about five years from the time Al was discharged from the service. He still had a governmental option to travel to the space city of Orant, so he went to the government travel board and applied for a space travel passport for his wife and himself. A couple weeks later, they took a shuttle from the city of Farna to the air station Losh, about ten miles from the city. All their papers were in order; they got on board with about two hundred other passengers. They were settled down and relaxed when they finally got the green light and took off like a gentle breeze. These new spacecraft were a lot more sophisticated—faster and smoother than the old spacecraft. They were also more comfortable, with a better view of the outside, to see planets and stars. The view was outstanding, with different color sunsets and sunrises as one started to orbit the planet.

These new crafts were designed so one would hardly feel any weightlessness once you're in outer space.

In a few hours they were ready to dock at one of the northern ports of the spacecity of Orant. Deton's wife, Taral, was amazed at the progress of the space city. Deton told her it was about fifty miles long, forty miles wide and ten stories high. They finally docked with hardly a bump. The protection shield was closed and everything checked out. They were given the go-ahead for the passengers to alight.

They got on a shuttle and traveled east down one of the boulevards to a beautiful garden-like villa, with a beautiful so-called condo. Everything was clean as a whistle. The city ordinance kept it that way. Taral could not believe how wonderful everything was—just like planet Thrae.

They planned to stay on the space city for about one month. They were having a very good time seeing the sights, going to movies, clubs, and operas. You name it they had it. They planned on taking a tour to moon Cona from the space city before they went back home. They said it was a spectacular sight on the moon. There was a very large colony that lived there. Some were stationed as scientists observing the universe in their observatories. They were supposed to take this tour in three days. Deton told Taral he was going to the observatory about fifteen miles away, to the east end of the city, to visit some of his buddies. Taral stayed behind so she could finish shopping with one of the friends she met while they were there, and would meet Deton back at the condo.

He got to the observatory just before lunch. He confronted the guards at the entrance and showed them his identification. They checked it out showing that he was on vacation and visiting some old friends. He was let in and walked down the familiar corridor, the same corridor he traveled down about five years ago. He still knew the entrance code. He pressed the buttons and the door opened. He walked in. He noticed a few new faces, whom he greeted. He asked for Adin, with whom he used to work. They told Deton he was at the new telescope to see how well it worked, and pointed in its direction. Deton walked about a hundred feet and there he was, busy as usual, writing down data. Deton called out in a soft whisper-like voice, so as not to disturb him.

Adin looked up and almost dropped his pen and shouted, "Deton, it is good to see you! My God, I have not seen you for two years, when I was on leave with my wife to planet Thrae. Where is your wife Taral anyway?"

Deton told him that she has a few things to take care of. "She said to ask you and your wife if you'd like to get together some evening?"

They went to his office and talked for an hour about old times while they had lunch. Adin told him about the new telescope and how much better it was than the old ones. It is all computerized, with a new type of lens that can gather things in space that the old telescopes would never pick up.

While they were talking, one of Adin's assistants came in to tell him about an object Adin discovered that was growing larger. Adin told his assistant he would be there in a few minutes. Adin told Deton to look at this object that he had been observing for about thirty hours. They got to the telescope to observe, and out loud Adin said, "Oh my God! Look at this."

Deton looked and said the same thing, "Oh my God!" Adin got on the emergency phone for a disaster alert. A meteor was heading directly for the space city. Usually meteors are small with a lot of specks that hardly do any damage, but this one was like a large stone about forty to sixty feet across. Adin was trying to read the speed and distance. It was traveling too fast. The computer was registering a very high rate of speed. The emergency jets were activated and started to move the space city from harm's way, but it was a little too late. It caught the east end of the space city Orant, and hit with an unbelievable impact. It was the last thing Deton remembered on the space city Orant.

It was dark, and pleasant. Deton was all alone. He did not know how long he was in this state of oblivion. It could have been seconds, minutes, or years. Then he started to see a pin point light, like the end of a very long tunnel. He wanted to move, walk, or crawl—anything to get to the other end. Then after the longest time, he started to move very slowly. It seemed like a year. He was hearing much commotion—screams and yelling of some foreign language that he could not understand. He started to move faster and faster and the light got closer and larger. Finally, he had physically emerged. There was no meaning, and he had no control of anything. What had taken place? Deton was born again, or simply put, was reincarnated to planet Earth as Al. He told his wife Rose (when back on Earth) all about this story from the beginning when he actually was a little boy on this other planet, and some of the episodes in his past life. She thought that he was only making it up, that he was having pipe dreams with a lot of piffle. He told her that one of these days soon, he would prove it to her. Of course, she does not dare quest to outer space and the other members personal episodes. He dropped the incident with his wife about his so-called piffle. They continued their vacation for the next few weeks in a harmonious manner, having a good time sightseeing and visiting friends.

They returned to Mayfield Heights the second week of August 1997. Al rested up for a couple of days before he headed back to the building at Future Vision in Chesterland, to see how everything was going.

The company was going quite well with an upswing of new subscribers. This meant expansion and the hiring of more personnel. They had quite a bit of acreage surrounding the cable site and the planetarium. Al had to get in touch with Paul the builder, to come out to survey this land. Plans had to be made for an addition including a parking lot and maintenance garage for the cable service trucks.

Al walked to the office of the observatory building, with astonishment, to find a new fence and a guard at the gate. He had to show some identification and still could not get in until his picture was shown on the monitor at the office. He finally got in, but was a little perplexed. When he reached the communication room, George and Bart were marking data down from distance messages. Al asked, "What the hell is going on around here? I could not even get in the place. Since when do we have a fence with a guard? God I cannot even go on a vacation for a few weeks, without there being any problems!"

George said, "You did not want to be bothered about anything while you were on vacation."

Al asked, "Why the security all of a sudden?"

George said, "You were not gone but three days, when someone broke into the planetarium office and stole some of the data we have been receiving. Whoever has taken it must know something. The only thing is, it is no good to them. We are the only ones that know the code. We could not let this happen again. You never know if whoever it is really might know something."

Bart said, "We were making a little headway with the code. The messages were a little unclear, but had some meaning to it. They left their planet three months previous with their newest spaceship. That is all we can figure out. They also said in a earlier message, something to the effect of—they did not get any message for a few weeks because of a violent cosmic dust storm across the ends of the solar systems, which caused blankness for awhile."

Al was so wrapped up in all the activity that was going on, that he completely forgot about his vacation and the vision he had. He remembered, however, when he got home. They had a Thorme meeting Friday evening, which was tomorrow. He would bring it up then. He was also satisfied with the progress of the building being built. Each meeting they had was always a discussion of new ideas for improvement of the company and any space material.

Two
Story of George—Club Member

It was about seven P.M. Friday at one of their meetings in the conference room in the Chesterland headquarters of the Future Vision Building. This meeting they were discussing their communications with planet Thrae. So far, the understandings are starting to have a little meaning to them. Al's memory was getting a little more refreshed, and certain happenings already popped up in his mind, including some of planet Thrae's language.

It started to rain when Al arrived at the station. He thought nothing of it. Then about an hour and a half later, a thunderstorm started. For awhile there were a few little flashes and a soft faraway rumble. It grew much worse when the lightning actually cracked very close by, which made everyone jump with the loud thunder. At this time, George excused himself to go to the bathroom. He sure was gone a long time. When he came back, he was as white as a ghost, like something scared the hell out of him. He asked if someone would drive him home, for he didn't feel well. He indicated that he would pick up his van tomorrow. He only lived about a mile down the road. Bart said he would take him home and be right back. Bart and George walked out of the room into the hallway as it stormed. George actually cringed as he fell against the wall. Bart held him up, escorting him to the car. Bart was driving him home, which was only a few minutes away, and it continued to lightning

14

and thunder. George would moan and actually try to get out of the car while it was moving. Bart was yelling and restraining him from opening the door. Bart asked what was the matter with him. All George said was to get him home. They finally got to the house. Bart felt it was like an eternity trying to control George. George got out of the car and practically ran inside of the house. His wife Ann came to the door and told Bart as it started to rain, with lightning and thunder, "This is what happens every time the weather gets like this." That is why Ann would call sometimes and tell them he would not be at the meeting when the weather is bad.

Bart got back to the meeting and told everyone what happened, that something was definitely wrong with George. Al asked Bart if his wife had him seeing a shrink. He said no because he was a hard head and thinks he can lick this thing himself.

The next time we saw George we asked how he was. He said he was fine and nothing to worry about, and that everything was well in hand. So we let it go at that. The next few meetings there were not any incidents because it did not rain.

Back to our communications. Every now and then we are getting some contact from space, and it seems to get clearer and louder. We have been sending messages every day starting with the quotes: "This is planet Earth. We are the third planet in our solar system from the Sun, out of nine planets." We also gave the English alphabet and numerals, to see if they can be deciphered. This has been going on for almost a year now, before they broke the barrier and deciphered and actually learned the English language and to code it and send it back. The only thing is we never received complete information from this other planet because of some sort of gap or void. It is believed the other planet's aliens are working on this problem, as well as the earthlings.

Now it is about the middle of August 1993. All the club members have decided to spend a few days on the company yacht with their families. They acquired this sixty-foot cabin cruiser so they could accommodate everyone and have a good time. They bought this yacht from the profits that were earned from the cable company. They also bought a company plane for business trips.

They ventured out on Friday and with intentions of returning on Monday, before the kids go back to school. They headed out of Mentor Lagoons to Pelee Island in Lake Erie for a day, and then across Lake Erie to Crystal Beach in Canada, Saturday evening and all day Sunday. Monday morning they headed back across Lake Erie and about half way they encountered a small storm. As usual, there was lightning and thunder. The weather did not bother the yacht, other than being tossed around a little. It sure bothered George. Every time it lightninged and thundered, George would be pounding the bulkhead moaning and screaming in some foreign language Al never heard before. George turned from side to side like he was asking for help. He was using gestures like he was trying to console someone else. Now this, Al would say, "Sure was some traumatic experience." This storm lasted for the rest of the way back to the Mentor Lagoons. George's wife Ann was trying to console him the rest of the way back.

When they got back home, they convinced George and Ann to see a shrink and hypnotist, to see what was going on in George's mind. Al set up an appointment with a shrink the following Monday, when the kids went back to school. Monday, George and Ann arrived at the doctors office about ten A.M. The receptionist took their names, and said Doctor Morris would see them in a few minutes. We

were led into the doctor's office and had George lie down on the therapist's couch, while Ann sat in the corner, out of sight. The doctor had George close his eyes and be still for a few minutes, then he asked a series of questions like—his name, where he was born, what he did for a living. Then he asked about the trip on the lake. George said he had a wonderful time. They went to Pelee Island, then across Lake Erie to Crystal Beach Park, and that they had a wonderful time. Then Monday they went back home. The doctor asked him about the storm across the lake on the way home. George said he did not recall any storm. When they left Canada, about half way across, he took a nap. The doctor asked where he woke up. George said he did not remember because he was at home by then. Doctor Morris said to be quiet for about three minutes and think carefully and try to collect all of his thoughts of any unusual events. Then he asked George, after a few minutes, why he clawed the bulkheads, moaned, cried, and carried on the way he did. George replied that he did no such thing and did not remember a thing. The doctor told George to open his eyes. Then told Ann that they should have another session.

"But first I want to set up an appointment with Doctor Bengal. He is a hypnotist. If anyone can get an answer, it will be him. In fact I will call him right now." The doctor dialed the number and the secretary connected Doctor Morris to Doctor Bengal. He told him the situation with George and to see what he could do. The appointment was made for that Friday.

On the way home, George and Ann had a little spat because George did not want to go Friday. Ann said, "You have to because we can't go on like this. If I didn't love you I would tell you to go to hell. Besides, the kids are beginning to think you're nuts. You do not know you are doing this." So George agreed to go.

17

Friday arrived, and on schedule we got to Doctor Bengal's office at ten o'clock in the morning. His secretary let us in the doctor's office, and a few minutes later Doctor Bengal came in. He said hello and told Ann to wait in the reception room. The doctor told George to sit in the chair that had the blue light overhead. George sat down and the doctor said, "Now look straight ahead," which George did. The doctor then put the back of his hand facing George, his ring finger had a ring on it, and it would glitter with the blue light when the doctor would give it just a slight movement. He did this for about twenty seconds. The sparkle from the ring was starting to put George into a trance. Then he told George he would count to ten, and that George would be completely asleep and not to wake up until he counted to three and snapped his fingers. The doctor started counting. By the time he got to ten George was out of it. The doctor immediately started to ask simple questions—his name, where he was born, where he went to school, things he liked to do, if he drank a lot of water, how often he went on vacation, if he liked to take a shower or bath, if he had any hobbies, or did he like swimming in deep water.

The doctor made a little progress because it seemed when he would mention anything that had to do with water, there would be a hesitant answer, as though George were afraid of it. Then the doctor mentioned rain, lightning and thunder. George then began to have a worried look on his face and told the doctor not to speak of such things. He was speaking his language and changing back and forth to some other language and then back to English. This went on for about forty-five minutes. Anything that had to do with water and the weather George would have an odd and worried reaction. He did not become frantic or out of hand. The doctor counted to three and snapped his fingers and George awoke from his trance. The doctor asked him if he remembered anything throughout the session. George replied that he did not remember anything. The doctor told George and Ann to come back the following Friday. He was going to try an experiment to get to the bottom of this mystery.

George and Ann left the doctor's office and stopped to have a little lunch at Bob Evans, and then went home. George was going to go back to the office at Future Vision, but Ann enticed him not to. She came on to him in such a way that he changed his mind in a hurry. Ann said, "This is a chance to make some serious love before the kids come home from school."

You talk about passionate love making. They were so wrapped up in it that they did not even hear the school bus drop off the kids until the door opened and one of their children yelled out, "Mother, we're home." Ann jumped up and said, "We will continue this another time." She put on her robe and went out to meet the children. Ann asked the kids how school was. They said school was fine. They inquired as to where dad was, because his van was outside. Ann said, "He didn't feel well. He's taking a nap. He will be out shortly."

The weekend weather was fine so there were no occurrences. Of course, George and Ann did continue where they left off Friday until they were both in ecstasy. George also got enough rest so he could go back to work Monday.

George got to the station early Monday morning to check the computers to see if any signals were registered on the tape from the beyond. There was not a thing registered. Then Carl came in and greeted George and asked how he was. George told him he was fine and everything went well at the doctor's, and that he was to go back the next Friday. Al had to check in at NASA, so he would not be in until later. Bart usually comes in the first thing in the morning, but had to take care of some customers at his office at an insurance company he worked for. Mike and Joe flew out West to check on some landing sites for the spacecraft when it arrives. They would not be back for a couple of weeks. Rosy and Tom always got to the station about eleven A.M. They are the ones that check out the whole cable company to make sure it is running smoothly.

All week it had been fairly quiet around the observatory and the station. They had not received any signals for about a week, which was very strange, because they always received something, at least every three or four days. The weather was tremendous all week except for a little drizzle, which hardly bothered George. They continued to send messages every day.

Friday rolled around. George, Ann and Al also came along taking one of his personal days from NASA to be with them, so he could witness and analyze the situation. They drove down to Doctor Bengal's office about ten A.M. They walked in and were immediately ushered into Doctor Bengal's office. He told George to sit down in the same chair as he did the week previous with the blue light overhead. Al and Ann sat close by in the shadows so they could observe. The doctor told them not to talk or make any unnecessary noise when George was in his trance.

The doctor went through the same routine as before. When George was asleep, the doctor asked all the same questions he did the time before and he observed all the same reactions. He put a tape in the stereo with speakers all around the room for a realistic effect. The doctor then told George that they were going on a sea voyage, and to put on his life preserver. George cringed a little and started to look worried. He said he didn't want to go on any voyage. But he was convinced that it was for the good of his family and his job. He reluctantly said okay. The doctor said good-bye to

George and his family while they were going on this cruise. We yelled, "All aboard!" About a minute later, he switched on the stereo. It started out with a lot of wind and you could hear the rain come down at first for a few minutes, and then a little harder. George's reaction was becoming a little uneasy and he mumbled, "Here we go again!" Then we heard a little thunder and then more thunder, George started to get up, then sat down again. The wind started to howl and little louder and then there was a loud crack of lightning and a rumble of thunder. Now George got up and headed for the wall as the lightning got sharper and the thunder, louder.

George was really frantic with his eyes insane-looking. He started scratching and pounding the wall screaming in an unrecognizable language. He was looking to the right and then to the left, as if talking and hollering to someone. He looked like he was trying to hang on as he was screaming and crying, pounding on the wall. His wife was watching all this, thinking, *I cannot bear to watch anymore of this.* She ran out of the room in tears and told us to get it over with. The tape had a few minutes to go so we let it continue, trying to figure out the language he was speaking so that we could figure out what the hell he was talking about. The tape finally ended. Everything was quiet. George quit pounding on the wall and ceased yelling. He was slumped on the floor, exhausted like he just came out of a boxing ring, and he was the loser. Finally, after about ten minutes, George arose to his feet and asked what he was doing on the floor. We told him he had an ordeal. He told us he did not remember anything but seemed to recall that he was speaking an odd language. He asked what language he was speaking.

The doctor recorded the whole incident on his camcorder, and told George he would show only part of it back to him; only parts where there was no lightning or thunder, so he would not go haywire again. In fact, at this time, he would only hear the language part to see if George knew any of it. The doctor put it on fast forward softly, until he came to the part with only the language, and turned it up so George could hear it clearly. The doctor turned it back again and ran it forward. George said he did not know that language, and could not recall any such event. The doctor looked at Al and shrugged his shoulders and said, "I do not know what to make of it." The doctor and Al both agreed that George was either trying to get in or out of something and never made it. But what was it. Then Al mentioned to the doctor on the side, telling him to ask George to wait in the other room with Ann. When George left the room, Al told the doctor, "I know this is all confidential. So what I say is between you and me. George an I are actually reincarnated from this other planet in another solar system. I believe we're from the same galaxy, but at different periods of time. I believe George is from a very early period on this so-called planet. I am from a more recent period, and we are trying to communicate with these other beings. When we can successfully communicate with them, that is when we are going to get some answers to this problem."

The doctor looked at Al with a rather quizzical look on his face, and asked, "Is this some kind of joke, or are you trying to make a fool out of me?"

Al said, "You can take it for what it is worth, but it is no sense having anymore sessions until I find out if I can get this language barrier broken. That is when we will get the answer to this riddle. I will need a copy of the tape with the language on it. As soon as I get the information I will be back with the answer." The doctor asked how long it would take. "It may take from today to a year, but I will get it, I know I will."

George, Ann, and Al left the doctor's office, since it was already twelve-thirty P.M. they stopped for lunch at T.G.I. Fridays. They stayed there for about an hour and a half, talking about a variety of things. They did not bring up anything that happened at the doctor's office, though it would be discussed at another time. Afterwards, they went back to George's house. Al said good-bye, and he would see them tomorrow at the station, since it would be Saturday. Al got in his van and drove down to the station. He walked in where Carl and Bart were at their desks, calculating the planets from the information gathered on the computers, to see if there was any variation from day to day. Bart was at the receiver, saying, "We really got something through the computer, but it did not make sense. The code was kind of broken up, like a blockage. We tried again and again sending messages. I think they are getting the messages alright. The problem is, we're not receiving their messages. I believe it is not in the equipment, but some other problem. The people on the other planet will tell us what it is." After a few more days, the messages received were getting clearer and clearer.

There was also a call from Mike and Joe from Tempe, Arizona. They were also club members of the Thorme. They are the ones who are flying the company's Club Cesna plane, looking for a non-conspicuous area for the spaceship from planet Thrae to land.

Three
Mike—Club Member

Mike was born and raised in the little town of Ramono, California, near San Diego in 1954. He graduated from high school in 1971. He was always interested in aviation to the point of being a fanatic, down to the model airplanes and anything that had to do with space travel. He always told stories of the visions he had about how he was some kind of pilot, speeding out through the galaxies, delivering his cargoes. Everyone told him he read too many science fiction magazines. However, they enjoyed his fantasies because they did seem so real.

After graduation, Mike received his greetings from Uncle Sam as he was drafted into the marines. He reported on the day for departures at the train station, and was transported to some marine camp in Georgia, with about two hundred other recruits. Mike took his basic training and then signed up for helicopter training. The Vietnam War was going on and they needed all the pilots they could train.

Mike spent a couple of years in Vietnam flying over jungles, villages and what have you. Sometimes he would get the strangest feeling, especially when the helicopter was hovering over an area in one spot. Mike had the feeling that he had done this before, but not in a helicopter. It was some kind of huge machine with a quiet whine. Mike usually did not hover too long over an area due to enemy fire.

He could not get the vision or feeling or whatever it was to find out if he was dreaming or if something really happened. These visions or feelings did not happen all the time. But when they did, Mike thought it was somewhat scary.

Mike's tour of duty was over and he did not have to worry about the "touch and go" with the enemy. He was lucky to survive some of the ordeals that he went through in the jungle. Especially getting shot at and almost going down a couple of times, but he always made it back to the base.

Mike was discharged and went back home to his family. He applied for a job at a cargo company at the airport. He flew all over the country for the company, including Canada and Mexico, for about a year. Mike then married his high school sweetheart and they had three children. He flew about five more years for this company, which was growing bigger every year. All the employees were stockholders in the company. Mike had about a hundred shares and got a fairly good dividend every six months.

On one cargo flight, on their way to Mexico, they had jet failure over New Mexico. They tried an emergency landing, calling in at the same time, giving location and time. They saw a clearing, but were not high enough to clear the gullies as they were coming down. They tried to give one more lift but barely budged any higher. They belly-slammed with such force, hitting some big rocks, which ripped right through the bottom of the fuselage, breaking up the pilot's and co-pilot's seats from their bracing, which swung them around in their cockpit killing the pilot, and knocking Mike unconscious. The plane was broken up with cargo strewn all over the place. There was not any smoke or fire, just a lot of noise and dust in the air. Everything settled down and was quiet for about a half an hour before anyone came around.

A rancher, his wife, and sixteen-year-old son saw the plane going down. It did look like it was in trouble after they noticed the burn out of the jet engine. They all jumped in their pickup truck, after his wife got the medical kit from the house. She called 911 for assistance.

The rancher and his family arrived at the scene in about a half hour, after traveling on the highway for a few miles. They left their son at the highway to wait for the ambulance. They proceeded up the road for about two miles, before they spotted the plane. The plane was one big mess, one wing broken off and the fuselage split open. The cargo was all over the place. You could see the skid marks for a couple hundred yards in soft dirt. The plane would have probably stayed intact if it had not hit all those big rocks, which tore the plane apart. The rancher and his wife looked into the fuselage in the big hole on the side. They kind of crawled in what space there was amongst boxes. They got to the cockpit and found the two pilots still strapped in their seats. Both seats were torn from their brackets because the bottom of the plane was ripped open. The pilot was on his side in his seat in a grotesque position. Blood was all over the place. It looked like he bled to death. Mike was still in his seat, but backwards. He was still alive but unconscious. He had a large cut on the side of his head, just above his right ear, and his left leg looked like it was broken. They comforted Mike the best they could until the air ambulance arrived, which took about forty-five minutes. Their son was still waiting on the road when the state trooper arrived. He got in the cruiser and followed the tire marks in the soft dirt.

They got to the plane and the rancher was still cleaning out some of the cargo to make room for the stretcher. The helicopter arrived a few minutes later on the scene.

The paramedics had to remove Mike carefully because of his broken leg, and lay him down on the stretcher. Mike was still unconscious. They also loaded the dead pilot. The emergency personnel thanked the rancher and his wife and took off while the state trooper questioned them.

Mike was flown to a nearby hospital in New Mexico. On the flight to the hospital, Mike was mumbling in two languages, plus English, but was still unconscious. The paramedics did not really pay attention to all the babbling. The delivery company and Mike's wife were notified of the accident. They arrived late that evening. Mike's wife, Connie, had to get her mother to look after the kids, while the company's boss had to notify the wife of the dead pilot.

They set Mike's leg and doctored up his head. They took X rays of his entire body. He was still unconscious and could not tell them where it hurt. The doctor said he was in a coma.

He continued to talk every now and then, first in one foreign language and then another. A couple of times he spoke English, which was a little incoherent. He would mumble about the spacecraft he was flying in Vietnam and could not find the landing strip anywhere in the vicinity of his calculations. His controls were all different, and he could not make them out. Then he would switch to a different language for a few minutes, but always in a calm manner. Then he would be quiet for a few hours. Out of the blue Mike would start to mumble again, but not in English or the other language. This was rather odd to those who observed him.

Mike's wife was by his side the whole time and used the bed next to his to rest. She ate at the cafeteria. This went on for two days. The third day Connie and Mike's boss used a tape recorder and taped the whole incident of all three of his languages.

They knew he was a helicopter pilot in Vietnam, but what did that have to do with any spacecraft and the controls he could not understand? "He must be having a pretty good dream somewhere." The other languages were played for a couple of professors. They said they had never heard anything like that.

A week later, Mike's wife woke up, startled to find Mike sitting up and talking to her. "What the hell happened and how come I am all bandaged up?"

Mike's wife, Connie, said, "You were in a plane crash in New Mexico."

He said, "What day is this? We have a schedule to meet?"

Connie answered, "There is no schedule to meet. Don't you understand? Your plane went down and crashed, and it is totaled!"

"Well where is Jim, the pilot?"

Connie was in tears and told Mike that he was killed instantly. "You were lucky to survive! If it were not for the rancher, his wife, and son, you would have died too."

Mike rested a few more days, then was released from the hospital. Mike's boss drove them to the airport and said he would keep in touch. They flew back to Ramona, California. He rested up for a couple months until he got the cast off of his leg, which left him with a little limp.

Mike decided to quit his job and with the money he received from the accident decided to open up a hobby shop in town. He also bought a twin engine Cessna. He still loved to fly, but not to be gone all the time on those out-of-town flights.

One night, Mike woke up sweating from a nightmare. He was in a spacecraft hovering over some landing sight with a cargo of black people, who were supposed to have immigrated from another planet at the beginning of time.

This is how different races on Earth began. Connie said that he did a lot of talking when he was in his coma, and also when he was asleep at home. "You spoke in two different languages, plus English." Connie told Mike to listen to the tapes that were recorded at the hospital when he was in the coma.

Mike listened to the English version of the tapes, especially the part when he's in the helicopter looking for the controls of a spacecraft instead of a helicopter. "I think I am half of another person, but not of this time or place. The other language is of a planet called Thrae. I am beginning to remember I used to live there at another time. When I died (but I do not know how), I guess I was reincarnated to planet Earth. Yes, I do recall. I was not born on planet Thrae. I was a pilot on a large spacecraft, which actually came from another planet in another galaxy. This is where the other language comes from. However, I cannot quite make out the context of that language. I will have to play it over and over again to see if I can figure it out.

"The three languages I believe I learned while I was stationed on Thrae for a few years. To the best of my knowledge, I feel that all this traveling is by the command of one God in the Universe. He created more than one planet, but a few planets with life on them with about the same purpose; with a sort of Adam and Eve and sustaining of life. Now the assuption is these planets were all also populated with different races and languages to test the people to see if they can harmoniously live together."

Mike said he was part of a crew that delivered these certain races to Thrae and Earth. "That is the only thing I can come up with," said Mike.

Mike's wife, Connie, had her doubts about his far-fetched story. After about a week it was dropped from their conversations, even though he still had a nightmare every now and then. Until a few years later, Mike read an article about a certain fellow who claimed he was reincarnated from a certain planet, namely planet Thrae. This is when Mike wrote back to Santini's post office box number and told his story. In a few weeks Santini wrote back to tell Mike that he heard from a couple of other people, deciding to get together for a meeting regarding their similar past experiences and lives. The place to meet was Yellowstone National Park, the last part of June 1984. A year later, Mike and his family moved to Pepper Pike, Ohio. He opened up a hobby shop in Mayfield Heights with one of the partners of Future Vision Cable Company in Chesterland, Ohio, named Joe Malita.

Four
Joe Malita—Club Member

Joe was born in British Columbia, Canada, on a farm in 1953. He lived a very stringent life with his two brothers and sister. Getting up early every morning, doing chores before going to school, Joe was the oldest of the children. He graduated in 1970. That summer he decided that he was going on a vacation to visit his Uncle Charles, who was a pilot of a seaplane up in Alaska, near Anchorage. After all these years growing up on a farm, where all he did was work and more work, it was time he got a break. Joe bought himself an old Ford jalopy, got himself a visa, and drove to Alaska to meet his Uncle Charles at one of the seaplane docks where British Columbia's border meets Alaska.

Joe had not seen his uncle in about three years, since Charles visited the family at the farm in 1967. They wrote back and forth a few times a year just to show that they still existed. Uncle Charles met Joe and had him follow the pickup he borrowed from a friend. They drove to the port where the seaplane was tied up. Charles introduced him to his buddy John, the person he borrowed the truck from. He told him that Joe was going to stay awhile and learn a few tricks about flying a seaplane. This surprised Joe, for he thought he was just visiting. But this made it even better. Maybe he had something to look forward to.

Joe loaded his baggage on the plane, then they both got in. The plane was checked over before take off. They made a clean take off and flew over the town of Sumdum heading for a little village near Anchorage.

Joe never saw such beautiful sights in his life, or should I say "this life." Joe claims he had never been in an airplane, but he had a certain feeling that for some unanswered reason he had been up in the air observing the Earth. Charles asked, "What the hell are you talking about?"

Joe said, "Never mind, I think I'm daydreaming from all this new excitement." He said he had never been any higher than the silo they have on the farm, but it still seemed strange.

Neither Joe nor his family ever smoked a cigarette in their life, but when Charles took out his pipe and lit it, Joe went into a mild trance from the lighter's flame. He made a tiny sound like he was tired. Charles looked over and said, "You must be tired from all this traveling. We have about a two-hour flight. Why don't you take a nap?" Joe said he wanted to see the scenery and did not want to miss anything. Charles said, "You will see plenty of sights while you are here."

They were silent for awhile and then Charles looked over to say something. Joe was sleeping, out like a light. In about another half hour, they arrived at their destination just when the sun was setting. Charles never liked to fly when it starts to get dark, so he times all his distances and how long each flight is. If he knows it's going to be too dark at the other end of his flight, he will cut it short, and stay over at one of the stops till morning. Charles landed the seaplane as smoothly as when he took off, and the porter was waiting to dock his plane. Joe woke up groggy and wanted to go right back to sleep. They took the baggage out of the plane and tossed it into Charles' pickup truck and headed for his cabin, about fifteen minutes away. When they got there, the first thing Joe did was head for the couch. He said, "The hell with the luggage, I will get it in the morning." Actually, Joe did not get much sleep the night before either, thinking of the trip to Alaska. Besides, farmers go to bed early and get up early.

Charles was up before daybreak. He had a cup of coffee, and left without waking up Joe. He left him a note, telling him to relax and enjoy himself around the cabin, or take a walk or whatever fancies him. Charles said he would be back later in the afternoon. Joe got up about six, read the note, then made some breakfast. He had bacon and eggs, toast, and some coffee. He sat around awhile and checked out the cabin. After he had a little lunch, he went out and took a little hike around the area. There was not much to see but trees and mountains and a beautiful river with a waterfall. Joe sat on the bank near the waterfall daydreaming of the things he wanted to do, like traveling and seeing the sights. It was getting late in the afternoon and the sun was beating down on him, making him doze off for a few minutes. He woke up and headed back to the cabin. He figured he still had some time before his uncle got home, so he decided to cook supper for Charles and himself. He got back to the cabin and headed straight for the refrigerator. He found a couple of steaks and got some potatoes out of the cupboard. Looks like Charles kept the kitchen pretty well stocked up. Joe started cooking the potatoes, made a salad, and then waited a bit until he heard his uncle's truck coming up the road. Then he threw the steaks onto the grill. By the time Uncle Charles messed around outside, then came in, he was totally surprised. He could smell the steaks cooking. He said hi to Joe. "Boy that sure smells good. I did not know you were a chef." Charles got cleaned up and sat down with Joe and ate their supper. He said, "That was sure good. I have not had that good a meal in ages."

Charles told Joe that tomorrow he was going to teach

him the ropes of the Alaska seaplane business. So the next morning, they had breakfast that Joe cooked, and left for the harbor where the seaplanes were docked. Charles had a partner named Jake, they owned two seaplanes in the company called the Brite Eagle Company. They delivered cargo and shuttled people to all parts of Alaska. It was a good business because there were not any railroads or airports in the remote parts of the state. Seaplanes were the main transportation for a lot of people.

Charles and Joe arrived at the seaplane dock about seven A.M., where Jake was fueling one of the planes. We got out of the truck and walked down the ramp to the dock. Charles said hi to Jake.

Jake looked over and said, "So this is the lad you were talking about. He is a nice looking kid." Jake finished fueling up and got down and shook Joe's hand, almost breaking the bones in his hand. Joe went "WOW! I shook hands before, but never got caught in a vise." Jake said he was sorry, that he did not know his own strength.

Uncle Charles said, "Jake used to be a professional wrestler and was champ for a while, until he got beaten by someone bigger and stronger. That's when he got out of it, and came to Alaska to work on the Alaska pipeline. That's where I met Jake running heavy equipment, clearing the land to make way for the laying of the pipe. We worked together for about three years and talked about staying in Alaska and pooling the money we saved to buy a couple of seaplanes and that's how we ended up owning the Brite Eagle Company. We make a very good living."

Jake was married with two grown children. There was one about Joe's age—Tim who was in college. The other was a girl named Christie. She worked for a law firm, and also did the paperwork for the Brite Eagle company with her mother.

Charles asked Jake, kidding around, about how we can make anything with Joe around here. Jake said, "We might, but be careful. He might want to take over the company."

Joe started to work around the dock preparing the cargoes for the next flights and checking the passenger list for no more than four at a time, depending on how much cargo there was to be delivered. Once in awhile, when there were not too many passengers, Joe got to go on a flight. There were between one and five flights in one day.

After a couple of weeks Joe got the hang of it and was beginning to like the job more and more everyday. He especially liked the flights he went on, which were very exciting.

One day Charles, Jake, and Joe were eating lunch at one of the local diners, when Christie walked in with some mail to be delivered in an emergency. This was the first time Joe saw Christie and thought she was very beautiful. He just kept staring at her. Charles made his hand go up and down in front of Joe's eyes and said, "Snap out of it, she is only a woman."

Joe said, "I know but what a beautiful one."

Christie said hello to Joe, and Joe almost choked for words, and said, "Hi."

Christie said, "My dad told me all about you. What a trooper you are." Then she turned to her dad and told him that Mom had invited Charles and Joe for supper on Sunday.

Charles said, "We will be there with flying colors." Jake took the mail and left, while Christie said she had to get back to the office. "Do not forget now, Sunday—bye now."

It was already Friday and Charles had to deliver cargo and pick up some passengers from Tyonek to bring them back to Anchorage. Charles told Joe, "While you have a little time on your hands, after you're done straightening out the dock, I'll give you your pay so you can go buy yourself some new clothes for Sunday. You don't know what might happen."

Joe cleaned up and made sure everything was in tip top shape before they got back. He went into town and bought some clothes, shoes, and got a haircut. He was all set for Sunday. Charles got back before Jake did, since his flight was shorter. They both went home and did not wait for Jake. There was always an attendant at the dock to assist the planes when they came in.

The next day, Saturday, after both planes were fueled up, Jake asked Joe if he wanted to take a ride with him, since he had cargo and no passengers.

Joe looked at Uncle Charles, and Charles said, "Go right ahead, you're pretty well caught up with everything here." Both Jake and Joe took off ahead of Charles because he was still waiting for another passenger.

They were airborne in no time at all, heading west to the coast. Jake asked Joe if he had ever been to the coast. Joe said, "No, because Uncle Charles' flights were always elsewhere."

Jake said, "You will love it because it is a lot different than inland."

After about an hour of flying, Jake asked Joe if his uncle ever let him handle the plane. Joe said, "No, I've never even thought of it, or if he would even want me to."

After about ten minutes silence, he asked Joe if he would like to take over. With astonishment, Joe said, "I sure would!"

Jake said, "I know you have been looking at the manuals and you're very observant. Get over here and sit." It was a tight squeeze but Joe managed. Jake showed him everything he had to know, how to read the gauges and keep control of the speed and altitude. Jake said, "Not bad, not bad at all."

Joe said, "It seems like I've done this before but not this type of plane, but that's absurd. I've never been up in an airplane before coming here."

They were getting near their destination, so Jake took over for the landing. He told Joe, "Some day I will teach you to take off and land."

They were getting close to a little town in an inlet of Angoon near Juneau, and would land in about five minutes. Joe said, "You were certainly right when you said it was different. It is actually beautiful. Remind me to buy a camera. I would like to send some pictures to my family back home." Jake put the stick forward a little with the wing flaps slightly down, and started to descend on a very easy approach until they started to skim the water. At the same time, he pulled the stick back slightly, and cut the throttle, which slowed them down to almost a cruise. He kept the engine at about a quarter throttle where it kept the prop almost feathered, and guided the plane almost to the dock before cutting the engine completely. They coasted to the dock and threw the line to the attendant who was waiting. The plane drifted to the side of the dock with the help of the attendant.

The cargo was unloaded and they had a couple of hours before heading back. They had to wait for two passengers and a couple of packages before heading back. So Jake took Joe sightseeing. They ate lunch and bought that camera Joe wanted, with a few extra rolls of film. Joe did not waste any time taking pictures.

It was getting close to one o'clock. They headed back where the two passengers were waiting. They greeted Jake and asked who Joe was. Jake introduced Joe, "This is Charles' nephew. He works for the company."

The attendant said, "Jake, everything is all set and ready to go." Everyone strapped in and they took off with no problems. They were airborne in no time and would reach their destination by four o'clock. Joe did not waste any time getting his camera to take pictures. The passengers had conversations with Joe all the way back asking all kinds of questions. Joe told them about the farm and school in British Columbia, and that he liked to travel. They asked him what he would like to do in the future. Joe said he likes to fly at this point in his life.

They reached their destination, and Uncle Charles was waiting by the dock at his leisure. He was smoking his pipe reading a magazine. We landed and everyone got out and unloaded the cargo.

Charles asked Joe how he liked flying with Jake. Joe said, "It is fun. He even let me fly the plane."

Charles replied, "Really!"

Jake popped in and said, "This kid is a natural. He flew the plane like he has been flying for years."

Charles exclaimed again, "Really. Well maybe we will have to do something about that."

Jake said, "On our slow days we will teach you to take off and land." Joe was thrilled and could hardly wait.

The next morning, which was Sunday, Uncle Charles and Joe woke up, showered, and dressed in their nicer clothes. Joe put on his new duds and looked pretty snazzy. They had breakfast, and left about nine o'clock to drive to the other side of town. While Charles was driving, Joe asked, "How come you never got married?" You could see on Charles' face the look of dismay. Joe said, "Did I say something wrong?"

Charles said, "Not really. I had a woman friend a few years back that I loved very much, and we were going to get married. But we were in a boating accident and she was killed. I blamed myself because we were partying and I was drunk. I ran the boat onto the rocks. Jake, his wife, Barb, and I, survived but Linda was killed. I've never touched a drop of booze since. It was not worth it. I spent a year in jail for manslaughter. That's the consequence you pay for being drunk. Didn't Jake tell you any of this?"

Joe said, "No."

"Well, that's what kind of a guy Jake is. He minds his own business and never gets in fights. He is honest and true blue. As far as women go, I sill have a few acquaintances I see every now and then."

They finally arrived at Jake's house, which was located at the edge of town. They both got out of the truck, walked to the door of the house and knocked. They walked in at the same time. "Is anybody home?"

Jake's wife Barb answered from upstairs and said, "Make yourselves at home and we will be right there."

Christie came down first, "Good morning! You guys are early."

Charles said, "No one said what time to come and you sure look all prettied up."

Joe said, "Yea-ah."

Christie said she was going to church, which she did practically every Sunday. She asked Joe if he went to church.

Joe said, "Not as often as I should, I surely have not gone since I've been here in Alaska."

Christie asked Joe if he wanted to go with her this morning. Joe said it would be his pleasure. They got in Christie's car and drove off. She asked Joe what religion he was. He said he was Presbyterian.

Christie said, "What a coincidence, I am Presbyterian also."

They got to the church, walked in, and Joe whispered,

"I have not been to church for so long, I hope it does not fall down."

Following the church service on the way back, Joe asked if she had any boyfriends. She said she had one and had been together with him for about a year, until he broke it off with her a few months ago, for another girl.

Joe said, "Was he crazy or just stupid? If you were my girl I sure as hell would not let you go for anyone. What a moron!"

Christie laughed. "Maybe it was just as well. I think he was the playboy type. I believe he was seeing other girls while we were going together anyway. He got mad at me because every time we necked he would try to get in my pants and I would not let him. That kind of pissed him off. I do not believe in sex until after I am married. So enough of me. What about you? I know you're from Canada and were brought up on a farm. Then you came here."

Joe indicated, "There is not too much more to add. I had a girlfriend or two when I was going to school, nothing serious. Where I lived, there was not too much to choose from. I thought it was a very boring life until I came here. I might never go back. Only to visit my family."

After that Sunday, Joe and Christie started to see each other every weekend and sometimes during the week. They fell in love, got engaged and set a date for the following June to get married.

Charles and Jake taught Joe to take off and land, which Joe learned quickly. They could not understand how Joe learned so fast, like he flew for years. Joe never brought it up anymore about having a feeling that he had flown before, maybe in another life. After a couple of months of training, Joe was flying like a real jockey. They had a meeting one day and decided to purchase another seaplane and expand the business.

Things went smoothly, now that they had three planes. They could alternate weekend flights unless there was an emergency. Joe started to earn pretty good money now that he made his own trips. Christie was happy about that because with earnings combined they put a down payment on a house a few miles out of town. June rolled around all of a sudden, they got married on Saturday in the church they attended. It was not a real big wedding, but enough people attended to make it look that way. All flights were cancelled until Monday morning. Joe's family was there, they arrived the day before. The ceremony went very well and finally they were pronounced man and wife. Some courier came in quietly and approached Charles with a message. The wedding service was over anyway, and out the door they went. Everyone was throwing rice, including Charles. Charles said, "What timing, I have an emergency in New Halen, I will be gone most of the afternoon. The Geromes have to get to the hospital, the missus is going to have a baby and it would take too long by boat. I shall be back in time for the reception this evening."

The reception was held in the new town hall that was built the year before. Everyone in town was invited. Charles did show up about seven o'clock. The hall was already half full. By ten o'clock, the hall was packed.

They had a hell of a band that played just about anything. Charles was a very good dancer. He really could cut a rug. Charles was tempted for a drink of booze, but he never touched a drop. The reception lasted well after the bride and groom left. Everyone had one of the best times in a long time in these remote parts, unless you went to Anchorage or some other big town.

Years had gone by, Joe and Christie had a couple of kids who were now in high school. Of course Christie had to quit her job at the law firm when her first child was born.

Now that they were in high school, she went back to work part-time for her dad, doing some of the book work. She was also very active in the community.

Joe kind of got used to the feelings he had been somewhere else in another life, but could not quite pinpoint it. There were also a few small fires he saw, that stirred his thinking, but he never figured out why it had anything to do with his flying. He brought it to Christie's attention a couple of times, but she said that maybe he had been dreaming these incidents. "Dreams do seem real sometimes."

Joe said, "But not this many times!" Then Joe said that he thought he had been reincarnated and came from another planet.

Christie could not stop laughing at that one, and said, "Boy you are dreaming!"

Joe responded, "One of these days it will come out."

A couple years went by, and no more was said about Joe's exploits. Their daughter Julie, was graduating this year and Jim the next year in 1992.

On a routine flight at about seven A.M. in July of 1991, Joe was approaching Lake Clark on his way to New Dalton, when he noticed smoke coming out of a cabin next to a lake. This was in a small village and most houses and cabins were scattered. He started to land the seaplane and call into the village, he reached the sheriff's office, which was about five or six miles away. Joe was close to landing when large flames started to appear at one end of the cabin. That is when it hit him, he was looking for a different set of controls that were not there, at the same time hitting the water with a bang, he got his senses back momentarily, until he got out of the plane and ran to the cabin to try to open the door, which was bolted on the inside. He got a big log that was nearby, and threw it through the window. He climbed in and opened the door, and hollered, and running to the bedroom. He grabbed a little boy about five or six years old and laid him outside. He ran back in when he heard an old man coughing and trying to get up. Joe pushed him onto the floor for cooler air and grabbed his wife and dragged her outside. She started to come to and Joe yelled, "Take care of your son. I'm going to get your husband."

The flames were already in the bedroom where he lay and the smoke was getting thicker. Joe got a towel in the kitchen, soaked it, and ran through the flames into the bedroom. He grabbed a blanket and threw it over him. The bright flames were making him remember a lot of strange things. Joe started to talk in a loud, strange voice, as he dragged the victim out of the bedroom to the entrance. The towel fell from Joe's face as the flames came at him, slightly singeing him about the face. He screamed in pain, yelling half in the foreign language and half in English. He said, "Lets get the hell out of here. The planet is doomed because the end has finally come."

He managed to drag the man outside, just in time because the whole cottage was in flames. Joe dragged him farther away from the cottage and collapsed alongside the unconscious person he saved. The man's wife brought her son too. He was coughing and throwing up.

At that time the ambulance and the sheriff arrived. Joe was half conscious, babbling about the end of the planet and to get out while you can. He also talked in "that other" foreign language. Joe said to take care of the other fellow, and he would be all right. They brought the other fellow too, who was about half dead. The sheriff told Joe that he was a hero.

"There are many that would not run into a flaming house the way you did. And what was the language you were speaking? You said something about the end of the planet?"

Joe said in a painful voice, "I do not remember saying anything; besides I have deliveries to make." Then Joe started to vomit, became dizzy, and passed out. He woke up about ten minutes later in the ambulance, on his way to the hospital in Anchorage, to be checked out. They had to treat him for smoke inhalation and the burns on his face and hands. Joe complained about his eyes hurting and his vision being blurred. The sheriff called Joe's wife and told her that he was in the hospital, telling her it was nothing serious, but to get there anyway. Charles just came in from a trip and Christie told him. Jake was still on a trip, so Charles flew Christie to the hospital.

Joe was sitting up in bed and said that he was all right, but his vision was blurred on account of his cornea being seared in the blaze. He said, "It sure hurts like hell!" Then Joe asked how the other people were—especially the little boy.

Christie said, "They were all right and could not thank you enough.

"They lost everything, even their pickup truck that was next to the cottage."

Joe said, "That is too bad! When we go to church next Sunday, we should ask the pastor for everyone to participate through the town and take up a collection for them. We will start by donating a thousand dollars. That should not hurt us any."

Joe could not fly for awhile. Charles and Jake had to go and pick up his plane, which was still anchored near the burned out cottage. Jake made the deliveries a day late, but the customers understood what happened. Jake and Charles told Joe to take it easy for awhile. They were expanding the business and buying three more planes for the new port they were opening up at Nayakuk Lake. They were hiring four new pilots so they had an alternating schedule seven days a week.

After a month's rest, Joe was getting cabin fever and had to get out. He had Christie drive him down to the dock because his eyesight had not improved since the fire. He was not able to drive, let alone fly a plane. That meant he could not fly until his eyesight was back to normal; and no one knew when that would be. Joe and Christie were not worried about their finances because they had a lot of shares in the Brite Eagle Company. They would do much better since the company was expanding, which would control most parts of Alaska, the Yukon, and British Columbia. Christie took a leave of absence for awhile so she could take care of Joe. She still did some of the work that had to be done. She did not mind it. It kept her busy.

Joe went down to the plane dock every day to see that everything was handled correctly and the shipments were secured into the planes, and that the passengers were checked out. He could see well enough to take care of those things.

The doctor was working on a pair of glasses that would improve his eyesight. This would take time, for he had to have a different strength lens made up every four months. It would probably take two to two and a half years before his eyesight would be almost normal. Joe already missed flying. He would get all tied up inside when he used to just go for a ride and could not fly the plane himself. He did not go too often. He got too stressed about it.

After about seven or eight months, Joe began to drive his pickup again. By that time his son graduated from high school, and was sent off to college. Their daughter had started the year before.

One day, Joe drove down to the dock. It was a pretty cool, brisk day and they usually had a fire going in a drum so the employees could stay warm when they were not in the crew's quarters. This time, someone threw too much of something in the fire and the flames were shooting out about ten feet. Charles was shouting, "What are you trying to do, burn the dock down?"

Joe got there about that time, looking at the huge flames and yelled out something that no one understood— some was in English. He said, "We have not much time; the whole planet is going up in flames! Hurry! The spacecraft is waiting! Come on, NOW." Joe hurried over, trying to get everybody away from the fire.

Charles had to restrain him. He yelled, "What the hell are you talking about?" Charles could see through Joe's glasses at his eyes. They were glazed and it seemed like he was somewhere else, far away. The flames died down, and Joe finally calmed down. Still in a sweat and mumbling, he sat for awhile thinking and remembering things that happened to come to his mind from way back when. A lot of the pieces started to fall into place.

His Uncle Charles sat down next to him staring at the perplexed look on his face for a few seconds. Then he asked, "Joe, what is all this bullshit about the planet going to burn up and to escape in a spaceship? You were carrying on the same way when you rescued those people at the cottage."

Joe said he did not want to discuss it right now and to wait until he was more sure about what was going on. "When I've figured it out, I will tell you all about it, and you probably will not believe me anyway."

About a month later there was a little ceremony held in town with the governor, the whole town, including a few people from British Columbia, mostly relatives in attendance. The ceremony was for Joe. The governor awarded Joe the medal of honor for his bravery, for saving the lives of the three people, and also for his unselfishness in starting a fund for helping them out. Everybody was proud of Joe, and always looked up to him.

For the next few months, things were fairly quiet around the dock, and the flights were as regular as clockwork. Joe was used to being grounded for awhile which gave him a chance to get everything reorganized. He also came up with a few new ideas. Joe did not let any moss grow under his feet. One day, on a brisk October morning, Joe was taking a coffee break when he noticed an article in a magazine he was reading titled, "Are You Here Or Are You There." It was a story of a fellow who claimed he was reincarnated from a planet named Thrae, which he claimed was in another solar system. He went on to tell how he lived on this so-called planet, and what he did. In fact, he gave quite a bit of information, which sounded all too familiar. He had a name and a post office box number, which was in Lyndhurst, Ohio. So Joe wrote back and explained what had been happening to him. This fellow wrote back, and said there was going to be a meeting at Yellowstone National Park on such and such a date, and a few other people were going to attend, who also claim they had similar experiences. He further indicated, "If you are interested, please bring your wife and kids if you have any. You can make a vacation of it."

Joe showed the response to his wife, and she was all for it. She said, "We have not been on a vacation in a long time. The company is well taken care of with enough experienced help anyway."

Joe showed Uncle Charles the article and the letter, and started to explain his actions that occurred when he was around large fires; sometimes even small ones. He told Charles that he believed he was reincarnated, and that he was saving a lot of lives on this so-called planet Thrae, at a particular time, which on Earth would be called the end of the world. This planet was destroyed by fire because of its wickedness, and only a few were saved and put on a large spacecity. I transported a lot of people, but I myself did not make it. I got killed in this big inferno. I do not remember when, but this planet was like Earth, with about the same problems.

That summer, Joe and Christie decided to go to the meeting at Yellowstone. Both kids were home from college, but did not want to go because they had other plans. Joe and Christie said it was all right. This would be like their second honeymoon.

They finally had the meeting at Yellowstone. There were five other people who attended. Christie said she would pick Joe up later with their rented car. She would see the sights and buy a few souvenirs. The meeting lasted about four hours. Joe Santini said that this was not his real name; that it was Al. He changed it for reasons such as being accused of being a crackpot. This is why he has a post office box.

They had a couple of meetings, when Al convinced them that he knew they were sending signals from far away past our solar system, for once in a while he would get very faint signals on his receiver that could almost be deciphered. "I do not know if they are trying to answer what I transmit, or what have you. I do not have enough of the code to make out what is said." Al said, "All of us should be in one place and start some communication center with better equipment."

It was decided by means of a vote that everyone was to move to Ohio in the Cleveland suburbs. The Yellowstone meeting ended the next day. They had a little picnic with the entire group, so everyone could be introduced to each other.

The next week, Joe and Christie left for home. Joe had

to convince Christie to move to Ohio. He said, "If we do not like it then we will come back." Charles did not like it very much but they moved anyway the next year. They said good-bye to Christie's parents and brother, who were not to happy about it either. The children stayed in Alaska until they finished college. At least they had a home to go to.

Joe and Christie packed what they needed for Ohio. They would stay at Al's until they purchased a house, which did not take long. They found one not too big or small in Gates Mills. They had it furnished and had the rest of their belongings sent. All the furniture stayed in the house in Alaska for the kids. They finally moved in and settled down.

Five
Al's Flashback

Chapter five is one of the scenarios about planet Thrae, which is almost identical to planet Earth, with the same type of lifestyle. A later chapter will define the history with the same similarity as planet Earth.

In the meantime, Al could not get the little episode out of his mind when he and his wife were on vacation driving through Pennsylvania.

One night late in August, Al was at home playing around with the grandkids before supper. He could not keep all the recent problems off his mind. After eating supper and getting all of the dishes squared away, the grandkids did their homework, before watching any television. (Incidentally the grandkids' parents have been detained for the last two years in Russia, for a mistaken espionage case that will hopefully be cleared up soon.) Al and his wife relaxed in the den watching a little TV, until Al started yawning. Al said he was going up to bed. Rose said she would be up later.

It was already ten o'clock. The kids went to bed after they said goodnight to them. Al brushed his teeth and got into bed. Lying there for a while thinking about the next day's events. Al thought they should send data continuously about all the planets in the solar system, especially about what to expect, when and if they reached Earth.

Al was in a twilight sleep, like a trance, when he started to get a clear vision of some episode he had in his other life on planet Thrae and the spacecity of Orant. As a little boy on planet Thrae, living with his mother and his sister, he remembered his mom's name, Verna. He did not remember his father too well because he was killed in one of the planet's stupid wars. Al's family got assistance from the country's government. His mother was a very religious person, who went to church regularly; always helping other people and participating in charity organizations. She was fairly strict in raising him and his sister with good moral standards; and keeping them out of trouble. My planet Thrae name was Deton.

When Deton finished his schooling, he decided to join the armed services and continue more schooling in space and astronomy. He knew the government wanted many pupils in that field. He chose the field of aeronautics, including schooling regarding spaceships and space stations. It was very hard to qualify for all three subjects. He passed the aptitude tests with flying colors. They also checked his background, and they were satisfied with his very clean lifestyle and religious record. He was based at one of the air and space control ports. The first year he learned weather, astronomy, and courses on flying different aircrafts. The next year, in 2007 planet Thrae time, he was one of the program's top notch students. There were nine of them chosen for the space program. He remembered the first flight from planet Thrae to the spacecity of Orant, which was almost complete. He was only a co-pilot then, still learning the ropes. They were shuttling some cargo and personnel to the spacecity. Deton just could not believe the size of the spacecity. It was really out of this world.

It took Deton awhile to find out what the spacecity was built for. He thought it was an experiment for outer space.

Then he learned it was going to be used as an exodus from planet Thrae; due to Thrae's evilness, wars, greed, lust, killings, and the like. Deton really could not understand what humanity really wanted. The planet's human inhabitants have everything—modern cities, beautiful parks, places to go, things to do, and all kinds of entertainment. He supposed some people are never satisfied with what they have, so they want somebody else's belongings, no matter how they get it. They will probably end the planet by nuclear war.

Deton and his crew shuttled back and forth from planet Thrae to the spacecity for about a year. He also kept on studying astronomy. He was actually obsessed with this subject. Back on planet Thrae, 2009, he was given a month's leave. He stopped at headquarters for his leave papers and they also handed him a dated confidential letter of when it could be opened—namely a week later. So he left, going back home to his mother and sister. They both greeted him with open arms and kisses. They were very glad to see him. He was glad to see them because it was such a long time.

There was another person in the room. Deton's mom and sister introduced him to his sister's boyfriend, Caston. They waited for him to come home on leave so he could attend their wedding. He was surely surprised with the announcement. Caston was a very nice, clean-cut fellow; and very intelligent. He spent three years as a missionary out in a remote part of the planet, until it became hostile. At that time, he was told to come back to his country of Sargasity. Their wedding was planned for the next year, 2010. However, the wedding was soon to be changed to an earlier date as Deton opened the letter of confidentiality. It gave him his orders of where to report, and to notify his family to get ready to evacuate with the belongings they would use on a long voyage. Deton's mother and sister were stunned to hear the news. They lived in the same place all their lives. This meant that his sister and future brother-in-law would be getting married within the month. After the wedding, Caston could automatically go on the voyage. As a married couple, they would have to obtain special orders to travel together—to be registered as another occupant on spacecity Orant.

Deton told Caston, his mother and sister that they would like this venture out into space on the modern shuttle. It is like flying in a dream with the most awesome sights that you can imagine. To live on the spacecity is an experience in itself. There is always something to do.

A few weeks later, Deton's sister and Caston had a small wedding ceremony with a few friends. Leaving her mother's house in the city of Baco, they went on their honeymoon to some island for three days and hurried back because Deton and his mom were already packed and ready to go the following week. When they returned and had completed their packing, the newlyweds were transported to the space shuttle station. Everyone was bid adieu, though they were just going on a vacation. The confidential instruction was not to let anyone know what was happening, because there were only about two thousand people chosen by the Lord's command. The end of the planet was at hand and most people did not think much of it. Even the tabloids contradicted the prophecies of long ago. They figured, "What can happen in this modern age?" Actually, they cried wolf too many times. There was always one Jesuit or another predicting the end of the planet at one time or another, and nothing ever happened. When they started transporting animals from all over the planet, people thought the high offials were really going to extremes.

Deton indicated, "After my family settled down on Orant, I was assigned to animal transportation. This was no easy task, even though the instinct of the lord was in them of when to depart. It still was difficult because these animals never flew anywhere. Each animal had to be tied down securely on the space shuttle because too much moving around might throw the shuttle out of control."

When they reached the spacecity, the docking station was on the bottom floor, with hundreds of stalls to accommodate the different species and their special needs. This area was also built with a miniature forest, so each group of animals would have a chance to wander around for a little freedom. They were each given a special marking so they could more easily be brought back to their stalls.

This modern spacecity was also equipped with a few dozen robots to facilitate and reduce the burdens of the humans. The robots were able to clean up the animal dung and kept the grounds clean and sanitary. The humans and animals were slated to live this way for the next twenty years until planet Thrae returned to normal from its destruction. It has been programmed for the next twenty years for anything that might happen, right down to the day when all the animals were transported back to planet Thrae. The regeneration in the life cycle of the humans and animals was also considered in the long range plan.

The shuttling of animals went on for most of the year 2009. There were also many spaceships transporting people and all kinds of supplies. This included thousands of items that were stored in large warehouses on the spacecity, for future use in expanding the spacecity. Some people were calling it "The Ark in the Sky."

Not much attention was paid to who was handling the animals on our initial trips. I always conversed with those with whom I was familiar, namely, the pilots or navigator. Every time I docked on the spacecity, I always had a day to myself to visit my family. Each time I would walk by the person that led the animals to their stalls I would notice a very beautiful girl of about eighteen or nineteen years of age. One time, when walking by when we were docked, she was letting one of the animals out backwards and stumbled right in my path. We collided and both landed on the floor, I joked and said, "Don't you observe traffic signals." She ignored me, got up and led the animal away. I thought to myself, *Boy, how stuck up.*

So a week went by, and I still noticed her every now and then. Then one day it happened again, I was going to the cafeteria, as I was going around the corner. She came around the opposite way and ran right smack into me with her tray and spilled food all over the front of my nice clean uniform. She was standing there with her mouth open, speechless. I said, "I usually eat my food not wear it." Then she finally started to utter a few words. Saying she was awfully sorry and would clean my uniform. She helped me scrape some of the food from my uniform and called for a robot to clean up the floor.

I told her, "Now that you did not eat any lunch, you could buy both our lunches, that will make up for my uniform." She agreed, so we ate lunch and got acquainted. She said her name was Taral and I told her I was Third Commander Deton. We started a very friendly relationship. Every chance we got we went out to some theater or just walked around. She was very good to be with and my mother and sister would just love her.

I asked her why she did not have a boyfriend. She said she used to have one a couple of years ago. His name was Ceikle, and they were going to get married. However, her parents said she was too young. He was much older anyway. "He wanted me to run away with him, to the enemy country of Jarconi, because he was going to join their military. I told him not to be so stupid, they were our enemy.

Then he said that they were going to make him an officer and that it was the beginning of a planet conquest." She told him to go without her, for he was going to meet his demise. He said, "The hell with you," and left. Taral said she loved him for a while, and then he started to change and be kind of bossy. "Another reason he left was because I would not have sex with him before we got married." She told him, "Well that is too bad, because I was not brought up that way."

It was two weeks, when one evening we were sitting in the park, by a pond, watching a couple of swans paddling by and a couple of robots keeping the landscape trimmed. I was holding her hand talking about just anything when my impulse could not stand it anymore and I just had to pull her over and kiss her, full on the lips.

It lasted about five seconds but enough to get your heart to pump faster. It made us both gasp for air. We looked into each others' eyes and she said, "What took you so long?"

I said, "I do not really know, maybe because you are so beautiful that I was not worthy of you."

She said, "Nonsense, I could say the same thing." Then she kissed me and would not let go.

Taral told me, when we got back to planet Thrae, that I will have to meet her parents. One of these days, I will meet her brother, who already lives on the spacecity Orant. Deton said, "My mother and sister are living here on the spacecity. You will have to meet them." It was another three days before they went back to planet Thrae, because of a malfunction in their spaceship. The crew finally got on board and ready to take flight. As soon as the outer protection shield was open, away they went. Slowly at first, and when everything was okayed they increased their speed. It was another pleasant flight, and before you knew it, they were landing at the spaceport on Thrae. You did not have to go through the formalities as in outerspace. You got your directions on where to land, and one, two, three, you were down.

Both Deton and Taral took a shuttle to the middle of town and stopped at a house that was next to a church. Deton said, "You sure live close enough to the church."

Taral said, "I know, that is because my father is the minister."

"Oh, how quaint, we do not have to look far for a minister to get married."

Taral responded, "Who said anything about getting married?"

Deton stopped short, and at the same time grabbed Taral's arm and turned her around facing him and looked her straight in the eye, and said, "I am." He went down on one knee, holding her hand and asking her if she would marry him. He said that he loved her with all his heart.

With tears of happiness in her eyes, she said, "Yes, yes I will!" Deton had a little ring on his little finger. He took it off and placed it on her ring finger, got up, and kissed her very gently on the lips.

They looked at each other for a while and Taral said, "Maybe we better go in and break the good news to my parents." They walked in and Taral's parents were sitting down eating lunch. Taral greeted both of them, walking over and kissing them both on the forehead. Her mother said, "You're just in time for a bit to eat," at the same time eyeing Deton.

Her father asked, "Who is this good looking fellow with you?"

Taral said, "Oh father, this is the most wonderful person you will ever want to meet. His name is Deton, or to put it formally, Third Commander Deton. He is the pilot of the spaceship I have been assigned to."

Taral was overwhelmed with excitement and could not hold back anymore. So she told her parents that Deton asked to marry her. Her mother was thrilled and said, "You will make a very nice and happy couple."

Her father asked if she set a date. Taral said no. "I suppose we will wait till everything is settled on spacecity Orant. We just got engaged and did not even think about the future."

Deton and Taral did not have to be back to the spaceport until the next morning for the flight back to spacecity Orant. Deton got to know Taral's parents and was shown around the church. He stayed for supper and had some entertainment of movies and news. Deton stayed in the guestroom while Taral stayed in her own bedroom, until her parents went to bed. She could not stand it anymore and snuck over to Deton's room and climbed into bed next to him. Deton was almost asleep when he felt her warm body next to his. His eyes opened wide and turned to her. Taral said she could not stand it and just had to be next to him. They kissed passionately, petting each other's entire bodies. After about a half an hour Deton was like a dog going after a female dog in heat and just exploded, losing his load. Taral said she was sorry. She wanted it as much as he did, but she obeyed her parents and she just could not. Taral said, "I know it was like a nasty tease, but once we're married we will make up for lost time." Deton said, "I understand, we will just have to wait." After about another hour of talking, Taral kissed Deton good night and went back to her room.

Early the next morning they had breakfast and called for a shuttle to take them back to the spaceport. The shuttle arrived, Deton said, "It was nice meeting you," and her parents said likewise.

Taral said, "We should be back in time for the weekend service."

Deton and Taral were about to get in the shuttle when her father called her back and said, "I have something to tell you."

Taral walked back to her parents while Deton waited in the shuttle, watching while they were talking. Deton could see some anguish come across Taral's face and then hugged first her father and then her mother for a long time. She then turned, waved and said, "I will see you this weekend," and ran to the shuttle. She no sooner got in when she burst into tears at the same time, burying her face into my shoulder. I asked what was the matter and she said choking, "Not now hon I will tell you later," and she continued crying until she fell asleep.

In a little while, we arrived at the spaceport and I gently shook her shoulder to wake her up. We got out and she did not say a word about anything. We checked in as she was ready to leave for her post. She gave me a kiss and said she would see me at lunch time in the spacecity. Man, that must have been the longest morning of my life. We finally got to Orant, we docked and she was busy unloading more animals. I asked her if she needed any help. She said, "No, I will meet you at the cafeteria."

I could see she had still been crying, so I did not push it any. I already sat down to lunch when Taral walked in and grabbed something to drink and sat down opposite me with her eyes all red. I said, "Aren't you going to eat anything?"

She said she was not hungry, with more tears in her eyes, and got up and ran out of the cafeteria saying, "I will see you tonight." Well I sure as hell did not eat much of anything either. The afternoon seemed even longer than the morning. Finally it was time to quit, with everything ready for tomorrow's flight back to planet Thrae. The spaceship will be inspected and anything being loaded with cargo or passengers will be ready for the morning flight.

I arrived at Taral's quarters about fifteen minutes later. It was located about two miles through the spacecity. I got to her quarters and pushed the buzzer. In a few seconds one of her three roommates answered the door. She said to wait in the very small living room while she got Taral. They have pretty good security. When you press the buzzer, your picture automatically comes on the screen inside the cabin and you have to show your card and say what your business is. Taral came into the room and gave a kiss and a hug and said let's get something to eat because she was awfully hungry. She looked like she calmed down. We found an eatery and ate, then took a walk in one of the small parks. When we sat down, she gave me a small kiss again and with some tears welling up in her eyes she said that her father told her the hostility was getting worse through the planet and the end was very near. Her father and mother were not leaving the planet for spacecity Orant. The people were going to need him and the church more than ever and he would stay there until the end. Taral said her father tried to persuade her mother to leave, but she would not. Her brother said their mother had been with her husband all these years and she was not about to leave him now. Taral said that her brother Garrah was also a minister, who graduated the year before from theological school (which I already said was on the spacecity).

The next weekend we both went to church where her father was preaching. He gave a wonderful sermon, "Heaven and the Hereafter." He spoke of the hereafter, where people became whole again, where there was no sickness and misery, and everyone got along with each other in a harmonious way.

Taral and I continued to transport animals from planet Thrae. Our job was almost complete. We decided not to wait until later to get married. Taral called her father from the spacecity and told him that we were ready and wanted him to marry us. So the date for our wedding was set for the first weekend of the month. This was the last month of the year, and it seemed to come upon us quickly. Deton took Taral over to meet his mother and sister, who were very surprised that Deton was going to marry such a fine girl; a daughter of a minister.

It was a beautiful day for a wedding. We arrived the day before from spacecity of Orant, with a few friends and the parishioners of the congregation. Taral's brother, Garrah, was already there. He took two weeks' leave to stay with his parents. Everything was set for the ten o'clock service. Everyone was present and the service began with a little music. Both Deton and Taral stood before the minister. Taral's father, the minister, looked at both of us, admiring how beautiful his daughter looked in her wedding dress, and how handsome I looked in my blue service uniform. He gave us both a little smile and started by saying, "I am about to bring together a new couple in Holy Matrimony, to start a new life, away from this troubled planet, to a new planet, free from all the turmoil and strife and hatred of this one. I believe they will be an inspiration to the people; upcoming leaders of righteousness. Their children will be leaders of a free and happy planet." He also said that he wished he could see this happen, but he had to assist in the redemption of many people who would not be going to the new planet.

Taral could hardly restrain herself from crying out loud. She held it in with a small trickle coming down her cheek. Even I had watery eyes. The minister finally said, "Please hold each other's hands and repeat after me: We are to become a union of one to love and cherish each other's company through sickness and in health, in all troubled and good times, as long as we both shall live. Taral, do you take Deton for your beloved husband?"

Taral said, "I will."

"Deton, do you take Taral for your beloved wife?"

Deton said, "I will."

"Deton will you place the ring on Taral's finger and repeat after me."

Deton placed the ring on Taral's finger and repeated, "Taral, I thee wed with all my love."

"Taral, will you please place the ring on Deton's finger and repeat after me?"

Taral put the ring on Deton's finger and repeated, "Deton, I thee wed with all my love."

The minister said, "I pronounce you man and wife; and go in peace. You may now kiss the bride." The music started with a beautiful hymn, and out the door they went where everyone was gathering. Later in the day, they had a wonderful reception. Her brother Garrah congratulated them, and said he would see them on the spacecity of Orant. Deton and Taral were going to stay at her parents' house the first night. Deton's mother and sister were there, congratulating both of them, and wishing them all the happiness.

When they left their parents' house, they were going on a honeymoon for about three days, at a resort that was like a big playground. The first night as Mr. And Mrs. was like being in heaven. We left the reception about ten o'clock, or should we say we snuck out. They will all be there having a good time, eating, singing, and dancing most of the night.

We got to the upstairs bedroom at Taral's parents' house, and I said, "Wait a minute, stand right there and do not move." I opened the door all the way, then I picked Taral up off the floor, kissed her and carried her over the threshold. I gave her another long passionate kiss, then I put her down gently.

We both looked at each other for a few seconds, which felt like a long, long time. Her eyes were pleading with mine, we could not stand it anymore. I put my arms around her and squeezed her gently and just held her for a few seconds, then I started to undo the buttons in the back of her wedding dress very slowly. I did not wait long to get aroused because I already was. I pulled her gown down over her shoulders and let it fall to the floor. She was still in her undergarments. I gave a little gasp, whispering how beautiful she was. She then said it was her turn. She reached over and took off my jacket and unbuttoned my shirt and took it off, and kissed me at the same time. Then she took off the sash holding my trousers and let everything fall to the floor, leaving me in my underwear. She could see the erection bulging through my underwear, looking as hard as a pony cock. That did it, we could not stand it anymore. We both attacked each other's underwear, and in no time flat we were in a heap on the floor. We were grabbing each other, hugging and kissing, and feeling each other like there was no tomorrow. At the same time, we moved rapidly toward the bed and both of us fell on the bed with a little thud, still embraced and kissing all the sensuous places imaginable. Her voice was getting very excited like she was pleading, "I cannot stand it anymore. Please do not let me wait a second longer, enter me PLEASE!"

Deton let go for a second as she got in a prone position with her legs slightly spread. Deton looked down at her, whispering how beautiful and sexy she looked. She whispered back to him, "Please hurry." Deton got on top, kissing her lips and neck, and then he put his manhood in very gently with a faint little thrust. Taral arched her body up to meet his with a soft ooowing sound of ecstasy that she never felt before in her entire life. Deton was in motion, in an uncontrollable motion of softness and warmth, which he tried to make last forever. After a few minutes, which felt like an eternity, they started to come to a climax like shooting stars all over the galaxy. They both finished in complete exhaustion in each other's arms. They stayed there in each other's arms for a long time until they both fell asleep.

In the morning they woke up still in each other's arms looking at each other smiling, and without a word continued where they left off from last night. This time it was longer and even better than the first time. It was getting close to noon and Deton and Taral decided to get up. They got dressed and went downstairs. Taral's mother was in the kitchen and said, "Hi there honeymooners. You want something to eat before you leave?" They both said at the same time, "Sure." Taral's father was at the church earlier that morning attending to some people, when he walked in saying, "Well hello! Welcome to what's left of the morning." Laughing at the same time, "I would ask how the night was, but I guess it is none of my business."

They finished eating and called for a shuttle. Taral kissed her parents good-bye. Deton shook her father's hand and kissed her mother on the cheek. "We will see you in a few days and have a good time."

Deton and Taral arrived at their destination in a couple of hours and checked in with two small bags. It was a nice little resort town, nice restaurants, a swimming pool, and very good entertainment. The first evening they had a little supper at a nice little secluded spot then went back to their room and just could not keep their hands, lips, and bodies off of each other. The second day they took advantage of sleeping late. When they got up they had a little love making while waiting for the lunch they ordered earlier. They ate, then got dressed and went out on the town. They had a very good time until about ten o'clock that night, and headed back to the hotel. They got to the door of their room and Deton said, "Something does not look right."

Taral looked at Deton with a puzzled look and said, "What is it?"

Deton said, "I do not really know, it is probably my imagination." He opened the door. They both walked in, Deton was ready to turn the light on, when someone grabbed Taral, putting his hand over her mouth preventing her from screaming. The light went on and Deton said, "What the hell!"

There was also someone sitting in a chair holding a weapon. He calmy said, "Please shut the door Deton." Taral was struggling to free herself but the assailant was too strong. There was another person with a gun looking out the window through the drapes.

Deton said, "What the hell is going on here?"

The man in the chair told the other fellow, "Let Taral go."

At the same time Deton said, "How do you know her name?" and almost simultaneously, Taral said, "Ceikle, what are you doing here and what do you want?"

Deton said, "So this is your old boyfriend! I do not blame you for dropping him."

Ceikle got a little enraged and said, "Do not get smart, you son of a bitch, or I will drop you right in your tracks. Nobody messes with my girlfriend."

Taral remarked, "I am not your girlfriend and besides we are married."

Ceikle yelled, "Bullshit! You are my girlfriend always. You think that little piece of paper and a few words mean anything? To me you never got married."

Taral was whispering to herself how were we going to get out of this. It sure looked like trouble. Taral asked Ceikle, "What are you going to do with us?"

Deton said, "You touch a hair on her head, you will not live to regret it."

Ceikle said, "I told you to shut up. And I am not telling you again." Ceikle said real softly, "Here is what I want you both to do. Pack up your stuff. We are going to check out early. You tell the clerk at the desk you are going to stay at some friend's house. Do not make any slip up or everyone will get killed, including the clerk and anyone in the lobby."

Taral told Deton, "We better do what he tells us, I think he is a little touched." Ceikle jumped up and yelled at Taral, "Do not start with your remarks. I had enough of you two. Now let's get going, and keep a smile when we get down stairs." They checked out and got into a six-passenger shuttle with the driver waiting. They drove to the edge of town where a large house was sitting back from the road, hidden behind the woods. They all got out and went in the house, which was well furnished with some pretty expensive furniture. They took Taral upstairs to one of the rooms, Deton assumed it was a bedroom. The two men came down right away, so I guess nothing happened. Ceikle told Deton to sit down so they could have a little chat. Deton asked, "Now what the hell do you want from me?"

"I will tell you want I want, commander."

Deton butted in, "Third Commander."

Ceikle said, "Whatever. I want all the scheduled flights to and from the spacecity, and the number of soldiers and personnel." Deton said, "I cannot give you that information because I do not have it. And if I did have it, which you would not know, I still would not give it to you!"

Ceikle went up to Deton and backhanded him across the face, quite hard. The sting made Deton reel his head back, and a little blood trickled from his mouth, down his chin. "We will see about that, get up and start walking up the stairs."

Ceikle and one of the other guys followed Deton and went in the room where Taral was lying on the bed with her hands tied to the bed post. Ceikle had a pair of shackles with a three foot chain. He unlocked the shackle and put the key in his pocket. Then he shackled Deton's wrists, putting the chain around the pole support that was holding up the loft on one end of the room. Deton had a full view of Taral lying on the bed. "When you see what is going on, maybe you will change your mind." Deton really got pissed off and tried to break loose. Ceikle said, "You're wasting your time." He told the guy with the weapon to leave the room, that he had everything under control. "Now are you going to tell me what I want to know about Thrae's spaceships, or are you going to watch me fuck the shit out of your new wife?"

Deton screamed out, "You son of a bitch. If I get loose I'll kill you, I will kill you."

Taral said, "Do not tell him anything because he had defected to the country of Jarconi, the enemy. Now he is back as a spy."

Ceikle laughed at both of them. "You're not going to tell me, well take a good look, Deton." Ceikle started to rip her clothes off, laughing at Deton, trying to break loose, Deton noticed one of the two bolts were missing, holding the post in place, leaving the post loose. He pushed it back and forth a little more and it moved a bit more. *If only I could get that other bolt out.* Ceikle had almost all of Taral's clothes off. Taral spit at him, calling him a stupid brutal animal. "When this planet goes you are going to go with it!"

"What are you talking about bitch? It will not be long before the country of Jarconi will take over the whole planet, you and everyone else."

Ceikle started to run his hands over her body when one of his cronies was pounding on the door hollering, "Konix is on the communicator. It is very important!" Ceikle said, "Shit! I will be right down."

"You mean to say Konix is doing business with you? Konix is as big a moron as you are Ceikle."

Ceikle said, "When I come back up, we will see who the moron is." Ceikle unlocked the door, laughing, saying, "Do not go away, I'll be right back."

His crony asked, "You want me to watch them?"

Ceikle said, "What for? He is chained up and she is tied down, so where are they going to go." They left and shut the door.

Deton said, "What a pair. Ceikle a fanatic, and Konix a rotten pimp gunrunner."

The next chapter is the story of Konix reincarnated from planet Thrae to life on planet Earth.

Six

Konix—Pimp on Planet Thrae

Konix was born in the city of Baco in the country of Sargarity on Planet Thrae. He was born in 1980 planet Thrae time. His mother was a single parent, and a prostitute. Konix observed throughout his young life all of the many men from many walks of life who slept with his mother. He originally thought this was normal, due to his naiveté. He went to school on and off, but he felt he really did not learn anything. He was always being taunted by the other guys. He tried to ignore them, but this only made him bitter. Konix grew to dislike everybody, especially himself and his mother. He endured this hate-filled way of life until he was about sixteen years old. He worked at various places to have extra money for himself. His mother bought some food, but usually blew the rest on booze and some kind of weed.

Konix's mother had three other girls working with her, until one day one of the girls contracted a disease. She passed it on to one of the customers, and probably others. One of the customers, who was a steady, went for a checkup where it was discovered he had the disease, and went berserk.

Konix was having lunch in the kitchen when he heard someone yelling and swearing. The door was kicked open. This guy stormed in and looked at Konix for a moment, raising his weapon. At that instant, Konix ran through the living room, and out the front door. The intruder ran after him. To the intruder's surprise, the three girls and Konix's mother were sitting around the table looking at the intruder with stunned looks on their faces. Before the girls had a chance to say anything or react, the intruder slew all four of the women so fast they did not even know what hit them. The intruder then turned the weapon on himself and blew his brains out. Konix had to clean up the bloody mess after the authorities had taken the bodies down to the morgue.

Konix was eighteen years old when this happened. He did not know exactly how to handle the situation, for he never lived anywhere else. At least his mother owned the house. Konix, however, really did not have much money to keep it up. He searched the whole house for anything worth money. He found some money, but it was nothing really to brag about. He also found a collection of old pictures. What really pissed him off was that a few of the pictures were of his mother and a black male holding a baby, who looked like he was half black. Konix read the back, which had the name of his mother, Monic, Jart, and baby Konix. That is when Konix almost flipped with rage. He ran to look in the mirror and said, "No wonder I always looked dark complexioned." Screaming and yelling, "You rotten sons of bitches, the both of you! Mother, I am glad you are dead! If I ever catch up with Jart, it will be his turn. I hate both of you."

After a so-called simple funeral, with almost no one attending, Konix noticed a tall light-skinned black male who looked like the person in the pictures. He walked up to him and asked, "Are you Jart?"

The reply was, "Yes."

Konix, with a hidden hate said, "Really, and I am your so-called son; but I do not care. I did not know you for eighteen years, and I do not care if I know you for another hundred and eighteen years!"

Jart said, "We might as well be friends because the house belongs to me. If you still want to live here, we might as well get along with each other."

Konix said, "Bullshit! This is my mother's house and it now belongs to me."

Jart said, "As long as I am your father, you will listen to me! We will both live here and I will show you how to make money." Jart brought in a few of his girls and told them I was his son, and to take care of me. They sure did that. I had sex just about every day, even Jart came on to me to suck him off, which made me feel like a pervert. I guess I did not know what I was doing because I was high on some kind of crap Jart was giving me. Konix still despised Jart because it was his fault for making Konix a halfbreed, and that he showed up when his mother died. Konix thought there was something fishy.

After about a year of this bullshit of pimping, gambling, and selling dope to people, even to young kids, I got tired of Jart taking most of the proceeds. Jart would say, "This is for you kid, for your future."

Konix would say, "What future? I am almost twenty years old, this is my future." Jart would always intimidate Konix, threatening to throw him out if he did not shape up.

One day there was a turn of events, when this guy knocked at the door. He looked about forty-five years old, good looking, and a little dark in complexion, like he came from one of the southern islands. He asked if Monic was home.

I said, "No, she died over a year ago."

This fellow said, "What?"

You could see some tears come into his eyes, he sat

71

down and was silent until Konix asked, "What do you want of her?"

He said his name was Unore and once was married to Monic over twenty years ago. "I happened to be in the city, and decided to say hello to her."

Konix looked at Unore and said, "You sure look familiar, because I resemble you." Konix was about to shit his pants and yelled, "That son of a bitch said he was my father."

Konix asked Unore, "How come you never came around before, and what happened?" Unore said, "It was like this. I came home one day a few hours early, and caught Monic in bed with this fellow named, I believe, Jart. Monic said she was already pregnant, that the baby would still look like me. I tried to fight this Jart fellow, but he was too much for me. He beat me mercifully, and threw me out of my own house. Monic did not do much of anything, just looked on in horror." Jart told Unore if he ever saw him around here again that he would kill him. Unore figured why fight it, she made her bed so she will live in it. I believe that Jart was a little touched anyway. Unore could not even throw them out of the house, so he went down to the law office and signed the house over to Monic and also stipulated, if anything happened to her that her children would receive the property, since she was pregnant with his child.

"Then I moved back to my native land in the islands." By this time Konix was at a boiling point, ready to explode. He started to talk but was so mad all he could do was stutter. Finally, Konix calmed down a little and said, "I really did not know Jart. My mother told me once that my father left on an out-of-town job when I was not even a year old, and got killed in a transport accident. I guess she was always a prostitute, and that's how she made money so we could live. When my mother got killed, Jart showed up claiming this house was his. He lied to me, this is not his house and he is not my father. What am I to do, this guy is a mean machine?"

We heard a transport pull up to the front of the house and a couple of girls get out, including Jart, laughing while walking into the house. The laughing stopped, and they just stood there momentarily until Jart finally recognized Unore and said, in a disgusting voice, "What the hell are you doing here? I told you if I ever caught you here again, I would kill you." But Unore beat him to the draw, because Unore had a satchel with an army projectile weapon, and before Jart could blink another eye Unore shot him dead, with about six shots, which splattered Jart all over the parlor wall and the girls who were standing next to him. The girls screamed and almost passed out. "Man what a mess," Konix screamed out. "Good you stupid fuck, you had it coming."

Since no one knew Unore's identity, they would not know who to accuse. Unore said he was glad to see Konix and to take care of himself, and said, "I may never see you again." Konix said, "Goodbye, I am glad I met you too." The police were called in and asked all the necessary questions. The girls said they never saw the man before and Konix said the same thing. "This man was in town and wanted to talk with Jart and shot him to my surprise." The police said, "Well that is one more bad egg we don't have to contend with."

The authorities called for the meat wagon and took Jart's body to the morgue. He probably will be buried in a potter's field. He had no friends, and Konix was sure as hell not going to have any funeral, or attend any ceremony.

Konix was mumbling to himself, "This is getting to be a habit, cleaning up all this blood again." This time he got the girls to clean up the place. He told the two girls he was going to run this operation, and if they wanted to stay they'd have to follow his instructions, and that goes for the other girls. Konix said, "I will show you how to run this business to make it look legitimate."

Konix rode down to the civil building where all the records were kept. He asked for a duplicate deed to the property. He showed his identification. They found that his mother did own the house and he showed them her death certificate. The house was automatically turned over to Konix. All Konix had to do was have his picture taken and sign a few papers, and legally the house belonged to him.

It was about three weeks since Jart was killed, and the girls were taking care of the customers. Some of the old customers did not come anymore since Jart was killed. Konix did not care because that shithead was gone. Konix had never been in Jart's room and decided to clean everything out and burn it. He did not want anything to remind him of that prick. Konix opened the door to Jart's room and about gagged. What a mess, and it stank. It looked like he had not cleaned this place since he moved in. Konix started hauling everything out and burning all of it in the backyard. He even hauled the rug down and burned it. In the corner wall where the bed was, Konix noticed a small three-by-three door that was nailed shut. The nails were not in all the way, like the door was removed a number of times. Konix pulled the door from the wall and his eyes got big. Here was a large cache of money, gold, jewels, and dope. Konix never saw so much money in all his life. He figured there was enough there to retire a couple of times over.

Konix got the money and put it in another hiding place, and a little at a time, he started to remodel the house. He made it larger with a few extra rooms, a few massage parlors, and picked up a few more girls, usually runaways. He had them cleaned up, and they all wore beautiful clothing. Once they got under Konix's spell, they were hooked. They were all intimidated. Konix really never touched the girls, but if they got out of hand or tried to cheat him, he would beat the crap out of them. They would be indisposed for awhile, but would never pull the same crap twice. Konix would shirk the issue, like it never happened. The girls did not run to the law because Konix had most of them paid off.

After a couple of years, Konix had half of the city of Baco in his control, and stole all the white prostitutes from the black pimps. Konix hated the blacks with a passion, since he lived with Jart. Konix would get his cronies, corner the black pimps and beat the living hell out of them—and leave them almost dead. If they retaliated, you might as well consider them dead. After a matter of time, there weren't anymore pimps to worry about. Konix thought about taking over the whole city of Baco in the near future. He really did not need anymore wealth, he just wanted control. His hate for black people got to be an obsession. He would beat a black person just for looking at him.

One day he took a couple of girls to the beach for a picnic and swimming. They played around all afternoon having a ball. There were a few people on the beach picnicking and swimming. Konix said, "We should have a big blowout one of these days with all the girls, and invite all the big wheels. We would have a blast."

It was getting late in the afternoon and most of the people left the beach. Konix and the girls were having too much fun to leave just yet. One of the girls said, "I will race you to that big tree at the other end of the beach." Konix said he would give them a head start. The two girls took off first, and Konix followed. They ran about a hundred yards and noticed a big bonfire and a bunch of fellows horsing around. They all had big physiques. They spotted Konix and the girls, and started to whistle and make remarks, not at the girls, but at Konix's body. All of a sudden one of them said, "Let's get 'em." Konix and the girls ran as fast as they could, but not fast enough. They caught up to them and dragged them back to the bonfire. The girls were screaming for help. It was getting dark, which made it worse and the beach was almost deserted. Konix was fighting back with all he had, but they had him overpowered. Konix finally realized these guys were a bunch of gays. To Konix, they were just a bunch of queers. Konix was hurting and said, "You do not know who you are messing with." The girls were scared out of their wits, crying and screaming.

The gays held all three down and took turns raping them in the ass, and jamming their penises in their mouths. There were about a dozen guys at this party, and the sodomy went on half of the night, until the authorities showed up, who were Konix's friends because he paid them off. They saw what was happening. The gays were all half in the bag and started running in different directions. The police shot down four and caught two. Konix and the girls were so screwed up they ended up in the hospital for a week. It did not take much more to get Konix on the loose end of his situation that was building up; any agitation and he would blow up. He really did not let anything get in his way. He even started to treat all the girls very badly, hitting them for nothing. He hated the blacks because Jart made him perform blowjobs on him, and now the gays. Konix never had anything against the gays, as long as they did not bother him. However, ever since the park incident, Konix hated them more than the blacks. Konix and his cronies would go out and look for gays, cut off their cocks and jam their cocks in their mouths, after they beat them up. Some bled to death, and the ones that lived were just cockless. Konix got away with it because he had the paid-off police on his side. They said it was the other gay gangs that were commiting the crimes. Konix continued these crimes for a couple of years. Everyone was afraid of Konix, and soon he controlled the whole city of Baco and its suburbs. He had a real business going with all his pimps working for him, and now he turned to gun running. He would buy all kinds of weapons and sell them to the enemy that came from Jarconi. He figured if Jarconi got control of the country of Sargarity, they would automatically control planet Thrae. The country of Jarconi had a lot of blacks in their military, and also spies. Konix did not care, he would have their asses kicked if they got near him.

They are now in the year 2010, and Konix just turned thirty years of age. The way his life was going, sometimes like a maniac, he began to look older, closer to fifty.

The bombing started on the west coast, from the country of Jarconi. Konix said, "This means war," and he was more defiant than before. He even started to ambush the military personnel of Sagarity. Konix heard and read of the warnings of the end of the existence of the planet, and dismissed it as a hoax. He said, "They are all full of shit," and went about his business.

In a couple of months, things started to get heated up. It was a very dry heat, with a steady wind blowing. Jarconi was sending missiles to the larger cities so the leaders of Sargarity would surrender to their demands. This was the beginning of the end of planet Thrae. Jarconi sent one missile too many, which started a chain reaction combined with the sun radiation going through the destroyed ozone to the planet; and the dried atmosphere, with a bursting crack of fire. The wind picked up speed and pushed and destroyed everything in its path with volcanic activity.

Konix noticed the planet trembling and getting hotter and hotter with explosions all around. All his girls were frightened, and they got on their knees, praying for forgiveness and crying with torturous pain in their eyes. Konix said, "Snap out of it. Jarconi is bombing the cities, and we naturally feel the effects. This should be over soon." Konix went out the door, stumbling over the shaking threshold, hanging on to the railing. "God damn, what the hell is going on around here," watching a huge fire ball as big as a mountain rolling toward him. That was the end of Konix, for he burned to a crisp from the heat before the fireball even hit the city or him, and destroyed everything in its path with quakes and volcanoes erupting. Buildings crumbled to the ground in a pile of rubble, and scattered all over the land, and the rivers and lakes dried up. All living things were gone. Konix never believed in space and the evacuation, or the end of the planet. He was a very naïve person.

Konix was killed in the big fire on planet Thrae in the year 2010. Konix was in limbo for a number of years. The heavens did not know what to do with him. They did not want to send him to hell just yet, until they tried something different.

Seven
Konix Reincarnated to Planet Earth

Konix was reincarnated to planet Earth, born to black parents, in Prattsville, Alabama, in the United States in 1943. His mother named him after the country's President Roosevelt, since he was doing a good job during the World War. Roosevelt Jackson knew from the beginning that something was amiss. He could almost feel himself not belonging to these people for the longest time. He looked at himself many times and said, "I am black like they are, so what is the problem?"

What Roosevelt did not know was that he was reincarnated as a black person, so he would learn from the prejudice he had toward black people in his past life as Konix. If this did not make him figure out the consequences of past actions, then he really was naïve. Roosevelt learned how degrading it was to sit at the back of the bus, and not to be served in white restaurants. Down South they were always called nigger by the white folks. Roosevelt went to an all-black school in Prattsville, because the schools in the '40s and '50s were all segregated down South. Roosevelt was a pretty bright kid, with good grades and with some sense and sensibility. He was the youngest of five children and his parents were sharecroppers, and rather poor. Roosevelt still had that strange feeling of something being amiss, especially when he was around white folks, like he was one of them.

One time there was a group of white kids playing ball. As he was watching, but ball was hit toward him on the ground, so he stopped it. He was ready to throw it back when they yelled at him, "Drop that ball, nigger." Roosevelt dropped the ball and started to walk away. Then the other white boys said, "Get back here." Roosevelt did not like that tone of voice and started to run. The whites started to run after Roosevelt and caught up to him. They started to beat him up. "Who told you to touch that ball. Now you got it all contaminated with your nigger skin." They continued to beat him until until he was motionless. While Roosevelt was being beaten up, he was between a rock and a hard place. He got this very far away feeling, like he did not know if he was one of the white guys beating on a black person, or if he was black being beat up. Roosevelt lay there for the longest time, he really did not want to move. His senses were a little jumbled up, and he could see a faint vision of his other life on planet Thrae, as Konix, looking down on one of his pimp victims after he and his cronies beat him up. After that incident, he felt too intimidated by the white folks, so he stayed away from them.

He was now a junior in high school, and a very good looking kid. A lot of girls had an eye on him. Roosevelt never had any interest in girls. Instead, especially in gym class and the showers, he would eye up the physiques of the other guys, wishing he could get close to them, but was afraid to try it. Roosevelt did not have too many friends, because they knew he was a little queer. But he was a very smart lad, with good grades. That was his forte, to study and learn everything about anything.

Roosevelt graduated in 1960 with honors. He specialized in journalism and received an award for swimming. After graduation, he got a job at the local newspaper as a copyboy, which to him did not amount to anything, unless they put him where all the main news was. He worked at the job for a couple of years without any promotion or raise. It seemed like there was no future in that field. He looked for another job and found one at a book company. He quit the non-promotional newspaper. They started him in the bookbinding department and he was told he could work his way up in other fields in the book publishing company.

He worked six months in bookbinding, when he met another black fellow who was just hired. They got to be friends, and to Roosevelt's surprise he was also gay. They kind of started a relationship, going out together and doing things that were unthinkable in those times. This other black fellow's name was Jason. He said the company told him he could work his way up if he was a good worker. Roosevelt said that is what they told him. After another year of this bookbinding bullcrap, Roosevelt went to the office and talked to the head supervisor, asking for a position in the printing department. He was told all the positions were for a four year training period; and because of the Vietnam War, Roosevelt was draft bait. Roosevelt was a little perturbed when he left the office, thinking of the almost two years wasted in the bookbinding department. He told Jason what happened and Jason said, "That figures." He said he did not think the war had anything to do with it, that it was because they were black. Roosevelt told Jason, "I guess we will have to try something else." Roosevelt said he knew a lot of journalism, but no one would hire him because he did not have a college education. I guess we're stuck here for awhile in the bookbinding department. It did not last much longer anyway. Roosevelt and Jason were caught kissing in one of the aisles in the stockroom by the foreman, and they both got fired. Roosevelt did not care anyway because he got his draft papers for the army, and had to report in a couple of weeks to the induction center. Jason was rejected because of a murmur in his heart. He said good-bye to Roosevelt, and told him to write, and that he would miss him. Roosevelt was sent to Fort Leonard Wood in Missouri for basic training, and then shipped out to Vietnam. He tried to hide the fact that he was gay, but it showed a little by the way he talked, and the way he moved around. He was a good soldier and did everything that everyone did. He made friends with a few guys, including the white soldiers because they were all in this together, and he found out that there was not too much discrimination. Of course there are always a few that do not like anyone. There were two white hillbillies who were always on Roosevelt's back. They were always calling him a queerball, and trying to pick a fight. Roosevelt would try to ignore them, but they were persistant to want to start something.

Roosevelt was a little more aggressive since he entered the army. He told them to get lost, and then it started. One of the hillbillies said, "What did you say?" and grabbed Roosevelt from behind with his arm around his neck.

Roosevelt gave him a quick elbow right in his ribs, and he let go in pain. The other hillbilly knocked Roosevelt to the ground straddling him and said, "I am going to beat the fucking shit out of you, you bastard queer." He had him pinned down when he felt a sharp pain in his nuts and rolled over onto his back in agony.

One of Roosevelt's buddies, named Arnold, kicked the hillbilly in the balls, and then kicked him in the ribs. He said, "You fuck with him again, you will not leave Vietnam alive."

The two hillbillies were mumbling in pain. "Do not have your back to us in the field, because you will not leave Vietnam either, you cocksucker."

Roosevelt's buddy put his arm around his shoulder and said, "Let's get out of here."

Arnold said, "We have known each other since basic training, and I know you're gay and so do the rest of our buddies; and so what, we're all friends."

There was a tear in Roosevelt's eye. He choked with emotion and said, "I really had not had many friends when I was growing up because of what I am, but I love you guys, as friends, of course."

Roosevelt told Arnold, "I have to tell you something, you may think I am full of shit, but here goes anyway; I believe I am reincarnated from a planet called Thrae. Throughout my life, I would get flashbacks of my being a white person. I was a pimp on this other planet."

"Aw come on Rosy." They started to crack up laughing.

Roosevelt said he was not kidding. "Whenever something would happen, like those two hillbillies beating me up, it made me feel like the aggressor, and I was beating up some gay person. I was a pimp in this other life. My name was Konix and I hated blacks and queers. I used to beat them up, and even kill them. The queers especially! Me and my cronies would beat them up and even cut off their cocks and jam them in their mouths. This planet I lived on was finally destroyed by fire, and I was killed, and then reincarnated to planet Earth as a black gay person for punishment."

Now Arnold was about doubled over with laughter. "Boy, that sure was a fairytale you told." He could not stop laughing.

Roosevelt said, "Laugh all you want, one of these days, you will see it was not a fairytale. Now let's go get something to eat before we go out on patrol."

Two weeks later, while out on a patrol of eight men, Roosevelt and Arnold were taking up the rear. They hiked about two and a half miles on and off the path. The lead man, or point man, was about fifty feet ahead of the rest of the patrol, when he stepped on a mine that went off. It blew him about twenty feet in the air with a leg blown off just below the knee, going to the left. Then all hell broke loose. They were being ambushed. The six GIs ahead all got mowed down and killed. Roosevelt and Arnold dashed off the path into the bushes as the Vietcong appeared to check over the bodies and take the weapons and other things.

There were six enemies. Arnold said, "Let's throw two hand grenades apiece and open fire at the same time." They did just that. They did not know if the gunfire killed the Cong first or the hand grenades. Whatever, they were all dead. Roosevelt and Arnold checked all the bodies on the ground to see if anyone was alive.

Roosevelt said, "They all look dead to me." Then they supplied themselves with more hand grenades and ammo from the dead soldiers.

Arnold figured that the enemy's camp had to be nearby. They were trying to decide whether to go ahead, or go back, since there were only two guys. Roosevelt said, "We're this far and probably closer to their camp. If we go back, they might find the bodies and go after us and find our camp." They figured to go ahead. They went about a half a mile and could hear screaming and cussing in English, and a lot of laughing and talking in Vietnamese.

We edged closer, and to our horror, they had four GIs tied up against some flat boards and were using them for target practice, with knives, like a huge dart board. They were not trying to kill them right off, just throwing these knives that looked like bowies, to see how close they could nip them. It looked like they were hit a few times.

Roosevelt could hardly bear to look, but to his amazement he said, "Arnold, aren't two of them the hillbillies that picked on me the other day?"

"Well I'll be damned," said Arnold. "We ought to leave them there, but we have two other guys to try and save."

Roosevelt said, "I do not care if the hillbillies were by themselves, I would still save them."

Arnold said, "OK, OK, but they do not deserve it."

Arnold said, "How do we do this, so far we see six Cong; four are sitting in a group eating, while two are using their victims for target practice? We cannot throw hand grenades. They are too close to the GIs. We'll shoot them. I'll take the four sitting and you take the other two. We have to do this fast in case there are others around. On the count of three; one . . . two . . . three." They fired simultaneously and got all of them in a few seconds. They ran to the prisoners and started to free them.

Arnold looked at the hillbillies and said, "We ought to leave you here." They did not say a word, besides they were moaning from being cut a number of times.

All of a sudden there was a blast of shots. One hit Arnold in the leg. Arnold bent down to pick up his rifle, and Roosevelt beat him to it and shot the Cong who was lying on the ground wounded. Arnold was pissed, and went around hobbling on one foot, shooting all of them over and over again yelling, "Come on you sons-a-bitches, try shooting me again." They finished untying the four GIs and they all hobbled out of the area. Roosevelt was the only one who was in good shape. They went back the same way, moaning and groaning with pain. It was slow going, passing the bodies where they were ambushed. One of the hillbillies said, "Oh my God what a mess." They went about another half mile and could hear talking and laughing. It was not English. They hid in the bushes until they passed. Arnold said, "Do not make a sound or we are dead ducks."

There were only three of the enemy. Arnold said, "Let

85

them go. We do not know how many others there are."

Roosevelt said, "They will find the bodies and they will be back. We still have about two miles to go."

Arnold said, "Let's take our chances." The three went by them, for about fifty feet when they stopped arguing with each other, as they looked at the ground where the trail of blood was, and one bent down with his finger and noticed the blood was fresh. They started to backtrack, following the trail of blood to about twenty-five feet, when Roosevelt jumped out of the bushes at the same time firing his automatic, killing the three, but not before he got one slug in the shoulder.

In pain, Roosevelt said, "Let's get out of here." It seemed like forever to get back to camp. They all collapsed to the ground. The medics had them all on stretchers, waiting for the choppers to pick them up. One of the GIs died on the stretcher from loss of blood. One of the hillbillies had been receiving blood plasma intervenously. He was bandaged up. They asked a few questions about what happened. Arnold told the captain of the ambush at the enemy camp; and how they fled. He said that Roosevelt was the real hero, and that he saw the three Cong face to face and that he slayed them.

The two hillbillies apologized to Roosevelt and thanked Arnold and him for saving their lives. They got to be very good friends. They also kept in touch after they were discharged. Roosevelt and Arnold were sent back to the States on a hospital ship. Their tour of duty was up anyway. The other three wounded stayed at an army hospital in Hanoi.

Roosevelt and Arnold were discharged from the army after a ceremony in their honor. Both were awarded the Distinguished Service Medal and Purple Heart for bravery in the line of duty. This made Roosevelt very happy, because he was finally accepted as a human being, and not because of what he was. He also realized the feeling of how it was to be black and gay; being picked on all the time. He figured he could never justify the wrong he had done to the other groups of blacks and gays on the other planet. However, he would give it a try.

Roosevelt did write regularly to his parents in Prattsville, Alabama. He wrote to his very best friend Jason, who was rejected from the army. In the last letter Roosevelt wrote to Jason, he said he had a couple of weeks to go before being discharged. He could hardly wait to be reunited with him. He indicated he would call when he got to the States. Roosevelt, with a group of other GIs were flown to Fort Leonard Wood for processing and left for home. Roosevelt got a ride from camp to Kansas City, Missouri, and took a train home. Roosevelt bought a ticket, but still had a couple of hours before boarding the train. He first called home and talked to his mother and father. Then he called his friend Jason, but got no answer. It started to get dark with a little drizzle, when Roosevelt boarded the train heading for Montgomery, then Prattsville, Alabama. Roosevelt sat down about half way up the aisle, next to some old man sitting next to the window. The old man looked up and without saying a word turned away, looking out the window. To himself Roosevelt said, "Fine, I will not ask any stupid questions and I will not receive any stupid answers." Roosevelt had a couple of magazines to read anyway. They traveled for a few hours until they hit Little Rock, Arkansas, for their first stop. Roosevelt got a snack and then phoned again, trying to get ahold of Jason. There was still no answer. Maybe Jason had something important he was doing. Roosevelt thought he would call later. He got back on the train and took a snooze. This time Roosevelt sat next to the window. The old man must have gotten off. It was like he was not there anyway. Rosey was asleep when the train pulled into the station at Montgomery, Alabama. It took him awhile to get his senses back when he woke up. He got his baggage and got off the train and headed for the men's room before his bladder burst. His thoughts were on and off, why Jason was not at home to answer his calls. Rosey called one more time, and still no answer. He called his parents to tell them that he was in Montgomery and was to take the next bus home to Prattsville. He said, "See you guys later," and hung up.

It took a little over a hour to get to Prattsville, where his parents were waiting for him at the station. Rosey got off the bus, hurrying toward them to give them both a big hug. Driving home, Rosey asked if they heard from Jason the last few days, "I tried calling him, but did not get any answer."

His mom said they had not heard from Jason for at least a couple of weeks. "Maybe you will get hold of him tomorrow, since it is the weekend." When they arrived home, Rosey tried one more time calling Jason, and still no answer.

Rosey's mother had supper already made and sat down in prayer and ate. Rosey's mother said, "Your brothers and sister are coming over Sunday to see you. They are all excited because they have not seen you for such a long time."

Rosey said, "I will be very glad to see them too. I'm going to bed. I've had a long day and I'm tired." It took Rosey a long time to fall asleep because Jason was on his mind. He thought maybe Jason did not like him anymore and would not answer the phone.

Rosey woke up about nine o'clock and went downstairs into the kitchen where his mother was making his breakfast. She said, "I heard you tip-toeing around up there, so I decided to start making you some breakfast. Your pappy was up bright and early and left to go fishing. He figured you were tired, so he let you be." Rosey told his mother that the food was delicious, and how he missed her cooking while he was in the army. He said he was going over to Jason's place to surprise him.

About an hour and a half later, Rosey's mother heard him come in the door half screaming and half crying, cussing something terrible. He ran up to his room and slammed the door behind him. Rosey's mother said, "What in the world!" She went up to his room, opened the door, and there he was, huddled in a corner mumbling in some language she never heard before. She thought maybe it was Vietnamese, but it sounded stranger than that. He was trembling and crying and had a very faraway look.

"Oh my God," she said, and put her arms around him. "Come Rosey, your mama's here, everything is all right." She was sitting next to him on the floor trying to soothe him.

Finally after about ten minutes, he settled down. She said, "What is the matter my baby? Tell me what is bothering you."

Rosey looked up into his mother's eyes, choking and sobbing at the same time, "Mama they killed Jason."

"Oh Rosey, what makes you say that?"

"Jason's landlady told me she had the funeral for him, since he had no kin folk. She said he was on the wrong side of town walking down this one street where some shooting broke out between some dope peddlers, and Jason got caught in the crossfire. He was killed instantly."

"Oh Rosey, that is terrible! What is this world coming to? You stay in your room and rest awhile. I will fix you a nice hot lunch."

Rosey stayed in his room for days, and would not come

out. His mother was getting worried about him. Even when his brothers and sister all came over on Sunday he stayed in his room. They had to go up to say hello to him. They all said they were glad he was home. All Rosey said was, "Me too," and kept staring out the window at the tree in the backyard.

His family was hoping he would snap out of it. It was like he never came home. Rosey was having all kinds of flashbacks of when he was a ruthless son of a bitch; always having his own way. Nobody dared oppose him, or they were in deep trouble. But these things were not on planet Earth.

Finally, after a couple of weeks of solitude, Rosey emerged from his room. He told his mother he was going out for awhile. His mother said, "Aren't you going to wear your civilian clothes? You have not shaved in two weeks."

Rosey gave his mother a kiss on the forehead and said, "I will catch up with myself later." It was about eight P.M. He took a bus into town to see what was going on, and maybe to check out a few bars. He thought maybe he would put his sorrows in a couple of drinks. He was going to go to Jason's grave site and figured, *What for? He is gone and nothing is going to bring him back.*

Rosey started to go to bars almost every night, still thinking of Jason and the good times they had. He could not believe he got caught in some stupid crossfire. Now Rosey's mother started to worry and told him, "Sooner or later you have to forget him. You have to get a job. You cannot keep asking your father and me for money all the time."

Rosey said, "I will get a job next week."

But next week never came around. His mother got mad because of his drinking. She said, "That is the last straw! As much as I love you, I cannot stand your actions anymore, and we are not giving you any more money."

Rosey had to get a job because he was out of money. He got a job at a local newspaper as a proofreader, which was better than nothing. Rosey went out only a couple times a month. He saved a few dollars so he could buy a car. He finally bought some beat-up Ford. It got him around. He even drove to Montgomery a couple of weekends. He was always back in time so he could get up and go to work.

One weekend he drove to Montgomery, had dinner at a restaurant, and took in a movie. At about eleven P.M., after the movie, he hit some dives that had a lot of people dancing to jazz music. There was so much smoke you could almost cut your way through. Rosey had to wait awhile before he could even get a drink. After buying his drink he stood up with it in his hand; sipping and watching the dancing and listening to the music. A half an hour went by before someone left the bar. He snapped up the stool in a hurry. Besides, his glass was empty anyway. He ordered another seven and seven. After another forty-five minutes, the couple next to him left. A creepy-looking guy sat next to him. Rosey did not care who was next to him. At this point he was a little high, so this creep started a conversation with Rosey, telling his war stories about Vietnam and how he killed all those Viet Cong. He explained how he was always high on dope, so if he got shot, it would not hurt so much. This creep was as high as Rosey was. He told Rosey when he came back to the States, nobody would hire him because he had no skills. The creep told all those employers that he fought in Vietnam. All they said was, "So?" The creep told all of them to go fuck themselves.

He said his name was Jimmy, and Rosey told him his name. Anyway, this Jimmy told Rosey he met a dope dealer and now he sells dope. He said he never saw so much money in all of his life. "I do not let anyone get in my way either." They both had a few more drinks until they were talking with a slur. At about two A.M., Rosey said he had enough and was going back home. Jimmy said, "Here let me give you one of these downers. It should make you sleep better. In fact, you can come to my place and sleep it off." Rosey said, "I don't think so. Besides I have my car, so I can drive home to Prattsville." Jimmy said, "That is a long way to go in your condition. I really do not know." Said Rosey, "We just met and I do not know anything about you." At that instance, this other fellow walked in. "Ah, there you are Jimmy. I was looking all over for you." Jimmy said, "Hi Leonard. I want you to meet a friend of mine." With his slurry voice, "Rosey, this is Leonard; Leonard, this is Rosey." Jimmy said, "Come on, just one more drink since Leonard is here."

"OK. OK," Rosey groaned. "Since it is only Saturday. I do not have to get up for work until Monday morning."

The bartender poured three drinks. Jimmy lifted his and said, "Cheers." Rosey and Leonard lifted their glasses and clinked them together. Rosey started to take a sip, staring at the ring on Leonard's right hand and almost choked. "What's the matter with you?" said Jimmy. Rosey said he was drinking it too fast. Leonard said, "You'd better watch that stuff."

Rosey kept looking at the ring on Leonard's finger. "What the hell are you looking at?" Leonard asked. "Your ring, I never saw such an unusual one like that? Don't they call that a cat's eye or something like that? I have to look at it a little closer." Rosey indicated that he liked it. "Do you want to sell it? Where did you get it? Maybe they have another one I could buy." Leonard explained, "I won it in a crap game, and will not part with it."

"OK, I just asked. Maybe I will take you up on staying at your place tonight. Besides, I don't feel like driving home tonight, or this morning."

"We will go with Leonard since he is more sober than we are. We will drop you off to your car when you get up. You will probably have a hangover anyways."

They drove a couple of miles to Jimmy's place. He lived on the second floor. When they got inside Jimmy said he was going to bed. Leonard asked Rosey if he wanted the couch or the bed. Rosey said he would take the couch. At this point he said he could sleep anywhere. Rosey really did not fall asleep that fast. He kept thinking about that ring. Saying to himself, "That ring belonged to Jason." Rosey knew because it had the same nick on the side, close to the stone. Rosey now had to figure out how Leonard really acquired that ring. He was beginning to think Jason got killed in a manner other than by crossfire. He finally fell asleep, but not for long. Rosey was listening to an argument in the other room between Jimmy and Leonard about money. Leonard was telling him to come up with the coke money.

"If the kingpin finds out we haven't got it, we are both dead. Besides, I am getting sick of your drunkenness."

Jimmy, with his slurry voice told Leonard to go fuck himself. Leonard said, "He should not have gotten in with you."

Jimmy replied, "Why did you, you dumb nigger."

Leonard said, "If you do not shut up, I will shoot you, like I did Louie and Jason. They were two dumb queers that liked to suck each other off."

Rosey's eyes got as big as saucers when he heard that. He started to tremble with rage. He ran in the other room, knocking Jimmy down to the floor. By Leonard's surprise, Rosey put his strong hands around Leonard's neck, choking the shit out of him. Jimmy staggered up from the floor toward Rosey, by the same time Leonard grabbed his gun out of his belt and fired at close range, grazing Rosey's side, and hitting Jimmy by accident, right square in the chest. Jimmy slumped against Rosey, and Rosey knocked the gun out of Leonard's hand as they were crashing to the floor. Rosey did not let go of the grip around Leonard's neck, squeezing tighter. Leonard was gasping and turning colors. Rosey was swearing every name in the book at him, until he went limp. He gave one more quick squeeze. Rosey was sweating so much, he could not see straight.

It was getting hot and smokey in the apartment. Rosey was getting flashbacks of the end of planet Thrae, when everything was ablaze. He kicked the door open to the kitchen. He figured the window opened and the wind blew the curtains to the stove, which must have been on. The whole room was on fire. He ran back to the other room, half dazed, speaking both English and Thrae, hollering, "Get the girls out." He grabbed the keys on the dresser and ran out the door into the hallway where a few people were coming. Rosey was screaming in Thrae language. Half way down the steps he got his full faculties. He hollered back, "Call the fire department and police."

Rosey sobered up in a hurry. He jumped into Leonard's car, and drove to the club in a calm, steady way, so he did not look suspicious. He parked Leonard's car about a block away from his car, wiped his prints off the steering wheel, and other parts. He walked to his car like nothing happened, and drove home to Prattsville, arriving about five A.M. Rosey's mother asked, "Why are you home so early? I thought you would be home tonight?" Rosey's mother screamed, "Now what is that blood coming through your clothing?" Rosey said, "I might be in a little trouble, I do not know." He explained to his mother what happened. How he choked this black guy to death, and how he shot Rosey. He was the one that killed Jason. His mother said he should stay home for a couple of days and see what happens. "I will call work for you and tell them you are too sick to come in."

Monday Rosey got up and took a walk to the drugstore for a paper. There it was on the front page of the *Montgomery.* "Two well-known dope dealers fought it out to the end." It told how one was choking the other until he was shot by the other, and both collapsed. They probably were also overcome by smoke fumes from a fire that was accidently started in the kitchen. Rosey could not believe what he read. This means he is in the clear. Unless there were witnesses that might change the story. Rosey told his mother the paper gave a different account of the story. Then he told his mother, "I have a friend that lives in Cleveland, Ohio. I think I am going to move out there. Besides, there is no future here. I will write to you, and I will come down to see you every now and then."

Rosey gave a couple of weeks' notice to his boss. His boss said he hated to see him leave, that he was a good worker, and wished Rosey lots of luck when he got to Ohio. In another week, Rosey had his bags packed and loaded into his rattletrap car. He hugged his parents and drove off to his new destination. Rosey arrived in Cleveland in a couple of days. He looked up Arnold who lived off Superior Avenue on 65th Street. He knocked on the door of Arnold's apartment, which was on the second floor of a two-suite house. A minute went by. Rosey could hear someone come down the steps. A nice looking white girl answered. What else, Arnold is white?

"I am Rosey. Is Arnold around, or is this the wrong place? I did not know Arnold had a woman."

She said, "Hi Rosey." They both walked up the steps into Arnold's place. "My name is Marie. Make yourself comfortable. Can I fix you a drink? Arnold will be out in a minute. He is taking a shower."

After about ten more minutes, Arnold came out. "You son of a gun. Rosey, how are you. I am glad to see you."

"I am glad to see you, too," said Rosey.

"How long are you staying in Cleveland?"

"I decided to move here and get a job, if they will hire me."

Arnold said, "A smart good-looking guy like you? Hell you won't have any trouble at all. Where are you staying?"

Rosey replied, "Nowhere right now. I have to find a motel or something before it gets dark. Then I will look for something permanent."

Arnold said, "Nonsense, stay here until you find a place, if that is all right with Marie?"

"It is OK with me," said Marie.

"Thank you," Rosey said. "I appreciate it." Rosey also told Marie, "If you find me a little strange, that is because I am a little gay. I told Arnold a story about that when we were in the army together. He cracked up and told me I was dreaming. I will not tell you about it, because if Arnold did not tell you before he sure will sooner or later."

Rosey stayed at Arnold's place for about a week. He got a suite in an apartment complex at 55th and Woodland Avenue. Also, he got a job with a local newspaper company as a copyman, until the newspaper went out of business. From there, he had no trouble getting a job with a larger newspaper company, this time as a journalist. He had a pretty good paycheck every week. He also found a new place out in Lakewood, on Clifton Boulevard near Bunts Road. It was a nice house where he lived on the second floor. After about two years of mostly keeping to himself, he met a black girl who lived a couple of doors down from him. He ran into her a couple of times when getting into his car. They talked on and off. One morning before going to work, she asked Rosey bluntly, "When are you going to ask me out?"

This put Rosey on the spot. Then he told her. "It is like this Angela, I will take you out this Saturday, OK? We will go out to dinner and maybe take in a movie. I might disappoint you in the evening's conversation."

Rosey left for work, saying good-bye to Angela. Rosey sat at his desk when his supervisor came in. He said, "I have something to tell you." With a serious look, Rosey thought to himself, *Oh, oh, here it comes, I am getting canned.* Then his supervisor, with a big smile, said, "Well Rosey you made it! You are going to be a reporter. You had your request in for over two years. Sam is moving to California in a month, and you are taking his place. Good luck in your new job." Rosey thanked his boss and said that made his day.

Saturday rolled around, Rosey picked up Angela about seven o'clock, drove to downtown Cleveland to one of the restaurants, and then to the State Theater. Afterwards, they went down to Short Vincent Street, doing the rounds at the clubs. At the second club, they got a table in a corner and ordered a couple of drinks. Rosey started the conversation, asking Angela if she was having a good time. She said she was having a very good time.

Rosey said, "I have to tell you this story, when I am done you probably will not even talk to me anymore."

Angela said, "Try me." Rosey told her the whole story about how he lived on this other planet Thrae, and how he was reincarnated on Earth as a black gay person.

Angela did not say anything for a couple of minutes. Then she said, "I think you're full of hot air."

Rosey said, "What do you think we're going to do when we leave here? I have no feelings for women. I like you, but I am not attracted to you."

Angela asked, "Did you ever try it with a woman?"

"Not really," said Rosey.

"Well anyway, let's finish our drinks and you can take me home."

They got back to Lakewood, Rosey pulled into his driveway. They got out and he walked Angela to her place. She said, "Come up for a night cap?"

Rosey said, "Okay, if that will make you happy."

Angela lived on the first floor. She unlocked the door and walked in the living room, turning on the light. She told Rosey to make himself comfortable on the couch while she got into something more comfortable and made a couple of drinks. Angela came out holding two drinks in her hands. The lights were low, but Rosey could see how beautiful she looked in the sheer lace light blue gown she was wearing. Angela put the drinks down on the coffee table revealing her goodies to Rosey.

"Wow," said Rosey, "you sure are beautiful!" He had to say something that would not hurt her feelings, even though it did not do anything for him. They both had a few drinks previously when they were out. So they were feeling pretty good. Angela sat down next to Rosey, snuggling up to him. Now Rosey felt he was in a very precarious position. He liked Angela, but his feelings were gay. He had to handle this in a finessed way.

Angela put on some mood music before she sat down. Now she was on him, kissing and fondling his clothes. Before you knew it, most of Rosey's clothes were off. He solved the problem by closing his eyes and believing he was with his late buddy Jason making love. They kept this up until they actually had intercourse. They were both in the clouds from all the drinks they had.

Angela said, "You sure felt good and made me spin around and around."

Rosey finally opened his eyes, realizing he was still on top of her. He told her it was very nice, just to make her feel good. Rosey looked at his watch. "My goodness it is going on five A.M. It is time I should leave."

Angela said, "What for, you are already undressed? So just stay here." She grabbed Rosey's hand and pulled him up from the couch toward the bedroom. Rosey was beat and just fell into the bed. He fell asleep in minutes. Rosey woke up about nine-thirty A.M. To his surprise, Angela was hugging him from behind. Rosey snuck out of bed without waking Angela. He got dressed, went home, and sat on the couch for awhile, thinking of the evening's situation. Asking himself, *What am I getting into? I like Angela, but I have no feelings for women. I guess this is my punishment from planet Thrae. I guess she really did not believe my story.*

Rosey had to tell her to lay off without hurting her feelings, and just stay friends. Since he was already dressed, he jumped in his car and stopped at a restaurant for breakfast. Then he drove down to Edgewater Park and sat in the grass on the hill, overlooking Lake Erie. He sat there for hours, thinking of the two lives he had: one on planet Thrae and this present one. He thought more of this one because it was starting to get a little complicated; especially now that he was going to be a reporter for the *Cleveland Plain Dealer.* It was the middle of the afternoon when he left Edgewater Park and decided to drive over and give Arnold a visit.

Rosey was just about to stop for a red light at Fortieth and Superior, when this guy behind him was speeding and flew by Rosey in the curb lane. He did not even slow down at all; going through the red light, hitting a car that just made a turn onto Superior Avenue and Fortieth Street. It burst into flames, about to engulf the whole car. In that instant, Rosey put his car in park so fast, jumped out of his car, ran over, opened the door, in spite of burning his hands and singeing his face. He pulled out two screaming kids with their clothes and hair on fire. He dragged them away from the flaming car, opened his jacket and threw himself, with his open jacket, on top of the children, smothering the flames. Rosey was hollering first in English, "What is happening girls? We must get away before it is too late." Then in Thrae language, on and on, he was speaking while a crowd was gathering. The children's mother came screaming over to the children. She managed to get out about the same time Rosey dragged the kids out. The driver from the other car managed to stagger out of his car with a cut over his right eye. He was too drunk to see straight or even do anything. Rosey finally came back to his senses, got up, and went over to the drunk and socked him in the mouth so hard he did not even know what hit him. He keeled over like a sack of potatoes. He hollered at the drunk and called him a stupid asshole.

The police and ambulance arrived about the same time. There were a few witnesses who saw what happened. They did not tell the police that Rosey socked the drunk. A fire truck arrived a couple of minutes later to put out the flames. The whole car was ablaze. Rosey kept staring at the fire, having a flashback of his end coming, speaking in Thrae language; and neither the police nor anybody else could figure out what he was mumbling about. The flame was finally out.

Rosey, still mumbling in the foreign language and getting back into his Earthly sanity, asked, "Is everyone safe from the planet's inferno?"

The police said, "Everything is fine. You know you are a hero, saving those children."

"How are they?" Rosey asked. "And when did they bandage up my hands? And where is that idiot drunk?"

The cop said, "You were a little delirious, hollering in a

foreign language when you got treated for your burns. A few seconds more, as a witness told, the girls would have been goners. The drunk was hauled to the police station. We checked him out and this is his third offense. The judge will probably throw the book at him."

Rosey gave a full report to the police, then got into his car and went back home. He took a nap until the evening news came on. On TV, there he was, being treated by the paramedics. There were pictures of the burnt car, and they talked to a few witnesses. They tried to talk to Rosey, but they could not understand what he was saying. All they said was, "We have this foreigner as a hero."

Half an hour later there was a knock at the door. Rosey answered it. To his surprise it was Angela. She ran into Rosey's arms sobbing, "Are you all right? Why did you leave this morning without saying anything?"

Rosey looked Angela in the eye and told her he was confused because he thought he was gay. He said he really did not have too much feeling toward women. Rosey told Angela he liked her very much. He said he just did not know.

Angela said she did not care what he said. She loved him, and was going to figure out a way to make their relationship happen. Angela said, "It is past seven o'clock, and I bet you are hungry. Let's see what we could dish up out of your kitchen."

She looked through all the cupboards and refrigerator. Then she came back to the living room, hollering, "What the hell do you eat anyway? There is nothing in that kitchen to even make a small meal!"

Rosey said, "I did not shop yet."

"Bullshit!" Angela exclaimed. "It looks like you've never shopped since you lived here. Well, you can just drag your ass to my place. We're going to eat, baby."

Angela had made supper. Rosey stayed until about eleven o'clock, and then told Angela that her cooking was one of the best meals he had in a long time, but he had to get back to his place because he had to get up early in the morning. Besides she was trying to come on to him again. He told her maybe some other time. He thanked her again. She kissed him good night saying, "I will see you soon; real soon."

For a couple of months, Rosey tried to avoid Angela, even though he kind of missed her. She was a lot of fun. Then it happened. Rosey was awakened with a startling pounding on the door that would not stop. Rosey said, "Okay, okay, I am coming." He said, while opening the door, "Are you trying to break the door down?"

There was Angela in tears, "You're in for it now Rosey. You are not going to get away with it."

Rosey said, "What in the Sam hell are you talking about?"

"Well I will tell you. I am going to have your baby, get it?"

Rosey had to sit before he fell down. "Are you sure?"

"I sure am sure, and you are the father."

Rosey said, "Can't you have an abortion."

Angela said in tears, "I do not want an abortion. That is murder. I want the baby, your baby."

Rosey said, "I have to think about this."

She said, "There is nothing to think about. It is your baby, we are going to get married, and we are both going to raise this here child. If my parents find out that you want to renege, then you've really had it."

Rosey figured, *Why not, it will be something different in life for me anyway.* They had a simple wedding with their relatives and a few friends. They had a beautiful baby girl. They rented a house close to where Arnold lived. After a few more years and two more children, which were boys, Rosey was making good money as a reporter. Rosey and Angela were able to buy a nice home up in Cleveland Heights, near Cedar and Taylor Road.

Every time Rosey would report on fires, prostitutes, gays, and the like, he would try to prevent himself from having flashbacks. He would hurry with his reports and then sit in his car for awhile, until the feeling was over. His assistant and cameraman understood him. Rosey told them what to expect. Rosey was a good reporter, he made it look so realistic. He was able to do this because he already went through the same feelings in his other life.

One day Rosey was reading an article about "reincarnation, or did you live another life?" He wrote to Santini, for information, and then he was invited to the meeting, which was combined with vacation with his family to Yellowstone National Park. The discussion at Yellowstone National Park was an agreement for their station in Chesterland, Ohio. Since Rosey already lived in Cleveland Heights, he did not have to make any transition. After the station was started and everyone was settled down, Rosey figured he would have to quit the local newspaper company and help run the station as their director for other reporters.

So Rosey is also another member of the Thorme Club.

Now, back upstairs where Deton is trying to get loose before Ceikle gets back.

Eight
Deton and Taral's Honeymoon, Continued

Deton, saying to himself, "If I only can get this other bolt out, I could move this post." He worked his fingers raw, jiggling the post and turning the bolt at the same time. After what seemed like an eternity, he got the bolt out. The post and loft were too heavy to lift, so he tried pushing, hoping the loft did not come crashing down. Deton looked up at the loft's end; it looked secured to the wall. The post at the other end should hold it well enough. Deton pushed again and again until it moved enough where he could slip the chain underneath. The loft only sagged about an inch. Deton, at first, was going to wait by the door and surprise them, then changed his mind. "I cannot fight both of them while I am shackled." So Deton struggled, lifting and pushing the post back in place. It was none too soon when Ceikle and his crony were coming in the door. Deton stayed down with his arms around the post and the chain exposed like it was still around the post. Deton also stretched his one leg out, covering the grooved marks the post left in the floor.

Ceikle told his crony, "Take the other transport to the other station to pick up a load of weapons, and hurry back. Luga will stay downstairs answering any calls that come in." Ceikle shut the door and walked about half way to Deton and said, "You have any information for me?"

Deton said, "Hell no, never."

Ceikle said, "You're stupid, I have a hard on anyway. I have to make up for lost time, when she did not give me any." Ceikle went to the bed and started to put his hands on Taral's breasts, feeling down between her legs, he cried out, "What is all this blood?"

Deton started to laugh, "You asshole, Taral was a virgin when I married her and I broke her cherry."

Ceikle ran over and kicked him in the side. "Do not laugh at me." Deton cried out in pain, but did not budge. He figured you cannot fight a madman. So he waited for the right opportunity.

Ceikle said, "Blood or no blood, I am going to fuck her anyway." He took his clothes off and looked over to Deton and said, "Just think, you get to watch a free floor show." Ceikle got on the bed and Taral kept her legs closed tightly. Ceikle said, "You better spread them and make it easier on yourself." He started to get on top of her.

Taral resisted, calling him a cowardly bastard, and under her breath calling for Deton, "Hurry I cannot stand it anymore."

Deton sprung up fast and quietly, and in great pain from the kick to his side. He held back his groan and went forward to the bed, wrapping the chain around Ceikle's neck, hearing gurgling and choking with his arms flailing with his naked body all over and his legs kicking. Deton dragged Ceikle off the bed backwards with the chain still around his neck, tightening it all the more. Deton rolled Ceikle onto his naked stomach, and with the chain around his neck, putting his knee into his back, gave one quick jerk, breaking his neck and spine at the same time. Deton told Taral to make noises, screaming at Ceikle like he was still in control. Deton got the key out of Ceikle's pocket and unlocked the shackles, and then untied Taral. She put on what was left of her clothes, put on Deton's coat, and said, "Now what?"

Deton figured there had to be more people in this big house. "We will have to go out the window."

Taral said, "We're on the second floor."

He said, "I know, I will go first and you do like I do. Hang from the sill and push yourself away as you jump. I will be waiting for you to jump so I could break your fall."

Deton jumped first with pain and hit the ground, which was a little hard. He made a little sound because his side hurt like hell from the kick. Taral finally let go, pushing herself away. Deton broke her fall, but got her elbow right in his chest, knocking the wind out of him. They both sprawled on the ground. Taral went to Deton, lying there, she started shaking him, "Come on honey, come on." After a few moments Deton opened his eyes and looked at Taral and said, "Are we always going to end up on the floor like this?"

Taral kissed him and said, "Let's get out of here." Deton got up in pain and hobbled with Taral to the front of the house. The shuttle was still parked in the same place. The house had plenty of shrubbery in the front, but you still could see out of the windows. It started to rain pretty hard.

Deton said, "That is what we need. We forgot to take our shower today." The both got on their hands and knees to the ground, which was starting to turn a little muddy. Deton said, "Now or never."

They crawled as fast as they could to the opposite side of the shuttle, opened the door and crawled in. This shuttle had two switches to turn on to activate the power. Deton told Taral, "Stay down while I get upright to step on the accelerator." Away they went. He looked at the rear scope and could see two guys coming out of the house, but they were too far for them to do anything. I do not think there was any other shuttle. We got on the highway, which was divided by a fifty foot median. It was raining a little harder, we had to put the window vaporizers on full blast to keep it clear, and besides it started to get dark.

We drove back to Taral's parents' house. We walked in and her parents were watching the news. They turned to look at us while getting up. "What happened to you two?"

Taral told her parents they had a little encounter with Ceikle. "He was a brutal person. You know he joined the forces of Jarconi, and was sent back as a spy."

Taral's father said, "What did you mean he was a brutal person?" Taral told everything that happened, and that Deton killed him. The minister said, "I cannot blame you at all for what you did. He had it coming one way or another."

Deton said, "We have to go back to headquarters and report this."

Taral's parents said, "It does not matter when you tell the authorities, because the end is upon us. I want you to stay with us, for this will be our last evening together. We shall have supper and have a toast and talk of old times, and then you can be on your merry way."

Taral was crying softly and said, "I know it is finally here, I will miss you both. Some day we will all meet in heaven."

Deton and Taral stayed for a few hours and said their good-byes with hugs and kisses. It was awfully hard for Taral to tear herself away from her parents' arms. We left with Ceikle's shuttle, driving to the spaceport headquarters. Taral was crying and I had tears in my eyes, because I felt very sorry for her. I was lucky my mother and sister went back to the spacecity.

When we got to headquarters we reported what happened and where the weapons were being stored. The military sent one vehicle to the site, fired one missile and destroyed the whole place. It went up like an erupting volcano.

It was now the beginning of the year 2010. Most of the planet was invaded by the forces of Jarconi. They started sending some missiles onto the country of Sargarity, which destroyed the west end of the country and killed countless people. Taral and her minister brother talked to their parents every day on the tela-communicator. Taral's father said it would not be long until they will be bombing this end. "It will be the last time I will be talking to you." Her father said, "I give you and your husband Deton, my blessing. Please let me talk to your brother." Taral's father talked to her brother Garrah and said to him, father to son, and also minister to minister, "I want to tell you that your mother and I love you and Taral very much, we do not want to leave you two, but there are many, many people; frightened people, who need our help getting through this crisis in their lives. As my son and minister, you must continue where I leave off, to get the new planet onto the right path of justice. Remember, you must keep your chin high and let everyone follow you in the right direction." Taral's mother also talked to both of them, also said a few nice words to Deton. That was the last we ever heard from Taral's parents.

The enemy sent a few missiles, too many. Then things started to happen. This was the beginning of the end. The spacecity of Orant had retrieved all personnel and vehicles, and vacated the prison that was away from the spacecity, so no one could live on it. They would make do with what they had for a jail on the spacecity. Everything was secured. The spacecity was closed up so there would not be any intruders trying to get in.

Taral was sobbing a little and praying for it to end quickly and without any pain to their parents. Everything was being recorded with the telescopic video cameras, and put on video screens throughout the spacecity. The whole destruction was to be put on microchips and stored in the library archives. Since the spacecity travels around the planet many times over, you can see all the destruction of the buildings, houses, and bridges just toppling over like a house of cards. Flames were starting to build up, and winds started to blow from all directions, fanning the flames. The winds were getting stronger and stronger, to hurricane force. We were watching building after building come crumbling down, and the closeup view of people looking like ants running here and there trying to get away from the flames and heat, and watching them disappear into the inferno. The rivers and lakes were so crowded with people you could not even see any water. A chain reaction from all the megaton bombs (in which the enemy of Jarconi was only going to destroy the country of Sargarity) started to combine with the radiation from the unprotected ozone. It became hotter from the sun and the many volcanoes, with their eruptions. The biggest wind ever imagined was whipping up the largest ball of fire and pushing it, slowly at first, burning everything in its path and drying up streams, rivers and lakes with all the ships and people in them, causing hot steaming tidal waves. Think of a huge dust storm in a desert, twenty stories high, and twenty-five miles long. That is what this looked like, but there were a few hundred of them throughout the planet, for months and months until there was not anything left breathing, and everything would be disintegrated.

Taral and Deton were watching all of this on the communicator with a group of other people in the stateroom. Most were in shock and crying, even screaming from what they were witnessing. Taral could not watch anymore, thinking of her parents down there. She ran out of the room crying, and disappeared down the corridor. Deton had to watch it and bear it and get the actual effect as an officer, so as to get the feeling. It must be imprinted in his mind, so he could teach and give the same feeling in teaching future generations what happens to evil people on a planet. But it is always an awful outcome for the innocent to suffer with the evil.

On the first Sabbath day on the spacecity of Orant, services were held in the few churches that were erected within the city. Most people attended in a very silent way, still in disbelief of what was happening to their planet Thrae. Taral, Deton, and his mother and sister went to the church where Taral's brother Garrah was going to preach. They knelt down and said a prayer before the reverend came out. Reverend Garrah started the service by having everyone pray for all the innocent people that were left behind to suffer with the evil ones, that they may be rewarded in heaven.

After the prayer, Reverend Garrah looked up with watery eyes. He could not say anything for a moment. It was very quiet, except for the few who were crying softly. He figured he had better snap out of it, or he would have the congregation bawling out loud. The reverend snapped back, and in a loud voice said, "There is nothing we can do for planet Thrae and the people who are perishing. They shall be rewarded by the Almighty. The evil ones will be judged accordingly. We, the chosen ones, are safe and sound on this spacecity. We follow the laws of God. There will be no room for evil, if there are any amongst us, they shall be cast out of the spacecity of Orant, into the void of oblivion. We will be out here for many years to come, waiting for planet Thrae to come back to life. In the meantime, we are to learn to prepare ourselves for when that time comes. Many of us, including the children that are to be born, will be starting a new beginning on a new clean planet. May God help us, Amen."

This inferno was to continue for a few months. It was an unimaginable havoc. If witnessed, it would be most unforgettable. After this holocaust, it will take many months for all the toxic gases in the atmosphere to settle and dissipate. Then it will take years before all the forests and streams and clean atmosphere will reappear. This rebirth will take be about twenty years.

After a couple of stressful months on the spacecity, getting used to new living quarters that were unlike those on planet Thrae. However, you get used to it after awhile. Everyone kept busy, including the children who still attended school.

After a few more months, there were still some spacecraft from from the enemy of Jarconi, orbiting the planet, demanding that the officials of the spacecity let them in. Of course, they were refused. They talked to us, saying after the flames died out on the planet, that a few tried to go back, to find out that there was nothing there. They tried to get back to space, instead their crafts disintegrated from the aeration of the contaminated atmosphere.

We tried to avoid any confrontation with them. The only ones that escaped the country of Jarconi were the government officials and their space personnel. They figured, to hell with the people. We told them their fate was probably sealed until future orders from the above. Of course, they did not know what the hell we were talking about. Now they started to threaten the spacecity. They had a few armed crafts with missiles, and demanded we let them in, or they would blow the spacecity to bits. We were well prepared for this encounter. We were far more advanced in anti-warfare than they thought. The city denied their request. They had about seventy crafts in space, about twenty were armed. They gave us until the next day, which was the same as night in space or other words twenty-six hours. The time came, for what they thought would be our destruction, but it was only their doom. Their spaceships were lined up abreast of the city, which spread a few miles. At the first sound of their demand, we let all hell loose at the same time with a hundred swooshes of missile fire, directed right at each of Jarconi's spacecraft. They could not get out of the way in time, for that was unexpected from the spacecity.

Every one of their warcraft disintegrated without a fight. The unarmed craft even tried ramming the city but to no avail. The city is protected with a shield from asteroids and small dust particles. We had to destroy some of those craft anyway, just in case they could cause any damage. All the other craft, after less then a year, started out aimlessly through outer space, knowing that they were all lifeless, for lack of food and oxygen. There were two spacecraft from the enemy left, which were built for about a year and a half endurance period. One landed softly on top of the spacecity like it was trying to be friendly. They told us their leader of Jarconi was in their craft, and that they had a malfunction and needed help. The leaders in the spacecity were not impressed or that stupid, and they knew how conniving they were. This was just a ploy. They were told that they could not be helped anyway, because the city was closed up until future orders.

Maybe they had a malfunction, maybe not. After about two weeks, they took off and and headed for our moon. We had a station on the moon that was built a few years back. The other enemy spacecraft were already there. All the personnel from the space station on the moon were back at the spacecity of Orant, for the duration of this great tragedy of planet Thrae. The enemy could stay alive at that station only for about six months, which was when their supplies would run out.

Watching the destruction of planet Thrae was enough to boggle anyone's mind. You did not ever want to see it again, the way all the skyscrapers crumbled down to the ground, bridges collapsed, lakes and rivers were boiling over; and especially, the people were charred to ashes. The whole planet was one big fireball.

Deton and Taral had their first child about a year later and two more within the next eight years. A few more years after the holocaust, the city was opened up, and all the enemy's debris was taken up. All corpses were disintegrated by a chemical. They took a crew to the moon station to set up shop as they did before, only to find most of the equipment was destroyed by the enemy. It looked like Jarconi's leaders were fighting between each other. They were killed, including about forty-five of their followers. The rest of about thirty men and women just starved to death in the space station, or died from lack of oxygen and cold. It took almost a year to rebuild the space station on the moon. They also installed one of the observatories on the spacecity.

The last few years, Deton studied advanced astronomy at one of the schools achieving one of the highest degrees. He was to be transferred to the moon station to help direct the dismantling of the observatory at the spacecity, so it could be transported to the moon and assembled. This would take about a month of transporting all of the pieces. This was Deton's baby. He made sure it was put together right. Deton communicated every night with Taral and was on leave every three weeks, for three days. This routine went on for a few years, until Deton got transferred back to the spacecity of Orant. They built a new observatory on the east end of the spacecity. Deton was promoted to chief astronomer. He ran the show.

In the meantime, Taral was in charge of the zoo on a

part-time basis. Even the animals were getting a little over-populated. In a few months, most of the population would be migrating back to planet Thrae. Deton and Taral's children were all grown up and graduated. All three had fiancées and were ready to get married.

The time had come for migration, and most people have transported back to planet Thrae. They were building as fast as possible. The planet had recovered fairly rapidly from radiation. There were quite a few pieces of machinery that were stored on the spacecity for this rebuilding occasion. Deton and Taral's children stayed on the spacecity for a few more years, then went back to planet Thrae after they were married, so they could raise their children on planet Thrae. Everything seemed to be getting back to normal. Taral received a high honor for her part in being in charge of the zoo and for transporting all the animals back to planet Thrae, which took almost a year.

Deton retired in a couple of years and moved back to planet Thrae so they could be near their children. Five years into his retirement, Deton and Taral went on vacation, back to the spacecity of Orant. One day, while Taral was shopping, Deton visited his old buddy at the observatory at the east end of the city, when it happened. A meteor struck the observatory and killed both Deton and his buddy.

Nine
Back on Earth

This dream or vision Al had of his other life on planet Thrae was something to ponder. If it had any connection to the future of planet Earth, we will all find out sooner or later.

The new building was almost complete and attached to the observatory with all lines linked to the tower with special antennas installed at the top of the tower. They had their own special frequency, so they could send their signals to outerspace with a special code. They knew for a fact that this code could be broken down by the technicians on planet Thrae, if the signal got that far. So far, after two years (it was 1992 Earth time) they had not received sounds or signals of any kind. They would have to try a different approach. They installed a different antenna on top of the tower and rejuvenated their transmitter with all the power it could stand. The signals were sent at different intervals, to try to keep in line with the sun and Earth's path in the solar system.

A month later they received their first signal. At first they could not make much sense of it. Mike took awhile to decipher the code. After a long while (a couple of months), it started to come much clearer to Mike, because they were getting more and more signals. Some were too faint to copy and some were strong. Al believed it was the rotation of the planets, which were not lined up all the time. Finally, some of the codes started to make sense. One message did mention planet Thrae. One stated a new spaceship that was on its way from planet Thrae to find out what was on the other end of their solar system. Sometimes they did not get any messages for weeks at a time. The aliens claimed they had received signals, but could not quite make them out. Al figured they still had not put together the right code or strong enough signals. They would try again until they got it. They acquired a new transmitter from one of their technology companies. They had been experimenting with different components and added some kind of a booster. It was installed in their station and everything checked out. So they started to send the messages. In about a week they started getting messages from planet Thrae. In the received messages, the aliens explained that they thought they lived in the same galaxy, but a different solar system. The aliens built a special spaceship, constructed big enough to withstand any long voyage when trying to find our planet.

Mike sent messages about the group of people that used to live on planet Thrae in another life, at different periods of time, who died and were reincarnated to planet Earth. Mike's messages were describing some of the incidents that were happening on planet Earth. Earth people were a hardheaded people. The end of the world was approaching, and more people seemed to ignore the problem. It was getting close to the year 2000, Earth time. There already were a few skirmishes throughout the world. The terrorist bombings were getting out of hand. Most people on planet Earth just lived from day to day and did not give a damn about what was going on or what might happen. They did not believe anything was going to happen. Al knew the end of the world was going to happen, for he knew what the Bible foretold: the archeological history of the world was also an indicator of what was going to happen; almost about the same way as it happened on planet Thrae. The only difference was, on planet Earth the people were not prepared for any destruction. They did not take heed to the prophecies and warnings. There were a few that believed in the warnings and tried to convince higher authorities of what might happen, but it went in one ear and out the other.

Friday's Thorme meeting at the Chesterland station was well attended. During the meeting they discussed the possibility of planet Thrae and the spacecraft they were supposed to send on its voyage. They spoke of how and where they would accept the aliens, and where they would meet without being conspicuous to the world, and not blow their cover. They talked about other matters; about their families and schools, about having picnics, baseball, and things like that. Even though, we knew some day the end would come.

Then out of the blue Tom came up with a dream he had. Actually it was like a nightmare. He told us he seemed to be shut up inside some container and his feelings had no being. It seemed to be the end of some tragic event, and his soul alone was closed up. He was traveling at some astronomical speed to infinity. He came to the conclusion that there was hardly any meaning to what was happening. He also confided to the group that he would not read or watch anything that had to do with medieval. When he was growing up and he attended school, the first few grades were not too bad. When he reached tenth grade, he had a report to make on medieval history and the Spanish Inquisition. He started to do the report quite well, until he got to the part about the dungeons and all the torture that took place. They were dismembered. Their eyes poked out, and then their bodies were burned at the stake. What really got him was their pouring of hot lead into their mouths and ears.

117

As Tom was reading all this, he broke out into a traumatic sweat. He trembled all over, and actually felt the pain. It made him wince with pain, and he moaned like he was really there. Actually Tom was there in his other life, on a different planet that was just like Earth that went through all the same type of torturing. He was falsely accused of holding information from the rulers in about the fouteenth century on planet Thrae, just like it happened on Earth. They tortured him to get information from him that he did not have. When they poured the hot lead down his throat, the pain was unbearable. He suffered for several hours until he died.

"After death I was reincarnated to Earth so I could react to something that humans should not do to any other human beings." After Tom finished speaking, there was not a sound in the room for a couple of minutes. We were spellbound. So Al called the meeting to a close. It was getting late anyway. They had a meeting just about every week, to discuss all the problems that they would encounter in the future.

Ten
Espionage

Father Carl was the latest person to join the group, about six months ago. He said a closing prayer before everyone left the Thorme meeting. Father Carl joined the group after an article he read in a magazine. He then wrote a letter to Joe Santini wanting to meet. Al responded, telling Father Carl to come to a meeting at the Chesterland station, since he was living in Cleveland anyway. Father Carl showed up at the meeting and everyone was introduced. Al told him he was using Joe Santini as an assumed name.

Father Carl told the group that he was also reincarnated from planet Thrae. He had lived there many centuries before there was religion. He was on a crusade, starting one of the first religions in a country called Sargarity on the planet. He tried to teach morality and good for a number of years. Everything was undercover because there was so much evil. They seemed to prefer it that way. There were a few hundred people that converted, but they did not live long. At one of the meetings they were attacked, and most were killed. Carl escaped and told the survivors to continue the work for he would not be around to continue. A few days later he died from wounds received during the attack. For a priest, Father Carl appeared rather knowledgeable about communications and space affairs. He revamped quite a bit of the system for better communications. It was strange that he would never ask about any messages that were received, as though he really did not care. Sometimes he would stay a little later than he had to during his own time when not at church. Father Carl would show up for a couple of hours, about two or three times a week. He also showed up for every meeting.

At one of the meetings, we discussed when the spaceship from planet Thrae would arrive and how we would handle it. Then we got on the subject of our reincarnation to Earth. Everyone came up with their unusual stories. When we got to Father Carl and asked him where in Cleveland he was born, to our surprise, he indicated he was born in Clearwater, Montana, near the Canadian border. As he was growing up, he learned all there was to know about electrical systems and loved airplanes, especially the space program. That was Father Carl's hobby, all the material he could get his hands on, he would study.

George asked, "Then why are you a priest?"

Father Carl said, "That has to do with my reincarnation to Earth. It is like the continuation of what I was doing on planet Thrae, the feeling was always there right when I was born. I have to try to save people from their own destruction." He continued saying that he graduated from high school and moved to Ohio so he could go to the seminary to become a priest. After he took his vows, he was sent to a church in Cleveland, and there he stayed. It was getting late so Father Carl said a prayer, and everyone left.

George and Al were still outside the station talking about the evening's events. George said to Al, "It seems a little strange that if Father Carl was born in Montana, why he has a very slight foreign accent? I wonder if he thinks we did not notice it?" George said he was going down to the church to listen to one of the Father's sermons to see if anything comes of it. George was a little skeptical about this situation. George and his wife went to Father Carl's church down in Cleveland and listened to his sermon. The topic was about sexual harassment and the New World Order. George and his wife sat in the back pew so he would not notice them. There were quite a few people in attendance. After the service, everyone walked out to where Father Carl was standing to meet the flock. Father Carl spotted George and his wife and said, "Well what brings you here to my humble church?"

George responded, "Well I was curious about how you preached your sermons. I was very impressed."

"Thank you," said Father Carl. "You have to come again with your beautiful wife."

George said, "Even though I am of a different religion, I will still come every now and then."

They said their good-byes and departed. George remarked to his wife, "There is something that is not right about Father Carl, especially that sermon on the New World Order. Catholics do not want to know about a New World Order."

George missed a couple of days of going to the station in Chesterland because it was thundering and lightning fairly hard. His wife called the station, so he stayed home in agony, crying and scratching the walls. Al was working in one of the rooms at the station. When it would thunder, he would notice a flash of light under the door from the next room where the transmitter and receiver were, and the adjoining room where the telescope was kept.

Al walked in the other room where Father Carl was, asking him, "Wasn't that some thunder and lightning?"

Father Carl said, "I was too busy writing notes to notice."

Al asked, "Anything new that we could add to the equipment?"

"Not at this time," said Father Carl. "I am just taking

notes in case I come up with something for the future. Well I have work to finish up in the other room. I will see you later."

On the way out, Al noticed part of a camera case hidden under Father Carl's raincoat. Al did not say anything to Father Carl and left the room. Thinking to himself, *Something seems fishy here.* You could hear a little thunder, but there was no way you could see lightning flashes because there were no windows in either room. That could mean that Father Carl was taking pictures of the equipment. He did not hide his camera case well enough. Al did not want to ask Father Carl until he shared this information with George. Al walked back in the room where Father Carl was, and said he forgot to get some things in the file. When he walked past his coat, he noticed the case was well hidden.

It stopped raining about four o'clock, Father Carl said he had to get back for supper and prepare for confessions. "I will see you in a couple of days."

Al left the station about five o'clock and stopped at George's house to see how he was doing. George's wife answered the door and said, "Hello Al, come on in. George is in the den."

Al walked in the den and greeted George. Reading, George looked up. "Oh, it's you Al. Sit down and have a beer."

"I do not want to get too full before supper, but I will have one beer anyway." Al reported, "I have something to tell you about Father Carl."

He told him what happened at the station. George said, "Even though he is a priest, I still do not trust him. I have a feeling we will have to keep an eye on him and do a little checking around." Al said he was going down to listen to one of his services this Sunday. George said, "He gives a hell of a sermon." Al thanked George for the beer and left for home in Mayfield Heights.

He got to his house in about a half hour, greeted his wife Rose and the grandkids, took a shower, and got ready for supper. They all sat down to eat. They said grace and everyone dug in. Al took a few bites, hardly chewing his food, staring at nothing, like he was somewhere else. His wife said, "Hello, Al are you still with us?"

Al snapped out of it and said, "Sorry about that. Something is on my mind that I have to clear up." Al told Rose he was going down to Father Carl's church services by himself. He said he had to check on something. Sunday came and Al went down early and waited for the second service to start. The two services were an hour and a half apart. Al sat about half way down a pew that was located next to one of the confessionals. He was sitting in silent prayer waiting to see if Father Carl would show up at the altar for preparations. While Al was deep in thought praying, all of a sudden he could hear talking coming out of the confessional, of course, trying to keep it at a whisper. *Well,* Al was thinking, *it is a confessional. The only thing is, it sounds more like a conversation between two people, rather than a person confessing their sins to a priest.*

Al tried to listen with closer attention, and was surprised that the language spoken was foreign, like Russian. Al knew there were two priests at this church. However, he could not figure out which one was in the confessional. Al decided to get up and sit farther back in the church.

About five minutes later, the confessor came out and walked by Al. He looked like he was about fifty years old and just immigrated from a foreign country. A few minutes later, the priest came out. It was Father Carl. He was ready to walk toward the altar, but looked in Al's direction, noticing him. "Ah Al, you are early. You have a half an hour before the service." Some people were already coming in and sitting or kneeling down for prayer. Father Carl said someone had a last minute confession to make. "I cannot exactly refuse anyone."

Al responded, "Well, you do what you have to do."

Father Carl told Al he had to get things ready for the next service. "Father Daniel is the preacher today. I have to help serve communion. I will see you at the station."

Al's brain was really whirling now. "Something is really fishy, and I am going to find out what it is." Al was standing in back of the church when the service started. He waited until it was time for the serving of communion. Al then skipped out the back, heading for the rectory where Father Carl stayed. He sat in the waiting room looking at the pictures on the wall. He spotted Father Carl's certificate of ordination. Al quickly reached in his pocket for a pen and a small note pad. He wrote down the information he read on the certificate—the name of the seminary, the date he graduated, and that he was ordained in 1972.

Al left the rectory and went home. His wife asked, "How did it go?"

"Father Carl did not preach this morning," he said.

The next morning, Al asked George to go for a ride with him to the seminary that Father Carl attended. It was located in southern Ohio. They arrived at the seminary within a few hours. When they arrived, they walked in the office and told the office secretary that they needed some information on Father Carl for a party that was held in his honor. They needed to get his life history. The secretary pulled his file with everything they wanted to know; when and where he was born, and the schools and churches he attended in Clearwater, Montana. Al and George left late in the afternoon with all the information they could ascertain for the time being.

While driving back to Mayfield Heights, they were

silent for awhile. George finally asked Al, "Well what do you think?"

Al said, "I really do not know. Everything seems to be legit." They were silent for another hour.

"You know what we ought to do, take a plane up to Montana and check on his family."

Al said, "That sounds like a good idea. What do we have to lose anyway? We will leave Wednesday by plane. We'll tell everyone we are going to look at a landing site up in Wisconsin."

So Al took a ride to Cleveland Hopkins to book a flight so it would not look too conspicuous around the station. They could not take their own plane because Joe and Mike had it trying to find a landing site for the spacecraft from planet Thrae.

Al and George, with overnight bags, drove out to Hopkins Airport and boarded a plane early Wednesday morning to Great Falls, Montana. They talked over the events of the previous few days. Al said, "When we get back we will have to talk to Father Carl in a roundabout way so he would not get suspicious that we were on to him."

They arrived at Great Falls, Montana, at about noon. They inquired about a shuttle to Whitewater and how far it was. The attendant at the desk indicated that Whitewater was about two hundred miles north, close to the Canadian border. "The next plane out is tomorrow at ten A.M.," said the attendant. "You can hire a private plane and pilot." She gave us the name of a pilot who was just landing. "You can talk to him when he signs in. He said he was not going out until two-thirty. He said he had two passengers going to Dodson first, and then to Whitewater."

It was already one o'clock so Al and George had lunch and lounged around until two-thirty. They carried their bags on board and were finally airborne. They arrived in about an hour at the first stop. The pilot took on another passenger.

Al and George arrived at Whitewater at about five-thirty. If there was such a thing as a one horse town, this was it. The airport was a one hangar, one runway establishment. They landed with a bumpity, bump, bump. They could not exactly check on anything at this time. The pilot said the next flight out of Clearwater was on Friday at ten A.M. They seemed to roll up the sidewalks pretty early. There wasn't even a hotel around, but they did find a rooming house that the pilot directed them to. They were even served supper at the rooming house. Al and George ate with the landlords and two other boarders. The one boarder asked where we were from. Al told him, "We are here on business."

Then George asked if they knew a Father Carl who was supposed to be from Whitewater. They all looked at George quizzically. Then the female landlord said, "The only preacher we have is a Reverend Downey, and he has been preaching in Whitewater for the last twenty years."

George said, "Oh," and with a suspicious feeling looked at Al. They ate the rest of their supper in silence. After supper, they sat in the living room for an hour reading some magazines and books. Everybody seemed to disappear, so Al and George went up to their room, which had twin beds. They each took a shower and got in bed. Both of them were in deep thought. At the same time they both said, "You know!" and started laughing.

Finally George said, "We might as well get a good night's sleep. We will find the answers tomorrow." George seemed to fall asleep quickly, and like a log. Al on the other hand, tossed and turned for a couple of hours with a million things going through his mind.

The next morning the town seemed to be awake

between five and six A.M. Al and George stayed in bed until eight. They got up, washed, got dressed, and went downstairs. The landlord said, "You missed breakfast. It was at seven. You could have a cup of coffee and muffins."

Al and George left their bags, since they had to stay another night anyway. The first thing they did was to go down to the town hall. It took all of five minutes to get there. Al said, "This is weird. It's like living in the Andy of Mayberry episode." The town hall was the jail, the court, and anything that had to do with the town.

George asked the clerk about Father Carl, so we could find any of his kin to talk to. The clerk looked like she was in her late twenties and homely, with a "duh" attitude. She said there was no such name and never heard of it. She looked through all the files and found absolutely nothing. We asked where the Whitewater High School was. The clerk started to laugh, and could not stop. Finally she calmed down and said, "How many people do you think live in this town? There is no high school. All we have is a small grade school. There is only one high school, which is in the town of Soco. The high school students from about five surrounding towns go to the high school at Soco. The deputy sheriff is going there about eleven A.M. Maybe he will take you there."

The clerk phoned the deputy. He came over about ten minutes later. The deputy said he would take them now, since it was already ten thirty. It took about forty-five minutes to get to Soco through all the dust, since most of the roads were made of dirt. If it ever rains it would cut down the dust. But George hoped it did not rain. The deputy dropped Al and George in front of the school and said he would be back in an hour and a half. They walked into the school and asked a student where the office was. The student pointed to the end of the hall. George said, "This is our last stop until tomorrow, then home we go."

They walked into the office where a young brunette at the counter asked, "May I help you?"

Al introduced himself and George and asked about Father Carl from Whitewater. "Hadn't he graduated from high school about twenty-five or thirty years ago?"

The girl went through the files and said, "There was nothing on any Carl Croyden, that is the last name that you mentioned, isn't it? We have all the yearbooks on file for the past fifty years." She took us to the stock room where all the yearbooks were on the shelves in order. George started looking through them from 1965 and up, and Al went through them from 1964 and back.

After over an hour, the deputy was back and asked if they were ready. Al said, "Yes, we are done here." They thanked the clerk and left. On the way back the deputy asked if they found what they were looking for. "Yes," Al said, "we are finished up here."

The deputy drove Al and George back to Whitewater and dropped them off in front of the town hall. George thanked him for his time. The deputy said it was his pleasure. "We do not get many out-of-towners up here. I am glad to talk to someone different for a change." George and Al spent the rest of the day doing nothing, because there was nothing to do. They would be glad when the next morning came around, so they could leave this place. It was the most boring day they spent in their entire lives.

After supper, Al and George went to their room early and discussed the matter at hand. George said, "When we get back, we will have to handle this situation in a delicate and diplomatic way, without suspicion, to see what Father Carl is up to."

Al said, "You know what we ought to do, bug his confessional in case that foreigner comes back again."

George said, "That is a good idea. We should be back home by Saturday for the confessions that usually start in the evening. I will have to find an inconspicuous spot in the confessional." It would be hard to find a bug anyway, because it is always dark in one of those things.

Al said, "We should keep this between us in case one of the others could be with Father Carl."

The next morning finally come around. They missed breakfast again and had a cup of coffee and another muffin. They paid their bill and thanked the landlord for the hospitality. They left with their overnight bags, walking the whole length of the town, which took about fifteen minutes, to that fantastic airport. They arrived at the one and only hangar where the surroundings seemed deserted. They waited for a few minutes and George said to Al laughing, "You think we ought to move out here for a little peace and quiet?"

Al said, "Sure, why not? We could die of boredom."

Then a door creeped open from the hangar, and some old man came out. "Are you guys the passengers who are going to Great Falls?"

Al said, "Yes, that is us!"

The old man said the plane would be there in about ten minutes. The two other planes were out and would not be back until Tuesday. "We have another plane parked in the hangar, but it needs a motor or the present one has to be rebuilt, if anyone ever gets around to it."

George asked, "What the hell do people do around here anyway?"

The old man said, "Well, I work here. Most people work in Soco. Some are teachers at the school and have offices at other businesses. Most of the people keep to themselves and do not really bother anyone else. It is a quiet life!"

George said, "We found that out!" It was a few seconds to ten o'clock. The plane was right on time, landing practically at their feet. Al and George said good-bye to the old man, got in the plane and away they went. In no time, they were approaching the airport at Great Falls.

They had a three-hour wait for their flight back to Cleveland, Ohio. They walked around the terminal talking about different things. They had lunch for about an hour just to kill time. Finally they got to board the airliner.

It started to drizzle lightly on takeoff. Al said, "Oh-oh, I hope what I am thinking does not happen." Al was sitting next to the window purposefully, and George was next to him. Both were strapped in. They were in flight for about five minutes when there was a flash of lightning. It made George jump a little. Al closed the porthole curtain, which did not help too much because the lightning would show through the other windows. The thunder was not loud because of the pressurized cabin. The plane was climbing so it could be above the clouds, away from the lightning and thunder. George already got the effect and started to moan in that foreign language. It did not last long.

Already above the clouds, George was still moaning when the flight attendant came over and asked what was wrong. Al said George fell asleep and was having a nightmare, but everything was alright. The flight attendant walked away. George was coming to. As he did he said he was tired and was going to take a nap.

A half hour passed when he awoke. He said how tired he must have been. Al told George, "You know it started to rain on takeoff, which put you in one of your moaning trances. We got above the clouds when you came out of it. Then you fell asleep."

Al explained, "When we get back, we have to contact our electrical contractor to see about a bugging device, so we can install it at the church. We will have to install it next week while Father Carl is at the station."

Al and George arrived back in Cleveland in the early evening. They drove home like they were in the upper states, investigating a landing site. Monday, at the Chesterland station they contacted the electrical contractor. In a couple of days he obtained the bug. By Thursday, while Father Carl was at the Chesterland station, Al drove down to the church. Since it was open to the public, he walked in. He was in luck. Not a soul was in sight. He sat down across from the confessional, like he was in prayer, looking around to make sure no one was watching him. He walked into the confessional, shutting the door. With the use of a pen flashlight, he installed the bug (which was the same size as a quarter). He found a good, inconspicuous spot. It was self sticking, so there was not too much trouble installing it. It was quite dark anyway, so it could not be found. When Al came out there was an old lady in the pews. She was too deep in prayer to notice anything. Al walked out of the church and drove back to Chesterland.

George and Father Carl were talking in the office. George said, "I am glad you are here."

Father Carl indicated that he might get transferred to Portland, Oregon, in a couple of months. "Is that so," Al said, kind of winking to George. "I guess we will miss you and all the help you have been giving us."

Father Carl said, "We will see what happens when the time comes." He said he had to leave then, because of a baptism at one o'clock.

It was thought that Father Carl was suspected of obtaining information from the station. He was supposedly the one who broke in, stealing information before he joined the group. We were wrong, the break-in was caused by the F.B.I., finding out through the grapevine of the intervention.

George told Al, "We have to watch what we say at the station." He thought the break-in was a coverup to make it look like a burglary, so they could plant a bug to see what we were up to. "As far as Father Carl, I think he might be a spy, even if we think he is a legitimate priest. We will have to take turns outside the church until that Russian shows up."

By Friday morning we were receiving new messages from the spaceship Ventara about some repairs that were made after landing on one of Uranus's moons. We also received information about an enemy other than from planet Thrae, that wanted to invade planet Earth. Good thing Al received the messages so no one would know at this time. Usually Father Carl would show up on Tuesday to see that everything is in working order in the receiving and sending room. Al told George to get our radio installer here right away. "Tell him this is a high priority job!" The installer was there at the station within the hour. Al met him outside the station to talk in case the station was bugged. Al told the installer to install a recorder in a inconspicuous place to the main transmitter and receiver. It will be our backup in case the first messages are lost or fouled up.

Tuesday Father Carl came in about two o'clock. He was tinkering around the equipment, pretending he was adjusting this and that. Al kept a glancing eye, noticing Father Carl always walking by the desk where all the reports were, and looking as he passed. Everybody was leaving, around four-thirty. Al and George said they were leaving also, for a dinner date. "How about you Father?" Father Carl said he would stay about another hour or so. He had a few things to replace on the receiver. "Okay," Al said.

George and Al said, "We will see you later." They left and told the security guard at the gate to call Al at home as soon as Father Carl left the station. Al told George, "No sense lying about the dinner date. Get your baby sitter, and you and your wife come over to eat."

"Good idea. We might as well continue planning the arrival of the spaceship."

They had dinner. Afterwards, the women sat in the living room chatting. Al and George sat in the den, planning the arrival of the spaceship. They did not get too far into it when the phone rang. Al said he would get it. The guard at the station told Al Father Carl just left in kind of a hurry.

Al said, "Thanks, we will be up later on to finish some things." He hung up. Al told George he was there almost three hours since they left him. Something important must have happened, because he said he left in a hurry. "We will wait an hour, then we will go up and check it out."

In an hour, they drove to the station and walked into the transmitting and receiving room. Everything looked the same. Then they checked out the hidden recorder. They ran it back, then on play. Al and George could hear the switch in frequencies. Then you could hear Father Carl talking in a foreign language. It sure as hell wasn't Russian. It was something not heard before. Seems like they were talking a long time, trying to get through all the static. Some of it was the same over and over, like the message was not getting through. Then George said the first thing tomorrow they better get to the church just in case he would get a visitor.

They waited all day Wednesday. Nothing happened. Al went home. George stayed all evening. Nothing happened. George called Al on his car phone. "It is late and I am going home." The next day, Thursday, Al went down by himself. All day nothing happened. George relieved him for the evening shift. Al went home, saying, "My ass is sore from sitting in that damn car all day. Good-bye."

133

About six-thirty, just before the confessions started at seven P.M. a strange looking foreigner walked into the church. In a few seconds there were voices. His confession was not in English. George recorded it anyway. He figured it was the wrong man. It was almost seven o'clock. Father Carl would be getting all kinds of confessors, because a lot of people were now going into the church for confession. The next person, to George's surprise, started out a little loud in broken-up English. "Blessed me Father I have sinned." George thought, *What an understatement!* He was loud at first, so the other people would think he was really confessing. His voice was soon down to a whisper, and it switched to the Russian language. George did not know what the hell they were talking about, but he sure got all of it on tape for translation. At some points in the conversation, they talked a little louder, with excitement. All in all this conversation lasted about ten minutes.

George started driving back to Chesterland, calling Al on his car phone to meet him at his house. When George got home, Al was already there. It was after eight o'clock. George's wife said, "It is about time! The kids and I already ate." George said he was sorry, then asked Al to have a bite also. Al said he was stuffed. George said, "At least have a beer!"

"Okay, but what happened?"

George said, "It is all on tape, but in Russian."

Al said, "Doesn't Miss Choa teach languages at Lakeland College? Maybe she knows Russian? Besides we have not seen her for a couple of months. See what she's up to. Do you have her number?"

George said, "It is here someplace. Here it is." He called and got the answering machine. "Great," George said. "She is probably out on a date, since she is not married anyway. We will call her in the morning."

Miss Choa Mio

Miss Choa was born in Hong Kong, of a Chinese father and an English mother in 1960, on Earth. She attended grammar and high school in Canton, China. She already knew Chinese and English from her parents. She graduated at age sixteen, and traveled through parts of China with her parents, who were missionaries. Choa loved being a humanitarian. She also liked learning languages. After two and a half years with her parents, serving the poor people of China, she was getting the feeling that she had done this same type of work in another life and time. She could not make sense of this feeling. After all she was just going to be 19 years of age.

Miss Choa left her parents and went to a university in Moscow, Russia. She took a course in Russian language and philosophy. After two years of study, she left Russia and went back to China. She found her parents in Peking, running an orphanage. Choa told her parents that in six months (in 1981), she was going to America as an exchange student. Choa had her Bachelor's degree, and wanted to pursue a Doctoral degree in America.

Choa was a very big help to her parents in the short time she was at home. The orphan children all loved her like a mother. When she left for America, everyone was in tears.

She arrived in America and settled down in Cleveland, Ohio, attending a well-known university. She already had two years of college in Russia, spent two more in Cleveland going to college, and worked part-time at an exchange company as an interpreter. After college, she continued working at the exchange firm. She also started a program to help the needy children throughout the world. The exchange company backed her up in every way necessary. The program was going well. Choa's mother regularly wrote to her, telling her how proud she made her father.

In 1988 she received a letter from Lakeland College to take a position teaching the Chinese language. Without much hesitation, she accepted the position. She told her boss at the exchange firm that it was time for a change. She said she would leave in a month when the college term started. Choa told her boss that she would still run the needy children program. That was her main goal. She told them to call on her if they needed anything at the office. Choa moved into a condo at Deepwood, in Mentor, Ohio. It was close to Lakeland College, so she was close to work. Miss Choa was a very beautiful woman. She looked a lot younger than 28 years of age. She was a hit right from the start with the students. After a few months of teaching, she got some of the students interested in "The Saving the Children of the World Program."

After teaching classes, she usually went home to relax after a bath and preparing dinner. But her mind was racing with visions of her encounters saving children of ravaged countries. That showed disregard for their people. Visions were also not of Earth. It seemed so far away and a long, long time ago.

One evening Choa was reading an article in a magazine, about reincarnation! She read the article, which mentioned people living on another planet and then being reincarnated on Earth. They continued the work they were doing elsewhere. Choa thought it was a very interesting article. It also stated that there was a group of persons with the same experiences.

Due to this finding and seeing Al's address in the article she wrote a letter to Al under his alias name and post office box number. She also gave her phone number. A few days had passed, then she received a call from Al. He asked if she wanted to come to a meeting out at the Chesterland station on Saturday at seven P.M. She agreed and arrived Saturday, a few minutes before seven. Al met her at the gate so she would not have any trouble getting in. Choa parked her car inside the gate parking lot. Al and Choa walked to the station. Choa was surprised when she realized this was the Future Vision TV Station. Al said, "Yes we run this enterprise, and a few other ventures."

Before everyone sat down for the meeting, Al offered Miss Choa a cup of coffee and introduced her to all the members. They all talked for a while about many seemingly insignificant things. The meeting started about seven-thirty P.M. Everybody was there. They discussed the success of the Future Vision Company.

George asked Miss Choa why she thought she might be reincarnated. Miss Choa talked about when she grew up helping her parents at the orphanage in China. She also set up a program to help the needy children of the world. Then, becoming emotional, she explained she was continuing the work she was doing from another life. She also said that when she read the article on reincarnation, the planet of Thrae was mentioned.

"That was when a bell rang in my head. It made a lot of memories or feelings come back in my head about the terrible situation that the children on parts of planet Thrae were suffering. They were homeless, and were starving, all because of a country named Jarconi that invaded and raped most of the smaller countries. They were going to take over the planet. We worked day and night trying to save the poor children whose parents were killed or imprisoned for not participating in Jarconi's plan of the conquest of planet Thrae. We appealed to Jarconi for help to no avail. Our hands were full, trying to feed the homeless children. What we did not know was that the end of the planet was at hand.

"I had just turned, I believe, forty-eight years old, when the end came. We knew Jarconi was using nuclear weapons, bombing cities to bring the planet to its knees. One day it seemed a lot hotter than any other. The next day it seemed even hotter. The third day the heat was becoming unbearable. The children were suffering terribly. We were a long distance from the cities, but still could see the skyline of tall buildings and a couple of big blasts that did not help our eyesight. The children started to die one by one. The last thing I recall were big thunderous balls of fire rolling throughout all the land, burning everything in its path. We saw the high buildings collapsing and falling toward the ground. The many fireballs that were as big as mountains were destroying everything in their path. We comforted the children who were left until the end. That is why I always had the feeling of sympathy toward all children. Why should they be punished for the stupid mistakes the leaders of countries make?"

Choa apologized for getting carried away. She said she strongly believed all children of the world could be helped. Bart spoke up. "That was a very touching story. Since we own a cable vision company, we could try a series on one of the channels about the needy children of the world. We would talk to some of the networks to see what they thought. In the meantime, if you wanted to join our group, you would probably be voted in after a few technicalities. If you want, there is an option to buy stock into the cable vision company. Everything should be set up for our next meeting, which is a week from now."

Choa showed up a week later for another meeting with the group. She was okayed at the gate, drove in, and parked. When she entered the building, she greeted everyone. George offered Choa a cup of coffee. After a few minutes, everyone was seated. The minutes were read and old and new business was discussed. Al, as chairman of the company, got up and told Miss Choa that the group was glad to have her as a member. He said she was in for a number of surprises that would be discussed from time to time at the meetings. Choa was offered the chance to buy stock in the company at twenty-five dollars a share. She was told the company was growing at a steady pace. Choa said she would buy ten shares and think about buying more in the future.

Choa got to be a regular at the meetings. She found out about the communications from beings from outer space, and how the company was being run. They also got her fifteen minutes on one of the channels. In 1999, Choa started to miss a few meetings every now and then. Between teaching at Lakeland, working with the children's program at her old company, plus preparing the program on television, Choa had been going out once in awhile with one of the other teachers at Lakeland. She kept saying she had to start slowing down. Most of the time she just went home, eating a takeout order or cooking something. Then she usually fell asleep while watching television. One evening Choa was startled awake by the phone ringing. As she woke, she found herself still on the couch with the television still on. She said, "This is a first. I hope I don't do this again." It was almost nine-thirty when she answered the phone. It was Al. Choa said, "What do you want this early in the morning, on a Saturday?"

Al said, "I am sorry I woke you up on Saturday, but we have a very important tape that has to be interpreted. It really cannot wait. George and I will pick you up in about an hour. We'll buy you breakfast at Bob Evans."

Choa agreed, "Okay, good-bye."

They picked up Choa and asked to drive her car for

security reasons. "Why the mystery?" asked Choa.

Al said, "We'll tell you later." They drove out of Deepwood, located across from the Great Lakes Mall onto Johnnycake Road to Route 306. They made a right and drove across Mentor Avenue, under a railroad bridge to Bob Evans restaurant. The parking lot was rather full, but they were lucky someone was just pulling out near the entrance to the restaurant. This was one of the larger Bob Evans, so it was just a few minutes to wait for a table. They sat down, and in a minute a waitress took their order.

Choa asked again, "What in God's name is going on?"

George spoke up and said, "Choa, there are things you don't know that are going on. We know that you can be trusted with what we are about to tell you. Let's keep our voices at a very low pitch?"

Al said, "Here is the scoop. You must know by now that we have communicated with beings from another planet, the planet Thrae. It is the same planet that you were reincarnated from. George and I are also reincarnated from there. There are a few things we have to tell you because you will find out anyway. This must be kept a secret between us three and in time, the rest of the group will know, except Father Carl. One of the reasons we had to get ahold of you, was because we hoped you can interpret this language."

Al took the tape recorder out of his pocket. "If this tape has recorded on it what I think it does, then Father Carl is in deep trouble. First, I am going to explain the situation. Then I need you to put the earphones on to listen and tell us what is being said." George said, "We believe Father Carl is a Russian spy, and also contacts aliens from outer space. It sounds far-fetched, but that is the way it seems to be. We also are awaiting for the arrival of a spacecraft from planet Thrae. It has been in flight now for about nine or more months. We figure it's in about two and a half to three months of its arrival. That is why Mike and Joe are looking for a landing site. The third thing is, the spacecraft has encountered an enemy who is in dealings with some countries like Russia and Iraq, and a couple of others. We have a tape from our cable vision station also, when Father Carl was by himself talking to someone, and the language was not in Russian."

All of a sudden the waitress was there with our order. Al said to listen to the recorder later. "Let us eat. I'm hungry."

After breakfast, they sat in the car and Choa listened to the recorder without the earphones. After a couple of minutes Choa said, "Very interesting." She continued to listen for another eight minutes (as her eyes got bigger), saying under her breath, "Oh my God!"

George and Al were getting a little antsy waiting for the results. Choa shut the recorder off for a minute, staring out the car window, did not say anything. Al and George did not know what to make of it and just stared at Choa without saying anything. Choa finally came out of it, clearing her throat. She said in a low, soft voice, "First of all, Father Carl's name is Konrad Krocha, and his counterpart is Konrad Troski. Father Carl, or Krocha, take a pick, contacted the enemy who is stationed on planet Uranus. He specified an attack on the main stations that were on one of Uranus's moons. He said that everything was destroyed beyond repair, and the mothership would not be back for at least two years. They did not know where the enemy spaceship came from. Few of the troops were captured. Then Father Carl went on to say that the invasion of Earth from planet Koton would probably be put off for another year or two until all the bases were built up again. There were not enough spaceships and men on planet Uranus to begin its journey to Earth. Konrad Troski said, 'Too bad, we cannot take over the Earth without the special nuclear radiation weapons.' Troski said, 'That will give us more time to build up our military and our new weapons, as long as we do not encounter stiffer inspections from the United States team.' Father Carl said he did not know how much longer he could stay undercover without being caught. He also said that there might be some suspicion now. Konrad Troski told Father Carl to hang on for a few more weeks. 'Get all the information you can from the station. You should have all the diagrams, plans, photos, etc. Then we will not need the station anymore. It will be easier once our stations are built.' Then Troski said he would contact the seaplane pilot up in Alaska, and offer him double the amount to take them across the Bering Strait to Russia in a hurry. He said he would contact them a week before they left."

Choa said, "That is it, now what?"

Al said, "Wow! What the hell are we getting into? We started out with a peaceful mission between two planets and a spaceship arriving to Earth, now turning out to be a world episode."

George said, "We have to think this out. Should we tell the others about it?"

Al said, "Not right now, we have to check them out first."

George said, "Well anyway, I think Mike and Joe are legit. Besides, we need Joe because he's from Canada and has stock in a seaplane company in Alaska. He also knows most of the other flyers in that neck of the woods. When they call in again, tell them to get their asses back here. It is an emergency. As a matter of fact, Joe and Mike called in early this morning at my house to say they located a site with all the information that was needed. They should be back home this evening. They will touch down about seven or eight o'clock at the Cuyahoga Airport."

Al canceled any plans that evening. After supper, he picked up George and headed for the airport to wait for Joe and Mike's arrival, which was about 7:25 when they landed, taxied to the hangar they rented. They got out of the plane to find Al and George waiting for them. "Well," said Joe. "What did you think, we skipped the country?"

George laughed. "Yeah, knowing you guys."

Al said, "We would not come down here, but we have a few crazy problems mounting up that cannot wait until morning. Let's go to the Red Baron. I will buy you guys a drink and give you the lowdown."

Al and George, explained the whole situation of what was happening. They explained about Father Carl and his crony. Al told Joe, "We have to contact your Uncle Charles and explain what is going on. We have to stop them from getting across to Russia."

Mike said, "Why don't we just nab them right here."

Al said, "We thought of that, but that would jeopardize our whole project. Besides, we think we are being watched by either the F.B.I. or C.I.A. We have to be cautious from now on, in what we do or say. Starting tomorrow, we will have to take shifts and stay at the station day and night so no one else, especially Father Carl, gets messages from the spaceship. After we check out the others in our group, we will have more help. So let's go home and get some rest, we'll meet at the station in the morning to discuss this further."

The next morning, Sunday, Al, George, Joe, and Mike arrived almost at the same time at the gate. Al told them, "When we go in, the first thing we will do is hunt over the whole area for any bugs. We will check every inch, and be careful not to make a sound. If anything is found, we'll leave it where it is. Do not mention anything more about outer space or Father Carl by mouth. Write it down."

After about an hour and fifteen minutes Joe motioned everyone over. He pointed to one of the venetian blind slats inside the valance. Al said, "Yeah, we got something."

They looked for another half an hour and found the second bugging device on the opposite side of the room in the seam at the bottom of the window drape. George said, "That's funny. They should hide it in the drape seam, because that's where they would look if they were looking for something." (It was said in a whisper.) When everything was checked out they all left about one o'clock for home so they could enjoy the rest of their Sunday.

The four of them arrived very early Monday morning ahead of the rest of the group. Al was outside the transmitting room in the hallway, waiting for Tom and Bart. Actually they were the controllers and operation bosses of Future Vision Cable Company, who kept everything on an even keel. First Tom came in. Al then said, "Hi. How was your weekend?"

Tom said, "It was all right. Just quiet."

Then Bart arrived asking, "What is it? Coffee break already?"

Al laughed. "Well something serious came up and you two will have to avoid the transmitting and receiving room for a couple of days. We will explain everything this week. So you can take your time checking out your employees and what have you."

"That is fine with us I guess," said Bart. "We will talk to you later."

George, Joe, and Mike came out into the hallway after checking everything again in the transmitting room, just as Tom and Bart left. Joe told Al he was going home to phone his Uncle Charles about the situation, and possibly fly to Alaska to decide what to do. George said he was going down to Father Carl's church to see if that other Russian showed up. Al went down to relieve George at six o'clock. This went on until Thursday. At three o'clock, this Russian walked to the church—up the steps and in he went.

After a few minutes, George could hear footsteps, heavy breathing, and a door shutting. George had the recording on for a good ten or twelve minutes. There were foot noises and a door opening and then shutting and then silence. George started his car and headed back to Al's house in a hurry. George did not call in, in case the car was bugged. He got to Al's house and beeped the horn. Al came out and George got out of the car and pointed to the van parked in front of the garage and said, "In case our cars are bugged." They drove down to Choa's condo in Mentor. George said, "We might have something, because they both sounded excited." They parked in the lot in front of Choa's building. Al got out and rang the buzzer, but there wasn't any answer. Al sat back in the van.

"She should have been home already. We will just have to wait," George said. Choa arrived about five-thirty. Al beeped his horn and she spotted them, waved and parked. Al and George got out of the van. All three walked to Choa's condo. "Now what trouble are we getting into?" George said, "We don't know, but we will soon find out when we listen to this tape."

They went into Choa's suite. George and Al sat down on the couch. Choa said, "Let me fix you guys a drink." Al said he would have a scotch on the rocks. George would have the same. "Now that you guys have your drinks, let us see what you have this time." Choa listened intentively. Then she said, "Wow! These guys are for real. The Russian Troski said, 'You gather all the information and do not go back to the Chesterland station if you think they might know something. Do not jeopardize the project. As far as the seaplane pilot, he won't know anything either. When he drops us off about a half a mile from the Russian coast, a Russian patrol boat will be waiting for us. When the pilot flies back, his plane will blow up accidently about half way back to Alaska. That will take care of any loose talk. We leave next Friday. Be ready.' "

George said, "Holy shit! These Russians are nuts."

Al picked up the phone and called Joe, hoping he was still there, and that his phone was not bugged. Joe was still at home. He said he talked to his Uncle Charles. He told him something important came up, and to take the company plane to Anchorage. He said be looking for him in a few hours. Al told Joe the latest message to convey to his uncle. He said, "I am going down to Father Carl's church Sunday, with my wife. We already know he is not coming up to the station anymore, so Sunday I will ask him why he did not come to the meeting Saturday."

Saturday, we received a message from the spaceship that was recorded so no one could listen in. They say they are between our planets, Saturn and Jupiter. They also say they are waiting for a message from us. Al said, "Tomorrow we will block off the two bugs and transmit our message so they know we are in contact."

Sunday, Al and his wife went down to Father Carl's church. They sat in one of the pews while everyone was coming in. At ten o'clock, the service started, but no Father Carl. The prayers were said and the priest got up to the pulpit and announced that Father Carl was called away suddenly last Saturday, for an emergency. Al and his wife stayed till the end of the service so they could talk to the other priest. Al said, "I am sorry I missed him, I really wanted to talk to him. Where did he say he was going, and for how long?"

The priest said, "He told me he had urgent business,

where he grew up in Montana; and would take a leave of absence for a month."

Al and George got ahold of Tom, Bart, and Roosevelt to tell them what the situation was. They were taking a flight to Alaska and did not know when they would be back. Al and George got on the next flight out of Hopkins Airport. Al said to George, "I know we did not get a chance to check out the rest of the gang. We will just have to trust them. Besides, they would have left too." Al called Joe in Alaska before they left, to look out for Father Carl and his crony; and to check for the pilot that would take them across.

They arrived early Monday morning, and Joe's uncle was waiting for them with a cab to take them to the sea inlet, where the seaplane was waiting. The three of them took off for the Bering Strait coast, where Joe was waiting for them. They arrived about the middle of the afternoon. Joe said they talked to the seaplane attendant and were told that Armand took two people with baggage up to the coast to do some fishing, about two hours ago. Al said, "Damn it, we missed them. Miss Choa, interpreted that they were leaving Friday."

George said, "It is not her fault they changed their minds."

The pilot Armand took off up the coast of Alaska for a few miles, and then banked left, heading across the Bering Strait to Russia, to avoid suspicion. The plane got close to the international boundary line, when the plane blew up. A fishing vessel, a little ways up, about ten miles from the boundary, spotted a flash in the sky and a plane blown to pieces. They radioed the Coast Guard of the incident and location. They arrived in about twenty-five minutes to the scene.

There were parts of the plane and parts of bodies scattered all over the water. The Coast Guard crew picked up what they could of the wreckage and of the bodies and an attaché case still floating intact. A few minutes later, a Russian patrol boat arrived wanting to know what happened. The Coast Guard captain told them a plane had crashed. It looked like a seaplane from Alaska. The Russian captain said to leave everything alone. "You are in Russian waters."

The Coast Guard captain told the Russian to check their maps and compass. "You are about five miles into the United States' jurisdiction. You guys better turn around and head back to Russia, or we will haul all your asses in." The Russian captain apologized, made a quick turn, and headed for Russia. At the same time, Al, George, Joe, and his uncle saw the Coast Guard cutter in a hurry and knew something was up. They took off and followed them to the scene. Uncle Charles was piloting and Joe was taking movies with his camcorder of the whole incident, including the Coast Guard sailors picking up the attaché case, and the Russian patrol boat. The captain of the cutter radioed to Charles and asked what he was doing there. Charles said he knew the pilot of the downed seaplane. "Is that so?" said the captain. "We have your plane number. We will talk to you later."

Charles continued to circle around and around so Joe could take enough pictures. Charles said, "To hell with them. We are not violating any laws, and besides, I want to know what is going on." They finally headed back to the Alaska coast, where the Coast Guard station was located. They docked their plane to wait for the cutter. Charles said, "We do not know when they will be back, so let us go and eat lunch until they arrive."

After lunch, they headed back to find the Coast Guard cutter was already there. Al asked Charles, "What story are we going to tell?" Charles said he would only answer the questions they would ask and nothing more.

All four got cleared at the Coast Guard gate. They walked into the office where Captain Gray was sitting with the attaché case on the floor by his desk. The captain got up and said, "I am Captain Gray," shaking Charles' hand. Charles introduced his nephew Joe and his friends Al Difiara and George Barns. "So you know the dead pilot Armand?" said Captain Gray.

"Yes," said Charles. "I have talked to him between trips and at the Seaplane Association meetings."

"I see," said the captain. "Who were his passengers?"

"That I do not know." The captain then asked, "What were you doing up here, just at this particular time?" Charles said that Al, George, and Joe came up to visit. He was showing Al and George the sights, because they had never been to Alaska.

"Uh-huh, well did you know that Armand was warned a few months ago about being in Russian waters. His excuse was he got off course."

Charles said, "The plane did not crash in Russian waters. He was about five miles from the boundary line."

The captain said, "That is all for now, we will get hold of you if anything comes up."

The four left, and Joe asked why the captain did not ask us any questions. Charles answered, "I do not know, but something does not jive here."

Al said, "You will find out sooner or later. The answer is in the attaché case."

Joe told his uncle, "Remember the story I told you at the seaplane station before I left for Ohio, about being reincarnated? Well these two guys are also in the same situation. The two passengers that were on Armand's plane were Russian agents. The one was disguised as a Catholic priest named Father Carl, who infiltrated into our club.

Armand was being paid a lot of money to take them across the Bering Strait to Russia. On the way back, the plane was to blow up with just Armand on board, but something went wrong, and the bomb went off prematurely."

Uncle Charles said, "What happens now?"

Al and George simultaneously said, "We do not know." No one said anything the rest of the way, walking toward Charles' seaplane. They all boarded and took off to pick up the other seaplane.

Al said, "Eventually, they will open up the attaché case. Because I think I know what's in it. Sure as God is my witness, we will hear from someone." He continued, "I will not tell you what might be in that case, because if they do ask you any questions of its contents, you will not have an answer."

"Well," said Uncle Charles, "we will drop the whole matter for now, since you guys are up here in Alaska anyway, you might as well stay for a few days at my place. By the way, Joe is a hell of a cook." The three stayed for three days while Uncle Charles checked on the company. Joe borrowed one of the seaplanes that just came out of the shop, with a brand new engine. Joe took Al and George on a sightseeing tour of Alaska, since he regained his vision. He said, "It feels good to fly a seaplane again." Joe said, "Do you guys know that I own part of this company? I have a number of shares that split twice already. I figure after we get this so-called spaceship landing and its outcome, I will probably get my family and move back to Alaska. Remind me later to phone my family in British Columbia."

On the fourth day, Friday, Uncle Charles flew the three of them back to Anchorage. The weather was clear and crisp, as they said good-bye to Uncle Charles. They took a cab to the airport where their company plane was ready for takeoff. They did not say too much on the flight back to Ohio. They made one fuel stop and finally got cleared at the Cuyahoga County Airport for landing instructions.

Eleven
Caught in a Vortex, Spaceship from Planet Thrae

This is the year 2095 on planet Thrae. The spaceship is about to leave our launch area at about eight-thirty A.M. It is a beautiful morning, with a blue sky and the temperature at about 75 degrees. All controls are go, and we're waiting for the green light for take off. Everything is always checked off three times, so we never have any errors. All our mechanical devices and computers have a backup, so when we're in flight and something goes wrong with any component, it automatically switches over to its backup. All these components are on a robotic system, so the component can be removed and taken back to the repair station on the ship. After repair, it is taken back immediately and installed in its place. When a component is being repaired, it is scientifically analyzed as to what went wrong. Then it is made stronger and better than the first part, so it lasts longer. They have checked different types of alloys in space. They seem to last indefinitely, because there isn't any moisture in space to corrode and deteriorate the metals.

Jarson is chief air and space controller at the station. He is ready for one of our many takeoffs. Now the green light comes on for a clear and safe launching. All nuclear power units are revved to the half point of our thrust, so it will have a smooth effect on takeoff. They gradually speed through the first sound barrier, which, if stood a few miles away from the ship, would give a loud crack. You cannot hear it inside the ship because it happens a few miles behind the ship. It is recorded through their sensor sound equipment, just like everything else that is recorded in the computers. This is so we can check our data to see if there will need to be any changes made. After a few miles out, heading for the stratosphere toward outer space, engineer, Ravus, sent the data to the chief. He indicated that everything was okay. His job is to check out the whole system for any malfunctions. Jarson then gave the data to Quamo, the map reader and direction finder. The course was set, and Jarson put all dials and instruments in motion. Our speed started to increase every second. They would need about 2,500 miles an hour to get away from the gravitational pull if they went straight up.

While all that was going on, Doctor Lamis, the coordinator, was inspecting all the records of every individual on the spaceship. He makes sure everyone and things are free from any disease or disorders. This particular spaceship has a crew of 175 and carries an additional passenger list of about 400 people. Incidently, not just anyone can go on this space journey. You must have a college education, with a course in atmosphere, astronomy, and space, which is a necessity for this trip.

Doctor Lamis and his assistants, all very well educated in their special fields, were ready for examinations and aptitude tests of all the passengers. All of this had already been done on planet Thrae. All the tests were done as a precaution, so there would not be any chaos when we reached our spacecity. Once in awhile on our trip to the spacecity, there are one or two persons who do not pass when we are in flight. So, when we get to the spacecity, they are sent back to planet Thrae.

The purpose of having knowledgeable passengers on

this trip was to promise the future education in the space program, for those who desire to choose this field. This program would give them a firsthand account and knowledge that they would not obtain on planet Thrae. Many have chosen this field in the past, and many could not persevere in it. In time, they were sent back to planet Thrae.

Now we have left the atmosphere, passed through the stratosphere, and into the ionosphere, heading for outer space. Our speed has increased slightly. We can now feel just a little bit of weightlessness, which automatically switches on our neutralization components. This magnetizes the entire spaceship. It gives the same gravitational pull that planet Thrae has. Everything on board is like a jetliner, but larger. It has minimal recreation and enough nourishment to last much longer than the trip to the spacecity. After landing on spacecity Orant, the spaceship, the crew, and personnel, took three weeks preparation before takeoff to the unknown venture to planet Earth. There were so many things to check over on the new spaceship, named Ventara. They had a few trial runs to make sure everything was working properly.

Commander Siro was in charge of the spaceship and the overseer of the venture. Captain Cham was head pilot. The takeoff was routine when they left the spacecity, with everyone wishing them good luck and a safe voyage there and back. They would be gone for at least two years until they returned.

We are in our first week of space travel, arriving between our eighth planet, Komo. Komo is a dead, cold desolate place. The ninth planet Mirna, is also in our sights. We will reach Mirna in a week. We are ahead of schedule, and we will make one orbit around planet Mirna to get some data on anything that might be of any consequence to our travels. Might as well make the most of this journey

154

because it might be a while before we make another, depending on what we encounter.

We have taken a few hundred photos of planet Mirna and its three moons. It is a very strange planet, with its awesome colors as though there is life on it. When all the photos are studied and analyzed, maybe we will get a better idea of its landscape, and if there is any kind of precipitation. Our schedule does not give us enough time for any exploration, or we would miss the line of this planet Mirna, which orbits in one direction. The tenth planet, Otamu, (or Earth's ninth planet Pluto) orbits in the opposite direction, which we discovered is in another solar system. This lineup only comes around about every thirty years, which gives us accurate data of the direction we are traveling. This is one of those chances taken, for we really do not know what to expect in the unknown. After the second day of observing and photo taking, we were back on track, heading toward planet Otamu. We will be leaving our solar system and entering a different solar system. This ought to be a new experience for the crew. It was calculated that time travel between the two planets Mirna and Otamu should take about two months.

Over a month ago, when we finally communicated with the other planet named Earth, we were given all kinds of vital information. We know now there is life in the other solar system. So, we should not have too much trouble locating their planet. They gave us the names of nine planets that are in their solar system. The ninth, and last planet of theirs, is called Pluto. We discovered Pluto as our tenth planet naming it planet Otamu (Pluto). Obviously, they are not as advanced as we are, because they did not know too much of anything outside of the planet Pluto. They still gave us enough information to show us that they did know quite a bit of space technology. They claim that there are hundreds of manmade satellites in space, probing their planets and their sun. They also have a very small space station, which is the size of a pin head compared to our stations.

We are now starting into the third week, and a third distance of the way toward planet Otamu (Pluto). This is sure a large expanse of pitch black, and the stars are so distant. It feels like we are intruding, and not supposed to be here. We noticed on the instrument panel we were getting off our course. At first, it was thought the navigator made an error. This was checked and double checked and there was no error. Then they noticed they were going at a very slow pace, but not on their own power. They tried to pull back on course, but the spaceship kept going in a direction, like an orbit, but around nothing. They tried to send a message out but all communications seemed to be dead.

As they got caught in a vortex, they noticed there were all kinds of debris from asteroids, and millions of dust particles, all revolving in the same direction. They sped up a little, you would think that if there were a centrifugal force, it would go from the center to outward. However, in this vortex, we were being drawn closer to the center, like it was by gravitational force. They cut their speed down a little more. They sure as hell did not want to get to the center. They were afraid they would disappear altogether. They viewed on their picture scope that something quite large was approaching them from the rear besides dust particles and asteroids. This object started going by them at a slow pace. They sped up a bit and got alongside of it. To their amazement, this was a large and unusual spacecraft, much larger than theirs. They tried to communicate with different frequencies, but to no avail. It seemed like it was lifeless. They investigated the whole craft for a way to board it. It looked like it must be caught in the votex also. They went underneath the foreign craft and noticed a large oblong seam, like it was made for an entrance. They anchored their ship to this strange craft, and beamed their lights and cameras on the underside.

While three of their crew got into their spacesuits and hooked up their oxygen lines, they were let out of the pressure chambers, hanging on their lifelines. They got to the underside of the other craft to see how vulnerable the hatch was. They knocked on the metal hatch, just in case there was any life inside. They did not get any response. Now they checked the seams to see if it could be opened from the outside, like their craft with a code. They tried electrical frequencies. They even tried to pry it with a flat bar.

Commander Siro was on the communicator, suggesting that the hatch might be opened by vacuum. "Try drilling in different spots," he said, "to see what happens. We cannot waste too much time on this craft, or we will be stuck in the same situation." They tried drilling in eight different spots along the seam. Commander Siro was getting impatient. "What seems to be the problem?"

They hollered back, "Do not know what kind of metal the craft is made of, the drill did not even scratch it."

Commander Siro said, "We will try just one more thing. These diamond tip drills will cut through anything." They tried it with no resistance, and drilled right through. They drilled a few holes around the seam until they got about half way around. A gush of air was heard coming out of the last hole they drilled. The hatch started to slide open just a little, and then stopped. They tried the pry bar again, but it would not budge. This time they drilled more holes on the seam of the other side, and another gush of air came out with blue dust. The hatch slid open very slowly, with a groan, like it had not been opened in ages. They told the commander that they could use more light, which was available to them.

They lit up the whole flight cabin. Not a soul was in sight. The cabin was lined with a beautiful velvet material. The control panels were all push buttons and the openings below the buttons were something on the order of microphones. "We will have to check this out later." Commander Siro kept asking what was happening. They told him the flight cabin was empty and they were about to check out the rest of the craft. They checked out about eight rooms. When they got to the ninth room, there were about thirty personnel all lying down like they were asleep. This room looked like a sacred place of worship. On one wall, there was only one object, which looked like the sun. It was assumed this was a mass suicide. They looked around for any information, and took pictures of everything possible, including the strange clothing they were wearing. A notebook was found, made of some kind of parchment. Finally the commander could not stand it anymore. He put his spacesuit on, and came in and asked what the holdup was. He told the commander, "This craft is eerie, with about thirty corpses wearing the strangest uniforms. The controls looked a little more sophisticated than ours. The people look like us. The language found in the notebook, I have never seen before. The markings in this book might be the ship's log. Maybe the scribes in our ship can decipher it."

The control room had to be examined to see what made it go. The commander told us we had exactly three hours and we are getting out of here. They checked out the control room and found a cabinet, which looked like hundreds of microchips stored inside. In finding these microchips, there had to be some kind of unit to show them. They looked all over the control room and found nothing. Commander Siro, "Your time is running out."

They said, "There are a few more rooms we did not

look into. The doors where the bodies are, give us a half hour more."

"Okay, okay, get going," said the commander.

They ran through the corridor, opened one door, guessing this was the power room for the craft's energy. In the second room, we hit the jackpot. Here were a couple of projectors or video-looking machines of some kind. They called out to the commander to give us a hand, and bring Norh and Trox. This was the storeroom for all the information we might need. We hauled everything out, and stored it on Thrae's spaceship for further analysis. They left the strange craft as it was, except for the data that was taken. They could not close the hatch because of the lack of power. One of the crew brought back one of their spacesuits, which was made of a very unusual material they had never seen before.

Everyone was back on Spaceship Ventara. Everything was turned over to the staff of scholars and engineers. The commander gave the order to detach from the strange spacecraft. After Ventara's detachment from the spacecraft, they decided to fall behind for awhile. They were afraid to go forward at any speed so as not to be drawn to the center of the vortex. After a long, slow orbit in this endless whirlpool, the crew started to hear very soft, eerie voices from faint, misty figures throughout the spaceship. The crew did not know what to make of it.

The voices were starting to get to some of them. Commander Siro was talking over the intercom telling everyone to keep their cool. Eventually it would pass. Doctor Lamis translated the moans and cries. He told the commander that the voices were saying we invaded their territory, and that we are in their power with no way out. Commander said, "We will see about that."

The commander isolated himself in a darkened room

to talk to the voices after getting the translations from Doctor Lamis. He told the voices of the mission to travel to another planet to save souls. The voices, after time, answered, "We are lost souls from troubled planets throughout the universe, waiting for the salvation of all souls to enter the kingdom of God."

All of a sudden, the crew started to hear hundreds and hundreds of whispers, getting louder and louder, like they were agreeing with the one voice. The commander came out of the darkened room and sat down, exhausted. "Was it that bad?" questioned Doctor Lamis.

The commander said, "It was downright scary! Listen to those voices. The crew's going to go nuts sooner or later."

Scientist Carta came busting into the room where the commander and Doctor Lamis were discussing the events of those eerie voices. Commander Siro looked up and said, "What is it? Don't you know better than to charge in here without being announced?"

"Yes I know," said Doctor Carta, "but I am too excited to go through formalities."

Commander, "Well, what is it?"

"We deciphered some of the log books from that strange spacecraft. It stated they departed from planet Shamo in the year 1284. They were positioned in the Galaxy Pro Carno, which was swallowed up by a gigantic black hole. A few thousand people escaped by spaceships to other destinations unknown. 'We knew there were other galaxies and solar systems, but truly unknown were the consequences that were involved to get there. We were of one hundred thirty-five people on this spacecraft called Merci. We were caught in a vertigo, and could not escape. We had been going around and around for one year, running out of breathing air.

'This is the year 1286, it is the end of our time. We have

launched all eight of our shuttle crafts, with twelve personnel to a shuttle. The thirty-five of us left on spacecraft
Merci, which lasted about a month. Also, four personnel
died in the last year while in this vortex. We would take a
sleeping medicine. Good-bye, Commander Torzo.'

"You will also be surprised to know," said Doctor
Carta, "that the spacesuit we acquired from their spacecraft, which we did a carbon test on, registered as about six
hundred years old."

"Commander, what you mean is that spacecraft has
been in this vortex for six hundred years?"

Carta indicated, "Not only that, all those microchips
are part of the archives and history of their planet."

The commander wondered if we ever get out of this
jam, on our journey back to planet Thrae, if it would be fea-
sible to venture and find that spacecraft and examine it
thoroughly. The commander could not believe there was
another civilization that advanced that far back in time. It
would be taken up at a more opportune time. In the meantime, we had to figure a way out of this vortex.

The whispering voices were getting louder and more
pathetic. Some voices had a low, agonizing moan of self
pity. Some voices were translated. A few in unison cried
out over and over again, "We are lost, help us." After about
a week of this monotony, everybody was getting a little concerned. They all got together every day, to come up with a
solution. If they did not get out of their situation soon, they
would be so far off course that they would be lost in space.
If that happens, they will probably never be found. They
figured out what happened, and came to a conclusion that
they got caught in a vortex or some kind of whirlpool. One
solar system was going in one direction and the other was
traveling the opposite way. It is like a stream running its
course. Sometimes the water along the bank keeps going

around the same circle all the time, not going downstream. This is what is happening to them. Twice they have already passed the halfway mark in this so-called whirlpool, then back around where they started.

The third time in this unauthorized situation they did not try to pull directly straight out, but followed the orbiting whirlpool around one more time. Using their emergency side jets, they gradually pulled out of this orbit to feel free from the whirlpool force. They were going at a fantastic speed. Pilot Cham said, "This ship has never gone this fast." What is worse is when the spaceship gets out of the whirlpool, they will be heading in the wrong direction. It has taken them almost a day and a half of tracking on their computer to get the bearing on planet Otamu (Pluto) and turn in that direction. They were off by a few degrees. That two weeks cost them a lot of distance. They had to plot their course again to the distance they were supposed to be from planet Otamu (Pluto). If they came across any other surprises, they really would have been in trouble, even though this spaceship was well equipped for two years of travel. It was supplied for an extra six months. Everything was supplied for the trip back. They had to avoid the whirlpool that they encountered.

Since they were not going to approach close to planet Otamu (Pluto), they had to plot the course almost in line with planet Zumi (Uranus), and bypass planet Tarquam (Neptune). This correction should put them exactly on course. They tried to observe planet Otamu, but it was too far for a good close up. After almost three weeks, they finally were opposite planet Otamu. If they did not get caught in that whirlpool, they would have been right on top of planet Otamu. They could have orbited the planet for a couple of days and took some photos.

"Maybe we will try it on the way back," said the commander. They were now three weeks behind, and did not know if they would make it up. By the time they got to the next planet, Tarquam (Neptune), which is the one they were bypassing, it would be too far in its orbit to take any decent photos. By the next week, they noticed they could get more speed with their magnetic gyros than when they left planet Thrae. It was believed the gravitational force away from our sun seemed to slow them down a bit. This was believed since they were in another solar system, traveling toward their sun, which was making them speed up faster. If this was the case, they might be a lot closer than was calculated to planet Tarquam (Neptune), which is possible according to their schedule and calculations. (It would give us a chance to orbit the planet, so we could record some data.) The calculated time between each planet was supposed to be about a month. At this rate of speed, we should approach these planets a few days earlier. Right on schedule, approaching planet Tarquam and ready to make at least one orbit, because this is a fairly large planet. We got half way around the planet and noticed on the video computer, a very small speck out in the distance.

Thinking it was the planet's moon, we sped up to get a closer look, when the communicator, Zomi, started to get signals from this object. The signals could not be deciphered. At the same time, the object was getting signals from the direction of the sun. This was put on the spaceship's decoder, but no results were obtained. They will have to try different codes until they come up with an answer. They caught up with this object that was orbiting the planet. It had some kind of flaps and gadgets. They looked like solar panels and three big markings, U.S.A. They caught up to this object, which was a manmade satellite.

Obviously, they must be on the right track to their

planet. They stayed alongside this U.S.A. object for the rest of the orbit, to observe what its mission was. We assumed it was taking photos of the planet. Only one difference, we were there in person taking our photos. Doctor Zomi was intercepting signals that were going to the satelite, bouncing off and going back in the direction it came from. We believed these were telephotos. They had to scan through the decipher computer for the right frequency, to see if it was an observation satellite.

In the meantime, Doctor Zomi's assistant, Darna, had intercepted the English language as we were coming out of orbit and getting back on track. We were at our normal speed, heading to our next checkpoint, which would supposedly be planet Zumi (Uranus). This should take, at the most, about a month. They had been sending coded messages since they started this voyage, and got very little response. It had no meaning because of too much static. They did not have the right frequency to correspond. We had been getting their messages on the spacecity Orant, because it had larger and more powerful generators to obtain such information. So we believed we were close enough to receive a clearer message. It became clearer, the closer we got to their world.

The voices were coming in faint, but a lot clearer than before. We were back on the voyage's track. Everything we picked up was recorded so we could study the language to try to make out what was being said. Everyone on the spaceship had to learn the English language on the spacecity Orant. We talked the language amongst ourselves. We thought it was the right pronunciation, spelling, and so on. One thing different was that Thrae's alphabet has twenty-two letters, versus Earth's English language alphabet which has twenty-six letters.

The messages we received were not long. They only

had a few words to identify themselves with names and location. These messages would come in about every four hours and they were usually the same thing. The message was played over and over again. They were also shown on our computer screen so we could analyze each word. We could not make it out at first, because we had to teach ourselves the assumed pronunciation. When we compared words, most of ours was way off with distinct accents. So if the case may be, when we sent an English message in return, they probably would not understand what we were talking about. We adjusted some of the words so to be enough for a simple message. Also we would send messages in our own tongue of Thrae. Just for curiosity, Zomi, the communicator, sent in English and Thrae language a simple message which read: "Traveling at a high rate of speed, will reach your world in about five months, the month of Dia, 2114." This message was put into the automatic transmitter computer and it would be transmitted every hour until we got a reply.

We cannot talk directly to our communicator on spacecity Orant, because we are too far away for any verbal conversation. We are at least communicating by code. So far the codes are clear, but the farther away we get, the less frequency control we have. Once we get to their planet, we should get our messages back to planet Thrae much clearer, and get our instructions on what has to be done. We should also find out what is wrong with their transmitters.

Some of our crew members are getting cabin fever, even though there is enough room and enough things to do. But how much of the same thing can one do over and over again?

We held our daily meeting, which was early in the day. We assume it is day, even though it is pretty much the same outside the spaceship, which really has no time at all. Our space clocks are marked with daytime hours and nighttime hours, so we know when to get up and go back to bed. We were up at the crack of the clock's dawn. We showered with the same water that was purified already a few dozen times, including that of our excreted urine, it was no different than on planet Thrae. The sun drew any liquid up into the clouds. It was purified on the way up, held in the clouds, then it rained a nice clean and pure water that was used over and over again since the beginning of time. Okay, now we had our breakfast. This consisted of eggs and other vegetables condensed from the galley of the ship, along with enough food to last longer than the trip involved.

All seven leaders gathered and sat down. Captain Cham started out inquiring how everyone was feeling. Everyone said, "Fine and dandy." We discussed the situation of some of the crew and passengers that were in a state of boredom. You have to remind all of them that this was to be expected when in training for this voyage. You have to look on the bright side. When we arrive on this other planet, it is not a spacecity like spacecity Orant. This is a real planet, which they call Earth. So while we still have about five months to go, rouse your people and the professor to refresh your training. Remember what your purpose is when arriving on planet Earth.

The leaders went back to their respective compartments where the training classes were held. They were not big rooms, you know. There was a limit to room space on a spaceship for a crew and men and women of a hundred and sixty. Each group of ten persons had their class at a different time schedule so everyone got a chance.

On our third week, after leaving planet Tarquam (Neptune), we were right on track to the next checkpoint. It would be just opposite planet Zumi (Uranus), when we started to get our first reply of English language. To us it was more of a jumble because we still did not quite understand it. We spent a lot of time deciphering the messages and making copies so everyone had it to study and got an idea of what they were up against. Each group of personnel had a class to listen to the audio and compare the words with their notes. Slowly but surely, it was starting to make sense. That meant we could send our messages in complete sentences.

The captain was giving the sender, Zomi, at least one message a day to send verbally. These messages were about the vortex or whirlpool between Thrae's solar system's last planet Mirna. It was their last planet Otamu (Pluto). "We got caught in a whirlpool going around and around for thousands of miles in a great circle, and could not get out for two weeks. When we did get out, we were almost lost in space, because we lost track of your last planet Otamu (Pluto). We could not observe the planet very well because of the two weeks we lost. We did gain speed which put us on schedual to planet Tarquam (Neptune). So we orbited the planet once, and accidently caught up to one of your man-made satellites, which had U.S.A. on it in big letters. In a few days we would sight the next planet Zumi as soon as it comes around in its orbit. We sent message after message of the progress of our space journey, hoping to reach the planet on schedule."

Zomi of spaceship Ventara, started to receive some pretty clear messages in English. They stated, "The last three planets belong in the Earth's solar system, starting from the last planet, which is Pluto, (you named it Otamu). Next is Neptune, (your Tarquam), and Uranus, (your Zumi). You now have to pass Saturn, which is beautiful with a large ring around it. Then you will pass Jupiter, then Mars, and finally you will hit your destination Earth, the living planet. We were the third planet from our sun."

Now that we were starting to understand each other, we were now negotiating on the rest of the trip to Earth. There was still about four months' travel time. They also told us from Earth that we would probably see many more man-made satellites from time to time, that our government and other governments had sent into space at one time or other.

Zomi sent messages to them to try and send videos of Earth or anything that would interest us. We wanted to see if we could program the videos into our system. In about four days, the astronomer caught a glimpse of the planet Zumi, which was Earth's named planet of Uranus. As spaceship Ventara approached planet Uranus, they came across one of the moons before going into orbit. It should take about twelve hours to orbit. As they started to circle the far side of the planet, one more moon was sighted. The astronomer said he saw another moon at a further distance. But something did not seem right. Either we were gaining speed, or that moon was moving toward us. The speed indicator showed that the ship was not at an increase. By the looks of that moon, it was traveling right toward our spaceship Ventara.

As it got closer, there were flashes of light, like lasers. It made a pattern from top to bottom and hit our spaceship on the port side. It caused slight damage, which threw the spaceship slightly out of control. The enemy whizzed right by and started to turn for a re-run.

The commander said, "What the hell is their problem; they gave no warning, no nothing. Land this thing anywhere. The planet is way too far, so head for the nearest moon."

We outraced him and maneuvered to the nearest moon, and landed with a little thud. The enemy finally caught up and shot another blast, which caught the same

port side, causing a little more damage. We were not prepared for any encounters with anyone, and they did not
even try to communicate with us. The spaceship Ventara
could not travel with the protective shield drawn because
the spaceship would lose its speed. By the time the enemy
could come around again, spaceship Ventara was ready for
them. The protection shield only covered two thirds of the
ship because of the damage on its left side. Spaceship Ventara had twelve nuclear powered laser weapons. Three on
one side and three on the other side were aimed by computer, as each laser would converge into one, at double the
distance the enemy could fire. The radar caught the
approach, and three seconds later, automatically fired with
both sets of three lasers, slicing the enemy spacefighter to
pieces before they could fire back. The enemy soared right
over and crashed at a distance in pieces.

We tried to communicate to planet Earth with no
results, because we were on the far side of Uranus' moon.
Three of our ten probes were sent out. Two for safety cover-
age of our spaceship in case of other enemies. The enemy
must of signaled back to their base. The third probe headed
for the enemy's crash site to see if anything could be found
in the wreckage. In the meantime, there was a crew repair-
ing the damaged side of the spaceship. It looked like a couple of days to complete repairs.

One of our probes caught four enemies on the radar
scope approaching from the far end of the moon. They were
still quite a distance away. We scrambled six more probes,
all equipped with laser weapons. That left us with one spare
probe. Five probes were sent the opposite way around the
moon to catch the enemy from behind. Two probes were
sent to head off the enemy, with the other two probes
already waiting and wanting them to chase the probes
while the other five probes approached from the rear. The

five probes gave the call to the four that the enemy were on the scope. The four probes made an abrupt turn. Then one went left, one went right, and one went straight up. The fourth one went straight ahead. The enemy became confused and did not know which one to go after, so they split up. Two after one and one apiece for the other three. They played right into the other five probes' hands. Two probes went after one of the single ones, three probes went after the two. The three probes shot at the same time and sliced through both enemy crafts, which blew up into pieces.

We turned to go after the other enemy. We caught a third one that blasted one of the probes to smitherines. The fourth enemy broke off in a different direction to get away from us. The eight of us took pursuit and followed the enemy leading us to one of the other moons. Two probes followed the enemy craft. Three probes went left and three probes went right to circle the moon. To our surprise, we found the enemy camp with two stations, and six more spacecraft on the surface. Three probes took to the stations, which were pretty large, and three probes took the six craft exposed. Simultaneously, we sliced up the parked craft to pieces. The other three probes shot up all the entrances of the stations. The enemy craft, with the two probes following, did not land right away. He circled the moon once more, deciding on what to do. As he approached his base, there was not any signal to land. So we surrounded him in the center of our group, forcing him to go with us to our spaceship on the other moon, where Spaceship Ventara emergencied to land.

We arrived with no resistance from the enemy craft. The doors were opened with the pressure curtains on. One probe entered at a slow pace, so the enemy had to slow down also before entering. It is a tight squeeze to enter two craft simultaneously. There was another entrance at the damaged side, which was out of commission until repairs were made. The commander sent three probes back to the other moon with caution for investigation. The one probe that checked out the crash site of the enemy that was knocked down earlier, was scattered over a large area and would take weeks to pick up the pieces. There was not time for that.

The three probes approached cautiously and landed a few hundred feet from the enemy station. There were three men to each of the probes. One leader and five of the recruits got out of their probes wearing equipped space-suits, clutching their weapons. We noticed a number of casualties on the ground, dead or dying from lack of breathing air and wounds. We did not bother to look inside the first station. It was in a shambles. The second station was in fairly good shape except for the entrances, which were blown open. There were about a dozen dead, lying on the floor of the station. There were about twenty enemies in spacesuits moving debris, so they could get the undamaged craft out. There were eight craft inside. The first three were damaged when the entrances were blown in.

We caught them by surprise. They were to busy try-ing to get the undamaged craft out of the station, until one of them noticed us and cried out in some unknown language. They started shooting at us, hitting one of the recruits in the leg. We all fired at once, killing six of them right on the spot. The other fourteen stopped what they were doing, put their hands up and surrendered. We huddled them outside the station. We tried to talk to them, but no one understood each other. We called back to Spaceship Ventara telling the commander that we needed more help, and to come himself to look over the situation. The commander arrived in a couple of hours with two more probes and eight recruits.

Every inch of the area and station were gone over for more survivors. They also confiscated some equipment, charts, maps, logs, and what have you. We did not get too much information from the enemy because we could not understand them. We talked in sign language. They pointed to two dead enemies lying on the ground by the one entrance. We walked over to the bodies, and the one pointed to the insignias and then pointed to our commander's insignias. In other words, their leaders got killed when we raided them. They do not know what to do. That is why they did not put up too much of a fight. Commander Siro said he was going back to the spaceship to get it repaired as soon as possible. We should be back with the spaceship in about thirty hours.

Back at the spaceship, one enemy was being interrogated. We tried to decipher the language. It would probably take a couple of days before anything was learned. The enemy did mention the name Koton a few times, like that was where he came from. The repair crew worked straight through, about twenty-two hours, getting everything in working order. The spaceship took off heading for the other moon, getting there in a couple of hours. The landing was near the probe so they could easily embark onto the spaceship. The prisoners were in a compound, which looked like they could just walk off, but could not because of the invisible fence. If you got too close, you would get zapped. The prisoners were loaded on the spaceship with some equipment, all the information we could find, food, and what oxygen was left. The commander said to completely destroy all their craft and buildings, and anything else that may be used. When that was done, spaceship Ventara got underway at a moderate speed with its protection shield still on, until they got back on course, away from planet Uranus. Then the spaceship would retract the protection shield and pick up speed rapidly. They were still a little bit ahead of schedule.

All the personnel really were going to be busy questioning all those prisoners, as soon as their language barrier was broken. In the meantime, there were services held for the pilot and the recruits who were killed when their probe was disintegrated by the enemy.

Zomi, the communicator, finally received a message from planet Earth since they got back on course. Earth said they did not get any messages for a few days and wanted to know if anything was wrong. The commander told Zomi to send a message telling Earth that we landed on one of Uranus' moons for minor repairs. We were back on course heading for planet Saturn. The spaceship should arrive in about three weeks. The time from this point on was well spent learning yet another language. We could obtain information from this enemy and study all their writings. More and more of the language was being translated into Thrae's language. We now found out that the name Koton was the planet they came from. Their business on Uranus' moon was to set up stations for the spacecraft. Each one that was questioned gave a slightly different story about developing colonies on the moon. We asked, "Are there colonies on the planet Uranus?"

They said, "No."

While all these questions were being asked, the enemies were being secretly x-rayed through the brain, in a form of a lie detector. About fifty percent were lies, especially when asked if they had colonies on the Uranus planet. "If you are building colonies, how come you are set up as being aggressive?"

They answered, "We are not aggressive. We are protecting ourselves."

The interrogator said, "Bullshit! You people fired on us

without warning. And another thing, if we were aggressive, all of you would be dead with a capital D."

It took a full week to question all fifteen prisoners. We got pretty much the same story. We studied the x-ray lie detector graphs, and to our findings, they were all programmed on what to say. Now, when we finally studied all the information gathered up from the stations on the moon, it gave quite a different story. The language from planet Koton was very simple to decipher. The information from their logs gave the account that there was a colony on planet Uranus that stated, "It was built up within the last ten years with personnel and equipment and the moon, with their stations that we destroyed. It was the first stepping stone to invading the planet Earth."

They knew of planet Earth many, many years ago, because of the races being populated, plus other living planets throughout the galaxy. It also gave the tally of all the equipment and aggressive crafts they had. We destroyed most of them, so that left the enemy only a handful on planet Uranus. The mothership left for planet Koton about two months ago, for more equipment and spacecraft. It took a little over a year to get back to planet Koton. That meant the mothership would not be back for almost two years before getting back to planet Uranus. The fighter craft that was examined was simply made. The whole craft was operated on an electro-magnetic gyro with a storage of nuclear protons. The craft checked out to be very low on energy and needed a recharge. It was made of a very lightweight, durable material for radiation protection.

The Spaceship Ventara continued on course and decided to head right for planet Earth, since we had less than three months to go. The spaceship was a little overcrowded at this time. Two rooms had to be vacated of personnel, and doubled up with other personnel in their rooms. The two rooms kept the prisoners until we reached our destination. They bitched and moaned how crowded it was. They were told that if they were not happy with the conditions, they would be let off the ship.

Doctor Trenta and his colleages deciphered planet Koton's notes and logs from their stations that were destroyed on Uranus' moon. All the information compiled read as, "Enemy from planet Koton in contact with Konrad Kracha, who is stationed in Cleveland, Ohio, United States of America, disguised as a Catholic priest, Father Carl." This Father Carl must be a spy on planet Earth. He has gathered information that reads as follows—"The buildup of spacecraft and troops with the latest sophisticated weapons will be at the disposal to the countries on Earth by the year 2004 Earth time. Landing sites are at Siberia, the Arctic, and the peninsula of Russia across from Alaska at the Bering Strait. From the headquarters on planet Koton, all details of invasion to Earth will be transmitted every month until time of actual departure. By the end of year 2003, at least one thousand spacecraft equipped with the latest missiles and manpower, started their journey to Earth. By the end of 2003, your country should be ready to merge with us; and within a year's time we should be in control of your world."

Commander Siro of spaceship Ventara was shaking his head in disbelief of what he had read. He told Doctor Trenta to inform the dispatch Zomi to send a message, in detail, to planet Thrae of the situation. "Send the two new spaceships to planet Zumi, which was named planet Uranus by Earth. Investigate for enemies on the planet, which is an enemy of planet Koton. The newer spaceship should be more powerful and faster, so it should take five months between solar systems and to watch for a vortex of an opposite in centrifugal force, which will draw the ship to the center the faster it goes. When you get nearer the area, slow down. If the ship feels like it's being pulled in, detour around it, even if you lose time. Zomi will explain the details.

"If there are enemies on planet Zumi, you are to commence and destroy them, and all their stations, and also check out Zumi's five moons for any other activity. Their mothership left recently for their planet Koton, and would not be back for almost two years. That meant our ships from planet Thrae should arrive on planet Zumi in ample time before they returned. When the job was done, we waited for the enemies' mothership or ships to return and destroy them or any other type of enemy crafts. If they invaded Earth, that would mean that they could invade any other planet including planet Thrae."

A message was also sent to the station in Chesterland in code to Earth, short and simple, "An enemy, not the people from planet Thrae, is planning to invade planet Earth. Will discuss when we arrive."

We continued traveling at our lightspeed, without further incident, for about three weeks, approaching Earth's next planet, Saturn. This looked like a beautiful planet with a large ring around it, with a couple of moons. We decided not to orbit Saturn or Jupiter or Mars. We did not want to lose anymore time than possible, especially with prisoners aboard. Besides, the people on Earth claimed they had already explored these three planets. As our spaceship Ventara was passing planet Saturn, we would be traveling about five weeks before we would get to planet Mars. As far as planet Jupiter was concerned, it was at the other end of the solar system, which meant it was out of our travel path anyway.

In our third week of travel toward planet Mars, our navigator, Jac, informed the commander that the ship was slowing down for reasons unknown. The outer scopes were checked, and what we approached was a greenish haze. It looked like it was getting thicker, the deeper in the spaceship traveled. This was slowing down the spaceship more and more. More thrust was applied to no avail, until the spaceship came to a complete stop. It was like being stuck in a large vat of glue. "Now what do we do? The spaceship will not move in any direction." Jac, the navigator, said that the instruments indicated the spaceship was moving with the green haze, about ten miles an hour out of the traveling path.

This is a hell of a space storm, if that is what you can call it. If we did not do something soon, we would be drifting out of the Earth's solar system and be lost forever. All communications going out or coming in ceased. One of the scientists named Hirga suggested we take some of the matter in for a complete analysis. The commander thought it was a good idea. The greenish matter was obtained through one of the safety tubes, and put under transparent casing. Different chemicals were applied to which all were negative. Scientist Hirga noticed when changing to different chemicals, oxygen was having an effect on the green matter. The commander was informed of what happened. The only thing was how much oxygen did we have to spare? Even though we did obtain some from the enemy. Scientist Hirga tried some H_2O (water). To his surprise, it dissolved the green matter even faster with a chain reaction. Commander Siro said, "Good."

First we had to get some around the whole spaceship. There were a number of volunteers. They got in their spacesuits, starting at the entrance mixed with some type of antifreeze spraying a thin mist, working their way around the whole ship, which seemed to be freeing it from its greenish prison. They had to be conservative with the water even through they acquired many gallons from the enemy. The volunteers got back in the ship. The power sprayers were positioned in the front weapons tubes of the spaceship, spraying a fine water spray mixed with some type of anti-freeze to prevent it from freezing in space. It took almost a week to spray a path through the green mist, and finally it started to pick up speed and went back to its normal course. They used a lot of water to get out of that mess. The enemy's water was used up, and also about two-thirds of Spaceship Ventara's supply was used up. Everyone was put on a water ration until they got to their destination. The ship was almost out of special anti-freeze. We were hoping planet Earth had the materials to make more. Some of the oxygen was used also, or there would have been hardly any oxygen at all. The commander thought we would never get out of that one.

While traveling these five weeks to planet Mars, it was decided to give complete examinations to the fifteen prisoners before landing on planet Earth, just as a precautionary measure. One prisoner at a time was taken under guard to doc's office. Doctor Pil gave a complete physical from head to toe. The doctor noticed a small scar about a half an inch behind the left ear. He asked the prisoner how he got it. The prisoner's answer was, he got it in a battle. The second prisoner was brought in and was given a complete physical and also had a small half-inch scar behind his left ear. The doctor did not ask where he got it so he would not look too suspicious. The doctor examined the rest of the thirteen prisoners. They all had the same scar behind their left ear. The doctor had a meeting with the commander and some of the other officers.

The doctor gave his report that all prisoners were physically fit. He stated that all fifteen prisoners had this half-inch scar behind their left ear. The doctor concluded by saying that he believed something was planted in or next to the brain on each of these prisoners. The commander asked how come it did not show up in the x-rays that were taken before. The doctor said, "The x-rays were not studied that carefully because we did not expect anything."

The commander said, "We have to find out before this ship lands on Earth."

The doctor went immediately to his office and studied the x-rays under the enlargement and he barely could make out the very small units blending in with the bone structure. It was hard to detect. This was reported to the commander. The doctor said, "That is why you get all the same answers when you ask questions. That unit is being brainwashed."

The commander asked how hard it was to retrieve the unit. Doctor Pil said, "It should be a simple operation."

"Take one prisoner at a time, take the unit out, and mark each one so we know which prisoner it came out of. Put each prisoner in the new room so they will not communicate to the ones that were not operated on."

These operations were performed. It took a good two days. The scientists on Spaceship Ventara spent a week inventing a decoder so the units could be analyzed. Finally they were able to decipher all the computer chips. The chips were placed in such a way between the skull and the brain, which were sensitized with the tiniest electric current with each pulse of the heart beat, so the brains were programmed on what to say and how to act. In checking out the waves from the microchips, one pinhead component was supposed to program the soldier to fight to the end and not surrender. The scientist found this component was malfunctioning. That is why they surrendered to us. Actually, the malfunction probably saved their lives. The commander instructed the security personnel to interrogate all the prisoners all over again.

This time the prisoners seemed like they were back to their normal senses. What was found out would blow anyone's mind away. They were all cooperative in telling us anything they were asked, once the chip was removed from their skull. They had families and land, and were happy where they lived until this large domain named Dalax, whose people were very devious, took over the planet Koton. They captured the population of the planet and made them like robots, with the insertion of the microchips into their brains. Now they were asking questions on where they were and where they were going. They also had deep emotions about their families. They asked what year it was. All we could do was guess the present time of planet Koton's calendar. One prisoner cried out, "My God, that was seven years ago!" Some prisoners were longer, some only a couple of years.

They were asked the same questions again, as when the chips were in. This time there were no recollections between the time the chips were put in and the time they were taken out. They were also told we were on a mission to planet Earth and did not know exactly when they were to be taken back home. The people from planet Thrae did not know where planet Koton was located in the universe, and they never heard of such a place. Thrae's interpreter was getting a little overwhelmed from all these unexpected answers. They told us they were from the galaxy Fraxt, and from this point they were lost.

The commander and crew leaders had a meeting to discuss what to do with these prisoners. Could they be trusted to be on their own or was this a trick they were playing so they could take control later on? Everyone voted to keep them locked up, since we were so close to Earth.

We passed planet Mars, which left the destination less than two weeks. We had been in contact with station Future

Vision with strict coded security on where to land and when. Scientist Hirgo announced his presence to the commander to discuss his finding of the green matter that the spaceship was stuck in. He said it was experimented with and the findings were of a negative nature. Different chemicals were tested with the green matter and nothing happened, only water and oxygen affected it. The commander said, "We will have to stay clear of any more green matter."

Scientist Hirgo said, "That is not going to be the problem. The green matter on most metals has a tendency to deteriorate the molecules that hold metals together when in contact with just plain air."

The commander said, "You mean, if there is any green matter on the spaceship that did not wash off and we enter the Earth's atmosphere, the ship will start to deteriorate?"

"That is right, Commander. Also, the faster you go in their atmosphere, the more metal will flake off."

Commander asked, "How long will this deterioration take place, once we enter the Earth's atmosphere?"

Hirgo said, "About one to three days, depending on how much green matter is still on the spaceship."

The commander called the communications room. Assistant communicator Darna answered. "Tell Officer Zomi to come to my office immediately please."

Five minutes later communicator Zomi arrived. "Yes Commander, how may I help you?"

"I want you to get through to the station on Earth and tell them we have to have the precise landing area and time. It will be crucial for our ship to land safely and in one piece. Scientist Hirgo will fill you in on the situation we're in."

After all the information was received, Communicator Zomi hurried back to her station and sent the message to the station in Chesterland on Earth. Spaceship Ventara should get an answer in a matter of time. In the meantime,

Jac, the spaceship's navigator, is getting a blown-up view of Earth through their viewing window. He called the commander to come over and take a look. Commander Siro said, "This I have to see," and hurried over to the navigator's room.

Jac said to the commander jokingly, "Looks like we are going back to planet Thrae."

The commander said, "I see, it looks so similar to our planet. Well anyway, it will not be long before we get off this ship and breathe some real air and stretch our legs. Looks like it is going to be kind of weird, but exciting when we get there."

Twelve
Landing on Earth

Communicator Zomi translated the message to the Chesterland station requesting a quick landing at the ancient landing strip before anymore skin covering peeled off. Al, George, and Joe were waiting in their twin jet looking at the radar scope, catching the first glimpse of a craft appearing on the screen. It was about twenty miles away. The communication between Al and the spaceship was loud and clear. Spaceship Ventara was zeroed in on the frequency of the twin jet Cessna. Also the communicator of the spaceship already had the landing site in their scope a number of miles back. George hollered out, "There it is, getting closer and bigger." George was getting very excited. "Man look at that! It is a monster of a ship." The spaceship hovered for a few minutes over the Cessna jet, then made a very smooth touchdown after six pads were extracted from beneath the ship.

The three were very anxious and a little frightened of this new adventure. Joe remarked, "When are they coming out? It has been ten minutes since touchdown." Al contacted Commander Siro on the spaceship asking what the problem was. The commander said, "We noticed when we were approaching land, there were vehicles with red flashers about fifty miles away. It would be very risky to fly too much longer. We have a damaged ship."

Al said, "We have another place down in Peru, South

America. It is an ancient landing site overgrown with vegetation, but obscure from everyone to see."

Commander said, "We will have to try it. We do not want to engage in any fighting. We do not want to be an enemy."

A large door opened and a ramp slid down to the ground. The commander and a few of his associates came down the ramp to meet the trio. Al, George, and Joe looked at each other almost in unison and said, "They look like people from Earth. No different from us." In a serious tone the commander asked, "What about those vehicles with the red flashers coming this way?"

Al said, "They must be the state authorities, investigating your strange craft. It will be another half an hour at least, before they arrive."

Commander: "We must leave at once!"

George: "What about our plane?"

Commander: "We will take it with us."

The commander gave the order, and then a large cargo door opened. Then with a magnetic force with strange looking grappling arms, very tenderly brought the plane into the spaceship.

Al: "Well, will you look at that!"

All three were amazed at the sight. Then they all walked up the ramp, and the ramp slid back up, the hatch shut. In no time, they were on their way.

The commander led them to the communication room so they could look on the telescreen for the approaching vehicles. The vehicles seemed to slow down and come to a stop as the spaceship left them in an instant. The commander asked, "How far away is this other site?"

Al said, "About three thousand miles southwest past the Yucatan." Al had the map he retrieved from the Cessna.

Commander: "That's not too bad. We cannot go full

speed because of the damage we have on the outer part of the ship. We should get there in about an hour."

George looked at Al with surprise. "An hour."

Commander: "Is it a safe landing site?"

Al: "It is a very remote area. It was an ancient civilization. For some reason or another, it is now extinct. You will have to find a clearing to land because everything is overgrown with vegetation."

Commander: "That is no problem. We land everywhere. You'll see what I mean."

They arrived at their destination in a little less than an hour, like the commander said. Al said, "This is approximately where the ancient landing site is." Sharta, the second in command, sent out the sensors to obliterate all the vegetation and obstacles for enough room to set down the spaceship. All this took about fifteen minutes. When everything was cleared and the dust settled down, the spaceship eased down to the clearing with her six struts extracted out with wide pads on the bottom, and then made a smooth touchdown.

It started to get dark, so the commander indicated we would take a look around tomorrow, and send out a few probes to see what to expect around the vicinity.

Commander: "Before we discuss any business and problems, we must all relax and have a nice hot meal." The Earthlings were shown where to get cleaned up before supper. Walking to and from clean-up, they sure marveled an the interior of the spaceship. It was like being in a huge shopping mall. They all sat down in the good sized commander's quarters. They were served food they had never seen before, and enjoyed it thoroughly.

George remarked, "For a ship that has been in space for a year, it sure seems like you never left your planet."

Commander said, "That is because we have overcome

most of the scientific problems of space travel. We found new ways to preserve most everything indefinitely. Like the food we eat—it still tastes the same as when it was picked."

After supper, the commander led them to his lounge so they could chat about serious matters. In the lounge, they all sat down in very comfortable easy chairs. George took out a pack of cigarettes, tapped a cigarette out, and put it in his mouth. When the commander asked what that was, George said, "It is a cigarette. You light it up and smoke."

The commander asked what it was made of. George explained, "It is made of tobacco."

The commander said, "That is like taking drugs. I will tell you right now, there is no lighting of fire or any kind of smoking on this spaceship. On planet Thrae, all are banned from taking any kind of drugs unless it is for a cure."

George put the cigarette back in the pack and back into his pocket. "Sorry," he said, "I did not know."

Commander: "Now back to the problem at hand. The spaceship's covering and parts of the structure are deteriorating because of some green matter that the ship encountered on the trip to Earth. We will not work on it tonight because we might be spotted."

Joe: "Won't it keep destroying the skin covering if you wait any longer?"

The commander said, "It is a very slow process, but speeds up when in flight against air friction. We need Kryon metal to repair this ship."

Al said, "We do not know what kind of metal it is, until we can get it analyzed. We will look for it tomorrow."

Then they had some beverages brought in. The topic was changed. Both sides brought up all kinds of stories from Earth happenings, to space journey from planet Thrae. They talked about and compared the two planets and could not believe the similarity of the two. Commander Siro said, "Planet Thrae is a little larger, with a much older civilization and it seems to be more advanced in its technologies."

Joe said, "That we suppose it may be true because we really have not been to your planet and do not know the difference."

Commander: "Well it has been a long day and we will need some rest. Tomorrow we will plan our future stay on planet Earth to find the pros and cons of life here. Tomorrow will be the first real sunshine in over a year for me and my crew."

The three Earthlings were shown to their quarters and everyone hit the sack, except the sentries that were on watch throughout the spaceship. Al, Joe, and George did not get much sleep just thinking of the excitement being on a spaceship from another planet, and the technology that they were going to learn from them. With all the thoughts in their heads, morning came quickly. About six A.M. Earth-time, a pager summoned the trio. They waited patiently until they were ready to follow him through the long corridor to the commander's dining area for breakfast. They didn't know whether to call the pager a him or it, because the trio could not believe they were being led by a robot. The good mornings were said and they were seated at the table ready to eat. Joe remarked to the commander, "We have a few robots on Earth, but nothing as well programmed as yours."

The commander said, "We have two robots on board to take some of the stress off the crew. And how was your night's sleep gentlemen?"

Simultaneously they answered, "Just fine. Thank you." Just like the meal before, the food was exotic and tasted different and delicious. They could not stop eating.

The commander said, "Do not eat too much. You might

get sick because you are not used to this type of food."

George said, "We cannot help it, we never tasted anything like it before."

Commander: "I understand, besides there will be many more meals to come. We will go into the next room for awhile and relax. We have our receiver on for a little music and news from your planet. Then we will tackle the problems of the day. We won't rush into anything, not unless it is necessary. There is no room for error."

After relaxing for about half an hour, they got to their discussions about planet Earth. As Commander Siro pointed out, "Your planet Earth sounds like the reverse tense of my planet Thrae. Enough of this political bullshit, as you Earthlings would say. We shall take a tour of the interior of Spaceship Ventara, then we will go outside to assess the damage that was caused to the outer skin of the spaceship."

It took about an hour to tour the interior of the spaceship. The three earthlings could not believe how advanced the technology was compared to that of Earth.

The commander pointed to the entrance that held the prisoners. "This is a makeshift prison compound. Right now we have fifteen prisoners in there."

Joe commented, "Are these the same prisoners that were captured on planet Uranus?"

The commander answered, "Yes."

George asked, "How come they were not terminated on planet Uranus?"

Commander said, "There was not any need to. They surrendered to us. We also wanted to interrogate them. Right now they are harmless." He looked at the trio for a moment and said, "We are not murderers, are you?"

Joe looked at the commander also and said, "No one in our group are murderers either."

After going through a few more corridors and rooms,

they finally entered the navigation control room. George, with his mouth hanging open in awe said, "This is simply fantastic! I never saw anything like it, even on *Star Trek*, or any of the science fiction movies."

Joe agreed. The commander broke in on their spellbound situation and said, "It is time we went out for a breath of fresh air." One of the hatches was open with a ramp descending down to the ground.

The commander's crew and scientists were already analyzing the damage to the entire ship. Sharta, second in command, told Commander Siro that they were in bad shape. It was said in Thrae language. Commander asked, "What has to be done and how long must we sit here?"

Sharta said, "Every inch of the spaceship has to be scoured with soap and water; I mean scrubbed thoroughly. Any of the green matter left on it will be agitated by air friction and will spread and eat the skin again. If we are lucky to obtain this material to apply to the ship, we should be repaired in no more than a year. Also, we need a lot of water. On our photo maps, accumulated while landing, there shows a small stream, about a half mile away to the north. We don't have a hose of that length to go that far."

"If we cannot get either one of these things, then we are in trouble," the commander remarked.

Al mentioned, "If we have to, we can purchase hoses from supply depots, almost in any city and fly it back."

Commander asked, "What about the metal?"

Al said, "We need a sample, so it can be analyzed as to where it might be obtained."

Commander Siro: "Let us take a little ride in one of the probes to check out a few things."

Third in command Exton was also a probe pilot for Commander Siro, waiting for the foursome to board. They took off through the portage tunnel of the spaceship. First they circled the area of the downed spaceship. Looking down, the commander said, "It sure looks vulnerable to any attack." He radioed back to the ship and ordered them to camouflage the ship and to be alert for anything approaching.

They flew around for awhile. "You were right, there's nothing around for miles except jungle foliage and some half hidden ancient ruins, and as remote as you stated," remarked the commander. "Well anyway, we have to get to your station in Ohio for analysis of the metal from our spaceship. The faster the spaceship is repaired, the better."

The commander motioned to Exton to head back to the spaceship. "First I have to get my people organized and sent on their ways all over your planet Earth to gather information on how you Earthlings are living."

The probe arrived at noon, just in time for lunch and relaxation. Joe mentioned to George, "These people take everything in a very calm manner. It seems like they do not excite themselves about anything."

Exton, the probe pilot, got the okay light to enter the spaceship tube for landing. The commander said, "After lunch and relaxation you people can attend the meeting with our officers, discussing the future events. Since most of it will be in Thrae language, it will be translated to you as best we can, even though you might know a little of our language. This will be very interesting to you people."

Joe: "You seem to trust us in the short time that you have known us."

Commander: "I had had enough psychology training to judge a person. So far, you three are no threat to us; you are too honest."

Before they sat down to lunch. Plorta, the officer in charge of weather and observation of skies and space, buzzed in. "Excuse me a moment, Sir."

"Yes Plorta," said the commander.

"Sir, we are in luck, tomorrow's forecast is rain all day, which we need badly."

"Thank you, Plorta," said the commander and switched over to Sharta, second in command. He told him, "When it starts to rain tomorrow, get everyone outside, including the two robots, and start to scrub every inch of this spaceship and assess how much metal skin has to be replaced. Thank you."

After another delicious lunch and relaxation, they walked to the meeting room just down the corridor. There were about a dozen officers waiting. The commander introduced the three Earthlings to the officers and then they got down to business. The meeting started at two P.M. Earth time, and went well into the evening: except an hour for supper at six P.M.

During the meeting, the topics ranged from: seven probes that are to go on special missions, to the environment, to countries, different languages, wars, enemies, politics, etc. The seven officers and their crews were, Officers: #1, Druce; #2, Enor; #3, Garsh; #4, Zell; #5, Rotz; #6, Osla; and #7, Ikoe.

"Each one of you will communicate at least once a week to the mothership, so we know you are still alive. Otherwise you may be summoned for one reason or another. I will be going to the Earthlings' station in Chesterland, Ohio, for a few days, for information and supplies. When we get back, the seven probes should be serviced and ready to commence to their destinations. So prepare your probes for whatever you might need. Good luck on your missions," said the commander. "Oh yes, one more thing, stay out of trouble."

The meeting was over about ten P.M. Everyone left except the commander and the Earthlings. Joe said, "This is getting more exciting every minute."

Commander: "You have not seen anything. The people on this spaceship are the cream of the crop, as you people would say. They have photographic memories. They can memorize a whole language in days, also disguise themselves to fit any profile."

Al: "What about the probes? Won't they be spotted?"

Commander: "Possibly, but not likely! They are fast and radar proof. In populated places they fly at night, and where they land, no one will never know. Let us all get a good night's sleep. We will discuss what to do in the morning before we leave for Ohio. Good night and pleasant dreams."

The next morning the Earthlings woke up on their own. They freshened up and joined the commander for breakfast. They chatted a little afterwards. The four of them went outside for some fresh air. It was not as bright as the day before, it was a little cloudy. They were walking around the spaceship in discussion, when all of a sudden there was a loud deafening thunderclap and lightning. It started to rain pretty hard. Then the inevitable happened which Al, Joe, and of all people George forgot. On the next clap of lightning and thunder, George went into a frenzy. He started to moan and groan, clawing and scratching the side of one of the landing pods that were extracted, and was quite wild George was swaying, looking side to side, hollering in that foreign language. Commander Siro asked, "What is wrong with him? Maybe we should get him inside."

"No," said Al, "get a translator out here and record this episode. We have been puzzled a few years about this. Every time it rains with lightning and thunder, he goes into a state of madness. I think it might have something to do with your planet Thrae."

Genus, the translator, not only recorded the event, but also took a video of it.

Al: "When he comes out of it, he does not remember anything, but he is worn out from the ordeal." After the recording and enough information was obtained, they took George back into the spaceship to a soundproof sleeping quarters so he could sleep it off. Al told the commander about the other incidents on Lake Erie. "We had a psychiatrist do all kinds of tests to no avail."

Commander Siro said, "If I know my doctors, they will find the answer and cure him. We will have to put off our mission for another day or two till we see George's outcome."

The next morning after breakfast, while the four of them were relaxing and talking about everything and anything, Genus, the translator, buzzed in.

Commander: "Yes Genus."

"I believe I have the answer to George's riddle."

The commander said, "We will be right down."

Genus was all set up with his unit, when the commander and the three Earthlings walked in and sat down.

Genus: "First I will show you the first version of what you saw yesterday. Then I will show you want really happened in English." When they saw the first version, the sound was turned down low so George would not go haywire. "I cannot believe that is me," said George, trembling a little. "I look like a maniac."

Genus: "Now this is a reenaction made by computer of what really happened. We put the perspectives in English."

Joe: "Like a movie made on Earth."

The movie showed a large ark in the water with huge waves. There were small ancient fishing vessels bobbing around in the rough water. A close-up view showed the vessels clinging to the side of the ark. A man was screaming and pleading, pounding and scratching, begging to let him and his family inside. He kept looking from side to side at his wife and son with a look of terror and doom. He gave one more loud frantic scream to be let in, but the water was getting just too rough. Finally a huge wave came down upon his little boat and the other vessels, smashing them to bits. They all drowned. That was the big flood on planet Thrae to end all evilness. This happened a few thousand years ago. Not everyone was evil. Only a handful were chosen to be saved. Some of the good had to die with the bad.

Commander: "Now you know why; that was a previous life on planet Thrae. The language was also one of the previous ones. He probably has a purpose here on Earth. That is why he is reincarnated to find the meaning of his occurrences to help mankind. I will have Doctor Mysca, the psychiatrist, look George over. I am sure he will cure him." The doctor looked him over for any other signs. Then he told George, "We will fix you up in the morning."

It was still raining, so the commander had them go over the entire spaceship again. He said, "When and if we ever leave, we should have no mishaps."

Doctor Mysca was prepared for George. He was very shrewd, studying all the notes and the movie with a very interesting scheme. Doctor Mysca took George outside the spaceship where the crew set a few props to look like a part of an ark, with a small boat next to it. He used a couple of crew members to represent part of his family in his previous life on planet Thrae. The scene was set up partly under the spaceship and it was kept rather dark. George was put on a small boat between his assumed wife and son, next to the ark. The doctor showed a projection of a blown-up version of the ark and everything, moving up and down with George in the middle.

There were sound effects of thunder, with made up

realistic lightning flashing, and the small boat started to rock more and more, with water thrown onto the boat for wave effect. George started to scream and scratch the side of the ark, pounding to let him and his family in. He was looking on both sides, at his wife and son and told them in that ancient language that they were doomed. Then to George's surprise, the boat started to calm down a little. A door opened on the side of the ark. A man with a long white beard with his arms opened saying, "Come on in my children." George, looking at his family, said, "Come we are saved." The three walked into the ark. The door closed behind them. George collapsed onto the platform behind the props. He was carried to the spaceship's infirmary, where he slept for many hours.

Al: "What do you think doc? That was quite a performance."

Doctor: "Well! It looks pretty positive. He seems to believe he and his family were saved. We will soon find out."

Al looked at Joe. Joe just shrugged his shoulders. "Don't look at me, I am lost in this situation. But it sure was a pretty good performance." Then Al looked at the commander. "Do not worry, the doctor knows what he is doing."

George finally woke up around suppertime saying, "Boy, am I hungry. It feels like I was working on a fishing boat since sunrise."

"You know," Al said, "this was the first time the situation was acknowledged by him."

George: "I had the strangest dream that I was living in another world, caught in the middle of a disaster, like a big flood, with everyone fleeing for their lives. My family and I were caught in the middle of this dilemma. Everyone was trying to get aboard this huge vessel. Their little boats were smashed and the people drowned. My boat was next to the vessel, so I knocked on it. I said, 'Hello may I come in, we love the lord.' A door opened. My family and I walked in, lay down on the floor, and slept for a long, long time. When my family and I woke up, we were still on the vessel and alive. I said, 'Yes, it was just a dream.' Then I woke up for real on this spaceship." George was actually cured. Now when it lightnings and thunders, and rains, he has no reactions whatsoever, because he believes it was only a dream, and he and his family were saved.

Commander Siro told his men there would be another meeting when he gets back with information and supplies. They also needed clothing and money plus identification for a few of the men, enough so they could get the rest of their own when they get out in the world.

Al: "How do we get our airplane back where we started, so we will not be missed. We have not called in for awhile. They probably wondered what happened to us. We cannot take off from the jungle, because we need a runway. It will take about ten hours to get back to the Chesterland station, with at least two fuel stops on the way."

Commander Siro: "Our probes are equipped with different types of towing apparatuses. Your plane will be attached to the bottom of the probe. When we reach the desired speed of your plane, we will release it. Then you will be on your own."

George: "We three have no passports to cross the border to other countries. Without a passport or identification, you might be held indefinitely." Al took a flight map out of the Cessna, opened it, and went over it with Commander Siro, so he would know how the flight pattern was in our world. Al was to go with the commander to show the way to the Chesterland station.

Everything got into preparation for the probe's liftoff. Sharta, second in command, took over the duties of the spaceship while Commander Siro and a couple of officers went as interpreters. A tracking device was installed in the Cessna for the probe to keep track. Joe and George got into the Cessna, waiting for the space probe to hook up. It was late afternoon when they easily went through the spaceship's hatchway and out as smoothly and quietly as could be expected. Picking up speed, watching the spaceship getting smaller and smaller as it lay parked in the jungle. Al mentioned to the commander that one cannot go too fast with the probe, because the Cessna might fall apart at too great a speed.

The probes camouflage cannot be detected by radar, but with the Cessna hooked up, there might be some doubt. It did take almost an hour to get to the point where they met. They did not land. The Cessna was released in mid air after the probe slowed down to the Cessna's desired speed. After the release, George throttled for a little speed, leaving the probe behind for a couple of miles. Commander Siro followed for a few miles to see if everything was all right. Then passing the Cessna at an astronomical speed, as if the Cessna was standing still, Joe said, "Holy shit, what was that?" All they saw was a blurred streak pass them.

The commander was on the radio. "We will see you guys at the Chesterland station."

George: "Okay, we will see you there sooner or later. Over and out."

The space probe was moving so fast that when Joe was looking through the portholes, it was like watching a movie put in fast forward. It took all of twenty minutes to cross the United States from New Mexico to Ohio. It was already dark when they arrived because of the three hour time difference.

Commander Siro: "We must be getting close to our destination by now."

Joe: "We certainly are. There is the Detroit River dumping into Lake Erie, one of the five Great Lakes of the United States. In fact we are here." Exton, the pilot, slowed down to almost a stop. They were going northeast, made a slight turn to go east.

Joe: "There is Cleveland Hopkins Airport. Now we're over downtown Cleveland." The commander asked what that pointed, tall illuminated building was. Joe said, "That is one of Cleveland's landmarks, the Terminal Tower. A few more miles." Joe said, "There is the Cuyahoga County Airport, where we take the Cessna for maintenance. Up ahead, where you see that tower with blinking red lights, there is a runway. The lights will be turned on when the Cessna arrives." The probe pilot had the infra-red sensors on so they could pick up the runway of the Chesterland station.

Commander Siro: "Why don't you just land at the Cuyahoga Airport?"

Al: "We like to be close to the station for news emergencies. We are going to invest in a helicopter so we can land closer to the news events. We will show you what a helicopter looks like later on. The station, including the landing strip, is all fenced in with electric and well secured. We will find a spot near the woods, so the probe will not be spotted from the air."

The probe landed as close as possible to the station, without being detected. A very smooth touchdown as usual. They sat there for a few minutes to make sure the surroundings were safe.

The probe pilot had the computer on for tracking the Cessna.

Pilot Exton: "The Cessna is now over Colorado, according to the map. At the speed they are traveling, they will not arrive for another three to three and a half hours."

Al: "They had about a half tank of fuel, so they will

have to make one pit stop; so figure another half hour. The Jeep vehicle is parked by the strip. We will drive to the station. They will call in when the Cessna is a few miles before landing. Also, we will get a call from the gate tower so we can meet them at the field, so we can drive them back to the station. Also, the guard at the gate will know because there is a tracking device for anything landing at the strip. Joe has to call in at the gate for the landing lights to be turned on."

Al drove the commander to the station office, while the commander's crew waited in the probe. They parked in a small reserved lot close to the club's entrance, got out and walked to the observatory office where Bart was at his desk working the computer, figuring out the financial situation of the Future Vision Company.

"Working kind of late?" Al commented. Bart answered, "I have to straighten out the company's records." Then asking, "Who may this be. You guys planning a costume party?"

Looking at the commander's odd clothing, Al and Commander Siro laughed. Al said, "I want you to meet Commander Siro from Spaceship Ventara. He arrived to Earth a few days ago from planet Thrae." Bart just stood there speechless.

"N-no shit. So they finally arrived," thrusting out his hand for a handshake, while the commander backed off, not knowing what Bart was doing.

Al said, "Do not worry, he only wants to shake your hand as a gesture of welcome. That is our custom." Then they both gave each other a warm handshake. Bart said, "Welcome to our world, I hope we will have a wonderful and peaceful relationship."

Al said, "Let us show you around the station. But first, you should wear one of these long scientist coats so you will not look so conspicuous to the studio staff." The commander put on the long white coat and they proceeded, first to the communication room with all the high frequency equipment. Al showed how it worked and the way they communicated to Thrae. The commander kind of chuckled a little, saying, "I do not mean to be sarcastic. What I am trying to say is, no wonder you had a hard time communicating with us with this equipment. It looks like it is outdated."

Bart spoke up, "This equipment is the newest made. It is the state of the art, invented by the top technicians of the United States."

Then the commander remarked, "Well, they have a lot to learn. When we get settled on this planet I will have our technicians look over all your equipment. He will point out the pros and cons. They are thorough."

"I see," said Al. "Thank you. Now let us go into the observatory to see what you think of the telescope to study the stars."

It was not in use at the time, so Al had to press the code numbers on the panel alongside the door to open it. When Al opened the door, the lights came on automatically, which was on a low dim setting. Al turned up the lighting so the commander could see the room more clearly. Al explained the operation of the telescope. It is computerized to get a clear, bright picture. You can look through a peep hole at the bottom end of the telescope for settings and have it put on the screen for better observation of the universe. Al showed how it works so he could look for himself. Once you start to operate and observe, the lights automatically dim for better observation.

"Not bad," said the commander. "It is a powerful telescope, but it seems like it is limited as to how far it can reach out into space."

Al said, "We are a pretty wealthy company, but still

limited to what we can afford. A larger observatory with a new telescope is a great cost. We were more concerned with communicating with the receiver and transmitter." Al said, "We will get into this another time."

They then took a walk down to corridor to the television stations in the next building. It took five minutes to walk to the studios. There was a security guard on duty who let the three in the first studio where most of the cable programs were being shown—soap operas, movies, documentaries, and the like. The commander was getting very interested in the setup, which was quite different from the system on planet Thrae and spacecity Orant. He told Al and Bart he was quite impressed. Then asked, "What are soap operas?"

Bart said, "They are stories in a series and usually the sponsors that sell soap products and the like pay for it with their advertising on the television."

They left studio one, walked a few dozen steps to the entrance to studio two. They entered quietly, where Miss Choa Mio was on the air showing documentaries and speaking to a couple of guests about the deprived children of the world; especially those who reside in the countries that have the worst poverty. She pleads to the public to help out, remarking, "How would you feel if these were your children?"

The commander said, "She speaks very well with a convincing attitude. But she does not look the same as you."

Al said, "She is Chinese, from another country, but lives here in the United States. There are many different races here on Earth. Her name is Miss Choa Mio. She will be off the air in a few minutes, then I can introduce her to you. She is also a member of our Thorme Club." They watched the rest of the program with interest until it was over. Al motioned her over. When she got to the three, the commander complimented her on a wonderful program. Choa said "Thank you" to the commander, then looked at Al. Al said, "I have a big surprise for you."

Her eyes lighting up. "What?"

"This person that complimented you is Commander Siro. Have you ever heard of him?

Choa was thinking for a moment, really not realizing, she said, "Is he from a spaceship that was supposed to arrive here?" Then with astonishment and great surprise, "You are from planet Thrae and you finally arrived." With a couple of steps, giving the commander a big welcoming hug, "I am glad you made it here safely, and very glad to make your acquaintance."

Bart said not so loud, "We do not want to expose him at this time."

"I am sorry," said Choa. "I am so excited, we have a lot to talk about." Then the four of them walked over to the planetarium office.

Bart put a pot of coffee on. They sat down at the snack table, discussing the trip and what the future plans were going to be. The intercom came on, and the gate guard said, "George called in and will be landing in a few minutes." Al told Bart and Choa to keep the commander company while he went to pick up Joe and George. "I will be right back," he said and left. Bart got up and went to the Mr. Coffee Maker, poured the coffee in three coffee mugs, and brought the mugs over to Choa and the commander. He put one mug in front of the commander, and one in front of Choa, while the commander was watching with a little skepticism. Bart sat down, taking a sip from his mug. Ahh nothing like a nice cup of hot black coffee. Miss Choa remarked, "Well I like cream and sugar in mine thank you." After a minute Miss Choa said, "Aren't you going to drink your coffee before it gets cold?"

Commander looked at the two of them for a moment. "I never had a cup of coffee. What is it?"

Bart said, "It is more or less a stimulant. It is supposed to keep you going all day. Most people have it with their breakfast, some people drink a few cups a day. Of course, there are some people who will not drink it at all. Try it. We are still standing."

The commander reluctantly took a sip, shaking his head, making a screwed up face. "It is bitter," he said.

"Try it with cream and sugar, it makes a difference. Put just a little of each in the mug and stir. If you still don't like it, then do not drink anymore."

In the meantime Al, George, and Joe walked into the office. Joe said, "I see you guys made your acquaintances." The trio grabbed a mug of coffee each and sat down. Choa commented about the commander tasting his first cup of coffee. "Well, how do you like it?" George asked.

"It is not bad, I guess. It will have to grow on me. But I will have another cup, if you please." Everyone laughed while Bart poured the commander another cup, also filling up the others.

Everyone was silent for a few minutes while drinking their coffee. Then Al broke the silence by saying, in a low whisper, "I do not really know if we should continue to discuss anything more in this room."

"Why not?" asked the commander, also in a low whisper.

Al said, "This room has been bugged once before."

"What do you mean by bugged?" asked the commander.

Al said, "Hidden microphones, so they can hear what we are talking about."

"Who is they?" asked the commander.

Al whispered again, "The authorities, they must think

we are spies for wrongdoing, but they must not have any proof because they have not arrested us." The commander then took a small box from his vest. It looked like a pack of cigarettes. He whispered, "Nobody make a sound." He got up from his chair, pressed a couple of buttons on the box and walked around the room, pointing the box all over from one end of the room to the other, up and down. Coming back to the table he whispered, "There is no setup anywhere except the telescope with the computer that operates it."

Bart broke in saying in a whisper, "The unit has been turned off for a couple of days until it was shown to you. Then it was turned off again."

Al said in a low voice again, "Let us pretend to adjourn the meeting. The commander and I will stay to investigate, so wait in the hallway."

Everybody said their good-byes and went out the door. Al even shut the door a couple of more times to make it sound convincing. The commander then checked out the unit again. The box showed a higher reading at the bottom of the computer where the grill was for ventilation. The grill was taken off as quietly as possible. There it was, a round looking button, about as big as a quarter, magnetized to the inner frame. Al took the bottom to the sink, quietly filled a glass of water, putting the bug in it. "Well, that takes care of that." The commander and Al checked over the whole room a couple more times. They told the rest of the guys to come back in. They all came back in! George whispered, "Any results?"

"Yes," Al pointed to the glass of water. "We smothered it."

Everybody sat down again. Al said, "We better make more coffee, I think we are going to be here for awhile. Is that okay with you, Miss Choa?"

"Yes," said Miss Choa.

"Okay with the rest of you?"

Everybody said, "Yes."

"What we talk about and do here tonight is confidential among us and us alone. When you are with other people, pretend this meeting never happened. One slip of the tongue means disaster." The commander spoke up about the incident that happened on planet Uranus, being attacked by an enemy who was supposed to be communicating to a country whose name he believed is Russia. "We destroyed one of their stations, on one of Uranus' moons, and all their spacecraft. The mothership, we were told, went back to their own planet Koton for more service and equipment for an invasion to Earth with the help of Russia and some other countries. We captured fifteen of the enemy and found out they were brainwashed with computer chips installed in their brains. They were supposed to fight to the end, but the microchips seemed to malfunction. We found the chips by accident when our doctor examined them. We removed all the chips from their brains, and in time, they came back to normal. They were all kidnapped at various times from their planet Koton, and brainwashed against their will to fight to the end. These few were lucky to be alive. There are some groups who would have killed them instead of taking prisoners. They gave us quite a bit of information about their own planet, and how it was taken over by the enemy. Now they are trying to take over other planets in the universe."

George spoke up, "So that is the country Father Carl was communicating with? Father Carl was a Russian spy, disguised as a priest so he could obtain information from that planet, through our station without our knowledge, until we caught him by accident and taped the incident and took some photographs with another Russian spy, who was taking the information back to Russia. They both were killed by accident trying to get back to their own country. Father Carl also infiltrated as a member of the Thorme Club."

The commander remarked, "Their mothership will not arrive back to planet Uranus for almost another two years. Planet Thrae already launched another spaceship, more sophisticated than the one that landed on Earth and should arrive at planet Uranus way ahead of schedule, before the enemy arrives. We will not destroy their main base on Uranus itself at this time. We will wait until their mothercraft arrives and attack both at the same time. If I know our leader on planet Thrae, he will probably send one or two more spaceships right after the first one is sent out. After the enemy is wiped out, we will have to find and invade their planet and stop their aggressive behavior toward other planets in the universe. Furthermore, you must keep your communication center open day and night. I will send a few of my men to help with the communications. They will advance your system with high tech knowledge of theirs.

"Now let's get back down to Earth. We people from planet Thrae will be stationed on Earth for quite awhile. To begin with, we need Earth clothing and money so we will not look like aliens. Any suggestions?"

George asked, "What do you want, new clothing or old clothing?"

"Probably both, so we can fit in with the different classes of people," the commander replied.

George's solution was, "For the old clothing, we can obtain all you want from the Salvation Army, an organization who helps poor people. Their items are old, but very clean, even look like new."

"Good," said the commander. "We need a few hundred items for both men and women. We also need identification, money, and all else that is necessary."

Al said, "I have a very good idea. Let me pick up a number of videos on life, organizations, language, history, and a number of other things that will give your people an idea of what to expect on Earth. There is also a lot of crime."

"That sounds good, how long will all this take?" asked Commander Siro.

Al said, "A few days. We will get on it at once so no time is wasted. If we have to make more than one trip back to the spaceship, we will do it."

George commented, "Since you learned our language quite well, I believe you would like to visit our library in Mayfield. It consists of most of the information you might need. I will take you there tomorrow."

They discussed many other things for a couple of hours, then adjourned till morning. Choa and Bart left for their homes, while Al, Joe, and George accompanied the commander back to the spaceprobe. They talked for a few minutes then left the commander and went home.

Early next morning, Al and George arrived where the probe was still sitting from the night before. The commander was already up waiting for them. They said their good mornings, Al asking if everything was all right. "We brought you some clothing of George's, assuming they are your size."

The commander tried them on. He said, "Not bad, but they sure feel strange. The shoes are tight. I will wear my own until I find a pair somewhere else." Before they left, he instructed his men in the probe to keep communications open, and to keep in touch with spaceship Ventara. "Tell the officers we will be back in a few days. I will keep in touch with the probe from time to time. If you have any problems do not hesitate to call and let me know."

They left the probe and drove back to the station. Al said, "We are going to switch over to the company van. Before we get to the gate you will have to hide on the floor in the back of the van. We have tight security. Whoever goes through the security gate into the compound, must be the same people that come out. Before we come back, we will get you a badge so you can get in and out without any problems. We also have to get you some identification. I will take you to this dress-up artist who will disguise you with a mustache, beard, glasses, and different hair."

They left the Chesterland station, drove down Mayfield Road to 271 on the freeway to Route 90, taking about forty-five minutes to downtown Cleveland. The commander was hanging on for dear life. "You people actually drive these things. Our vehicles are a lot different on planet Thrae. They look much safer. And what is that musty odor that is choking me?"

Al said, "What odor?"

"The fumes," remarked the commander.

"Oh," said Al. "That is probably the exhaust fumes from the other vehicles around."

The commander was now complaining, "Planet Thrae has a clean air law. Anyone violating it pays the consequences."

Al said, "Really? We have a clean air or pollution law also, but it does not do much good."

The two spent the day stopping at various places, gathering some of the things that might be needed. They went back and forth to the station a number of times until the probe was loaded. A couple of days later, the commander was ready for takeoff. He invited Al and George to come along. George took up the offer after he called his wife to tell her he would be out of town for two or three days. He told her to have some change of clothes and a toothbrush ready, for he would stop to pick them up later.

Choa stopped by to tell the guys there was a very good movie at the movie studio at seven P.M. called *Schindler's List*. Al asked the commander if he wanted to watch a movie before they left. Al told the commander it was about a concentration camp in Nazi Germany in World War II. "Why not," said the commander, "I have not seen any movies on Earth." Bart called Master Pizza and ordered a pan pizza to be delivered to the station. Forty-five minutes later the pizza arrived. Al told the commander, "This is the country's tradition, eating pizza." They all had slice after slice. The commander said it was a little spicy, but good. "We do not have that on planet Thrae." After they were done, they walked over to the movie studio to watch the movie.

Thirteen
Bart's Past Ordeal

About a third into the movie, Bart was mumbling under his breath in German. George, who was sitting next to him, turned and looked at Bart with a puzzled look. Then he looked back to the screen. About half way through the movie, and hearing all the many times they said *Heil Hitler* in the movie, Bart got up from his seat, raised his hand in a Nazi salute, with a trembling voice saying out loud, in unison with the Nazis in the movie, "Sieg Heil, Sieg Heil." The commander and the group members turned to look at him. Bart caught himself with embarrassment, and walked out of the movie studio back to the meeting room.

Bart was waiting in the station meeting room for everyone to come in after the movie. Everyone sat down in silence for awhile. Then Bart said, "I have to tell you this story. Take it for what it is worth." Bart said he was a Nazi commandant in a prior life, in World War II, and the story went like this.

"Heil Hitler," Commandant Kraus raised his hand in the Nazi salute to General Bohn, commander of all concentration camps, who was getting out of the staff car. The commandant was in charge of a concentration camp in Poland, which was also an extermination camp for Hitler's final solution for the Jews, and other undesirables to Germany.

The general, holding his handkerchief over his nose,

asked, "Why is the stench so much greater at this camp than at the others?"

Commandant Kraus replied, "Because they built this camp in the wrong area. When the wind blows in the wrong direction, like today, there is a downdraft from the mountains blowing the smoke from the crematorium across the whole camp."

The general said, "I see. Why is the prison yard still full of prisoners?"

"We can only get rid of so many a day. Besides, they are arriving too fast and too many every day," commented the commandant.

Finishing the tour of the camp, they walked to the commandant's office. The general, with a strict commanding voice, "So you cannot keep up with the demand huh? We will fix that. I am calling to the supply depot to put the order in for all the material you need. When you order for the enlargement of the camp you will order at least four more gas chambers and four more crematories. I want this done at once, starting today! When I come back in two months or so, I want to see this camp in full operation, day and night."

The general clicked his heels and gave a Heil Hitler salute. Before the commandant could Heil back, he was out the door and gone.

The commandant, looking at his orderly, Lieutenant Karl, asked, "You believe this? For a year I have called headquarters, begging them to enlarge this camp, and all they gave me was a runaround. The general shows up, and looks around like we have not done anything. I am glad he came. Maybe now we can get rid of the vermin faster and more efficiently."

Commandant had very few friends. Of about fifty guards that ran the camp, almost none liked him, because he was a real asshole. He not only screamed at the prisoners, he screamed at his own guards for being stupid about how they would perform their duties. There were not too many mistakes with Kraus around.

One evening, while having drinks with his comrades in the office, he was chatting about different things, like when they will win the war and take over the world. The commandant told his comrades how he was reincarnated from a faraway world he believed was called Thrae. He was a high-ranking leader, and they were going to take over the universe. One of the comrades butted in, "Then what happened?"

The commandant said, "Well, the last thing I remember was a big battle in the middle of nowhere, against an enemy whom we thought was weak. Before you could figure what happened, there was this big flash and I went numb. So I guess I was killed and was destined to be here on Earth. I hated everything. I started when I was very young, killing little animals. When I got older, World War I started. I wasted no time joining the army. I wanted my chance to kill the enemy. I don't know why. I just loved to kill. When the war was over, I was bored to death. I had a few meaningless jobs and was mostly out of work. When Hitler got into power, I did not hesitate to join the Nazi Party and worked my way up. Now I am commandant of this camp."

Everyone might have been afraid of the commandant, but the commandant was afraid of the visiting general. So he put out an emergency order to all the guards of the camp. All the prisoners who are waiting to be gassed or put to death (of course the prisoners did not know they were going to be exterminated) were to be put to work at once, starting to clear ground for the four new gas chambers and crematoriums. It was already the end of October 1943 when the construction started. Things went pretty smoothly for the first two weeks. Then there was a cold snap. That was when all hell broke loose. The prisoners were not clothed for cooler weather, let alone the cold. And there was not enough food to keep them alive. The SS guards worked the prisoners until they fell to the ground from exposure and exhaustion. The other prisoners had to drag them away to the adjoining court, stacking the frozen bodies like cord wood ready for the crematory. There was no problem replacing the workers with newer and fresher prisoners, who came by train daily.

The SS guards made their reports daily to the commandant's nice warm office, which he hardly left because of the cold weather he hated. The reports the SS guards gave seemed to be satisfactory, and the building was on schedule. "Good! Good!" said the commandant. "In another month we ought to be finished and everything will be in operation when General Bohn arrives."

But everything was not all right and on schedule. Every time the prisoners got used to knowing what they were doing, they would either freeze to death or die of exhaustion, or they'd get shot by an SS guard for not working fast enough. When the dead were replaced, it was like starting over again, showing what to do and how to do it.

It was a little over a month since the project was started. There was a warm spell for a few days. This is what the SS guards were afraid of. As long as it stayed cold, the commandant would stay away. It was the middle of December 1943 when the commandant decided to see the progress of the project that his SS guards were bragging about. Yes, it was a lot warmer and he started to inspect what was done at the site. The building site was about half a mile from his headquarters. His driver was holding his car door open until the commandant emerged from his quarters. He got in and they rode the snowy road. They were just short of a hundred yards from the site, when the commandant yelled at the top of his lungs to stop. He flung the door open, getting out very slowly. His eyes were as big as saucers, and he was trembling. In a low, and almost shameful voice, "Is this all they got done?" He stared at the site for a long time, recollecting his thoughts. Finally he left the car and started to walk through the slush on the path made by the vehicle tires. Now he was walking faster and faster, practically running toward the first SS guard. The guard, not noticing at first, turned around just when the commandant was a few paces away and gave the *Heil Hitler* salute. The commandant was so pissed off, he yelled, "Don't give me that Heil Hitler shit," grabbing the SS guard by the front of his coat and pulling him toward himself with his face in his. He started screaming at him with every name in the book. "Is this all you assholes got done? The building should have been up." He was so mad he could hardly talk, with saliva splattering in the SS guard's face. All the SS guard could say was "Yes, sir, yes, sir."

"I am going to have all of you guards replaced. I will have all of you sent to the Russian front. You morons did not get anything done! Most of the material is still sitting on the ground under the snow. Where is Major Kiel, who is supposed to be in charge here?" snapped Commandant Kraus.

With a half-afraid voice the SS guard said, "He is at the depot, checking out the rest of the material."

The commandant yelled, "Go get him and bring him here, now."

The commandant started walking back and forth all over the place mumbling, "I cannot believe it, I cannot believe it." His pacing went on for about a half an hour. The other SS guards were directing the other prisoners like nothing happened, but still glancing at the commandant out of the corner of their eyes. Finally, Major Kiel arrived. To his surprise, the commandant looked as calm as could be. The SS guard told him the commandant was like a maniac. The major said, "Heil Hitler." The commandant just stared at him. The major could see the killing hate in his eyes.

The commandant, in a normal voice, "Major Kiel, I am taking over all operations in this camp. You are relieved of your command. Your transfer papers will be ready for you in the morning."

The major asked, "But, Commandant, what is the problem?"

Commandant, starting in a low voice, "You idiots all lied to me with your reports, saying we were on schedule. You lying son of a bitches!" he screamed. "Get out!" Commandant, motioning to the driver, went back to his quarters. He drank a hot brew, and put on heavier boots and clothing. He went out the door, slamming it. He told the driver to get him back to the building site. Commandant Kraus muttered out loud, "I will show them how to get things done." The car hardly came to a stop when he jumped out, and started walking all around the site, telling the guards to get them to work faster. He looked at all those pathetic prisoners. "They do not even know how to work." Then he said, "And they are supposed to be the chosen race," laughing hysterically. He was near a group of working prisoners. One of them carried a load of bricks on his shoulders and happened to trip and fall, spilling all the bricks. The commandant screamed, "You stupid Jew." He pulled out his pistol and shot him in the head. "From now on, if they fall, shoot 'em and replace them with able workers."

The commandant took over the whole project when he

got rid of the major who was in charge. He stayed on the job, making sure everyone was working. If any of these Jews slacked off, he would have them shot on the spot, or shoot them himself. He would then replace them just as fast. As long as the weather was still warm for a few days, progress was being made on both the gas chambers and crematories. No one dared slow up on their work, even the SS guards. They were more afraid of the commandant than before.

It was now the middle of January of 1944, and it started to get colder and colder. The workers worked slower and slower, and the commandant grew meaner and meaner. They were already behind schedule. Now the commandant started to worry that the general would be back before the job was complete. The commandant was there in the morning as soon as he got up, screaming as usual, why the workers were so slow. That is because they were freezing to death, in addition to starving. The commandant was getting so obsessed with the project, that he was pacing morning, noon, and night. He hated the cold with a passion, with temperatures ranging from twenty degrees to zero every day. He developed a persistent cough that would not go away. The more he went out the more he coughed.

One morning he did not get up, because he was burning up with fever. The doctor showed up and checked him out. He asked him when he ate last. He tried to holler back in a weak, coughing voice, kind of delirious. "Eat? Who's got time to eat. This project has to be done before the general comes back for inspection."

The doctor said, "You keep going at this rate, and you won't have to worry about the general or the inspection." The doctor gave him a shot and a sedative. In a few minutes, the commandant fell asleep. The doctor told the orderly to keep an eye on him. They both said their *Heil Hitlers* and the doctor left.

The commandant slept for most of the day until late in the afternoon when he was awakened by the smell of food that had just been prepared. He managed to get out of bed, a little shaky, but felt better. The orderly noticed him out of bed. "Sir, I was going to bring you the food to your bed."

Commandant said, "Nonsense I will eat at the table." He felt like he arrived from a great journey, and not eaten in days and finally arrived at his destination. He remarked how famished he was, with nothing on his mind, but to eat. He devoured everything, like a hungry animal. When he was finished eating, the orderly to his surprise, was commended by the commandant, which was very unusual, for he never commended anyone for anything. He sat back, taking out a brown looking cigar from his case, at the same time, the orderly with a lighter lit his cigar.

He was half way through his cigar, and just starting to relax staring out the window, watching the snow coming down, then noticing the smoke from the crematorium. His eyes got big with fright. He got up screaming as he threw his cigar to the floor. "What am I still doing here?" He headed for the door. "We have to get these buildings finished."

The orderly had to stop him at the door. The orderly said, "The doctor said you have to rest for a few days, and besides you are still in your night garment."

The commandant yelled, "Get my clothes. I feel fine. Tell my driver to pull around." He hurried himself dressing, and practically ran out the door to the car, hopped in, telling the driver to step on it. The tires spun around in the snow, and in no time they were at the site.

Everyone knew he was coming, so they looked very busy, even though they were hungry and cold. One prisoner remarked to the other, "At least it was quiet for one day."

The commandant was out on the site three times a day to make sure everything was being done. The buildings were almost finished with the furnaces in place. But the prisoners were dropping like flies from the cold, which fell to about five above zero. The commandant walked back and forth at the site for about six days, when he started to cough again. What was even worse, he started to cough up blood. The more he yelled, the more he coughed. Then it happened. He went into a rage at one of the prisoners because he dropped a hammer from his frozen fingers. The commandant pulled out his pistol, ready to shoot the prisoner in the head, when he had a massive pain in his chest. He dropped the pistol from his right hand, while clutching his chest with his left, gagging and choking. He crumpled to the ground unconscious. Everyone stopped what they were doing, just staring wide-eyed, their mouths agape. No one bothered to run over to him. One SS guard told another guard to fetch the doctor, while he went over to see if he still had a pulse. He told the prisoners to get back to work because nothing really changed, only the screaming and noise he made. He was still alive but with a weak pulse. By the time the doctor arrived with the meat wagon and took him to the infirmary, he was gone. The ironic part of this whole ordeal was that the general did not get back to the camp for another six months.

The commandant died in January of 1944. He should have been sent directly to hell, but was held in limbo until the spring of 1945, when he was reincarnated and conceived by a female Nazi guard named Helga. No one knew she was a Jew. Her birth name was Elsie Kline. At least everyone thought she was a true German. She helped kill enough Jews, so she herself could stay alive comfortably during the war. She became pregnant by one of the German SS guards. When the war was over and Germany lost, she was finally caught two months later and was about seven months pregnant. Investigating her past records, the authorities discovered her parents were Jews. Elsie also had a sister named Anna, who survived from another concentration camp. Anna Kline at first did not know if her sister or her parents and a brother were still alive. Later she discovered her parents and brother were killed by the Nazis.

Anna was stunned and could not believe, after reading a local newspaper, about some of the quick trials that were had, and to find her sister's name among some of the war criminals. Anna was in shock to realize her sister committed such atrocities. Anna went to the prison where Elsie was held and begged the authorities to see her. After a little red tape from security checking Anna's past, they let her in. The door was opened to the small, dark, cold cell, with a small window with two bars, about eight feet from the floor. There was just enough light to distinguish someone sitting on the floor in the corner. Anna, with a loud whisper called Elsie's name. She did not get any answer. Anna stood three for a moment until her eyes became used to the darkness. She noticed her sister's outline in the corner, and Anna took a few steps to where Elsie was crouched. "It is me, Anna," she whispered a little louder. For about a minute, not a sound. Anna could hear her own heartbeat. Then Elsie looked up with tears in her eyes, and still did not say anything. Anna then said, "Oh Elsie, how could you have done a thing like this?"

After another minute of silence, all Elsie could say was, "Survival." Then she said, "I am having a baby soon."

"Who is going to take care of it!" Anna remarked. "I was not prepared for anything like this, but whatever happens I will." Anna asked, "What happened to the father?"

"Hans got himself killed resisting arrest."

That was the only time Anna saw her sister. Before Elsie's trial was over, a baby son was born, who in turn was turned over to her sister Anna. A month later Elsie was hung as a traitor and murderer—a disgrace to the Jewish people.

Anna had her sister's baby and no place to go. It was bad enough when she was by herself trying to feed herself. She walked through the countryside asking the peasant farmers if there was any milk for the baby. She at least could get goats' milk, which helped tremendously. They slept in barns or wherever they could. This went on for a few months, until she met a man named Isaac Brosen, while waiting in a breadline by the charities from England and the United States. He remarked, "What a beautiful baby you have." Well, one thing led to another and they got to be good friends. Anna lied and told him her husband was killed in the concentration camp near the end of the war. "I was pregnant when I was captured, but survived the ordeal. The Nazis did not know I was pregnant at the time. Good thing we were liberated."

Anna and Isaac's relationship grew until they finally got married. They could raise the baby, whom they named Barton Brosen. They seemed to get along as a family for about a year, when a strange thing happened to alter the course of their marriage. Isaac got a job with the United States armed forces working as a clerk in one of the offices locating missing Jews lost during the war, for the survivors to be reunited with their families. One day he came across the name of Stella Kline, who was a survivor and the aunt of Elsie and Anna Kline. Isaac did not tell Anna until he located the aunt, Mrs. Kline. About a week later he found her. He talked to her, and was astounded at what she said. Isaac said, "I do not believe, are you sure?"

Stella replied, "Yes, I am quite sure, because I was at the same camp where her parents were killed. I survived because I worked as a seamstress. I said nothing of my niece being a Jew. To my dismay, I found out she was killing our own people, but I still did not say anything. I do not know if I could face her sister. Anna is taking care of the baby for her since she was executed."

Isaac, with surprise, "What? You mean to say that is not Anna's baby? She told me her husband was killed in a concentration camp and she was liberated in time, so the baby was saved when he was born."

With sarcasm, Stella said, "That is a laugh, she never was married and cannot have children because she had a hysterectomy a few years ago from an illness."

Isaac was so dumbfounded he could not speak for a moment. Finally he told Stella, "Thank your for your time. Here is Anna's address. It is up to you if you want to see her." After he left Stella, Isaac could not hold it anymore and really hit the ceiling, cursing and yelling. When he finally calmed down, he went through all the files he could get ahold of, until he found Anna's sister. There it was, in black and white. Posed as a Nazi guard and the baby's father was Hans Kietel, another Nazi guard. She was hanged as a murderer and traitor. "What a disgrace!" said Isaac.

Anna was wondering why Isaac was so late coming home. He walked in the door, not saying anything. While sitting down at the table, he just stared. Anna asked what was the matter? He just stared at Anna for awhile with contemptible eyes. Anna said again, "What is it?"

Finally Isaac said, "You lied to me. Bart is a born Nazi. I hate Nazis, and now I hate you for not telling me. I am leaving you because I do not want a Nazi son for the rest of my life." Isaac got up and went to the bedroom, packed a couple of bags and left. Anna did not say a word. She stood in the far end of the room in tears.

She had some money put away that Isaac did not know about. She sold all of what furniture she had, and took the baby. She used her old identification, went to the immigration center and put in for the displaced persons waiting list to the United States. She had no friends, her husband left, and her Aunt Stella never looked her up. Obviously she had no future in Europe. Anna and the baby wandered from place to place, sleeping wherever they could for almost four months, before she found out she had a passage to the United States. She looked at Bart and said, "We are finally free!"

Anna was seasick for almost the whole trip to New York. Passing the Statue of Liberty was a big welcome and a new life. They had no trouble with the inspection at Ellis Island. Their papers seemed to be in order. They got in this line and everyone was sprayed with DDT white powder. Bart started to cry and would not stop until they were out of the building. They walked, following the others, to another building that had long tables and benches. Then they all sat down and were fed lunch. The next day they were ferried across the New York Harbor to Brooklyn, where they were welcomed by a Jewish committee. They were given shelter at a synagogue. Anna was introduced to a man named Shy, who owned a plant that manufactured clothing. He gave her a job that she could begin in a few days. He also helped her find a place to rent in one of the tenement buildings.

When Bart was growing up, he had nightmares of people being murdered, and heard agonizing crying and screams. Bart would wake up once in a while in the middle of the night screaming and having cold sweats and shivering. Anna would go to him in his room and try to comfort him, asking what was wrong. With a trembling voice, he would tell Anna about the dreams, of many, many bodies, all standing up like zombies, with no clothes on, and eyes closed. This was happening on and off until he was twelve years old. Anna took him to a psychiatrist to see what he could do for him. He told Bart to wait in the waiting room while he talked to his mother. Anna told him his whole background.

"I see," said the shrink. "It is going to be rather difficult to assist him." Anna took Bart to a few sessions, then discontinued it, because it was too expensive. Bart continued his schooling in Manhattan, working after school, saving his money for college until he was eighteen. He stayed with Anna, who he thought all along was his real mother. The shrink never got to the part about who his real parents were. Bart continued to have nightmares more often, with the same crying and screaming, and a sharp voice of someone shouting. Most of the time, it sounded like a muffled sound. All the time Bart would say he had to get to the bottom of these nightmares.

Bart worked for another year after he graduated from high school. Then he chose to go to a college in Cleveland, Ohio for the fall semester in 1964. He majored in business and psychiatry. The years in college where he stayed in the dorms, he was still having his nightmares, talking and yelling in his sleep. This occurred about once or twice a month. His roommates could not make heads or tails of it. Even when he was studying his psychiatry course, learning about peoples' backgrounds and their behavior, Bart could not find the answer to his own behavior. He checked his whole background from time to time of his life, tracing it back to Germany and up to the present in case he missed something. He thought there was a piece of the puzzle missing. The situation still continued, after three years of psychiatry. That is when a girl named Esther, who was mastering to be a music teacher came along. They went together until they both graduated in 1968. Bart's mother, Anna, took a plane from New York for the graduation and met Esther, whom she liked right off. Bart told his mother they were getting married in a couple of months. "We decided to get married in Manhattan where my old friends are. Then we are going to travel for a month on our honeymoon. We are then going back to Cleveland, Ohio, where we have new jobs waiting for us."

Bart and his wife lived in an apartment for about three years, then purchased a home in Beachwood, in the suburbs. They lived there for about ten years and had three children.

Then a strange thing happened. While the children were in school, Bart and his wife were shopping at South Euclid supermarket. At the checkout, Bart noticed the woman cashier looked at lot like his mother Anna. Bart told her, "You know you look a lot like my mother Anna."

The cashier, a little stunned and stuttering asked, "Is your name Bart?"

Bart a little puzzled, "How do you know my name?"

The cashier said, "I believe I am your great aunt Stella, and your mother is my niece."

"Well I'll be damned," Bart said. "This is my wife Esther." Esther said hello in a surprised, but cordial way.

The person in line behind them remarked, "Have your reunion some other time and check me out!" Esther apologized and finished checking out.

Stella said, "Wait for me. I am on break in about twenty minutes."

They got together and talked about old times and got to see each other from time to time. Stella lived in South Euclid with her retired husband, Aaron. One day Bart went

224

to see his Aunt Stella and began talking about the Holocaust and what happened to the rest of the family. Bart remarked how he had nightmares, that he had been having them since he left Germany with his mother, from the time he was a bay. Stella asked, "Bart, did Anna ever explain to you your birth and where?"

Bart thinking back said, "One time we got in an argument. She told me she was not my real mother. Then after, she said she was just kidding. After her remark about not being my real mother, I got to thinking. She did seem strange sometimes."

Stella said, "I am going to tell you something you're not going to like. The last time I saw Anna was before the war. Anna is not your mother. She is your aunt. Your real mother was in disguise as a German guard at one of the concentration camps in Poland. She was pregnant with you in prison. Your father was a Nazi guard and was killed when the camp was liberated. Your biological mother was executed after you were born. You were given to Anna to be raised."

Bart could not believe it, and said, "I don't believe it!"

Stella said, "It is all on record at the embassy files in Germany. Now all these years you lived in the United States and had a good life. I will not tell anyone what I told you, but you had to know sooner or later. I know you are a good person, so we will let it go at that."

Now this was a new scenario for Bart. He did not expect this in a million years. He might find the reason for his nightmares. He tried not to think of his past and his real parents. But the nightmares continued to remind him.

One Saturday at a booksale, which was held at the Mayfield Regional Library, he came across a very old book from the 1920s. He bought it for fifty cents and took it home. He put it on the bookshelf in the study. It sat there for a year before he actually opened it. Bart flipped through it to see what kind of subjects it might contain. He stopped about half way through, at chapter thirteen, which was entitled, "Psychiatry of the Unborn Child." This sounded interesting. He sat down and read about the baby in the womb, who was trapped in its own little world, with a psychogenic problem. In other words, everything that was happening outside the womb was heard by the baby inside the womb, which caused a trauma to the unborn child psychologically. In the end it caused the baby to have a sleep disorder after its birth. This seemed to shed light on the subject of Bart's nightmares.

Bart called his Aunt Stella and told her that he thought he found the reason for his nightmares, but that he needed more answers. Bart went over to her house the following evening and told her what he read. He wanted to know the activity his real mother went through.

Stella said, "Do you really want to hear this?"

Bart said, "Yes, if it will help the situation."

"Okay, brace yourself. In the concentration camp during the war, the Nazis killed the Jews as a necessity for Germany. First of all their possessions were taken from them. Some were shot, some were experimented on, gassed, and cremated. The Jews were forced to do all the work in destroying their own people. This went on day in and day out. People were always crying, screaming, and moaning in agony. Your mother took part in this extermination while she was pregnant with you."

Bart asked, "So do you think it was possible that I could have heard and felt the events of that time, storing them in my subconscious before being born?"

Stella answered, "Yes, I believe you could have."

So Bart finally got the answer he had been looking for. After hearing about such atrocities, and also seeing videos, and reading about it, things did not get any better. He not only had nightmares, he was also having trance-like visions of a past life from another world named planet Thrae. He was a leader, always in battles with the enemy, trying to take over planet Thrae and the universe. The real clincher was the recent past of being a Nazi, actually enjoying the killing of people until he met his fate.

Since Bart was brought up by Jewish teachings, and the good there was in life, he just could not get it out of his mind that he was that kind of a person in his previous lives. He kept a journal on most of his nightmares and the visions of the past so he could analyze the situation more clearly.

Bart joined a Jewish organization, whose job was to track down Nazi war criminals from World War II. They had tracked down a few Nazis from about 1980 to 1990. They were sent back to Europe, tried, and were either executed or sent to prison for their crimes. Bart was working for an insurance company for the last few years and now ran his own office.

One day in February 1996, he was reading an article on reincarnation in one of the psychiatry magazines. It was very interesting. Bart wrote back to Santini's post office box number asking to meet the reincarnated people, which in turn helped form the Thorme Club, which brought Bart up to date on the functioning of the club and the Future Vision Cable Company.

Commander Siro said, "That was a strange but fantastic story," and he would remember it. "But before we fly back to Peru, where the Ventara spaceship is, I would like to tell you about the history of planet Thrae, which is similar to the history of planet Earth. There are a couple of differences, though plant Thrae has a large spacecity which was built when planet Thrae came to an end for the second time." Commander Siro had his assistant bring it to the studio from the probe to show a documentary of planet Thrae. It went something like this.

Fourteen
Planet Thrae's History

We left the atmosphere of our planet Thrae heading for the stratosphere and the ozone layer. At this time we were traveling twice the speed of sound. In a couple of minutes, our speed was increased to about six times the speed of sound. Our scientists had discovered new and improved ways to control magnetic waves for obtaining speed in outer space, called electromagnetics.

We figured on spending one year traveling to a practically unknown destination. We believed there was life on another planet within our galaxy, in another solar system farther out than the imagination could conceive. We first needed to stop at our spacecity, named Orant, which was constructed many years ago. At this stop at the spacecity we would prepare and map out our direction and the speed it would take on the exploration. It would take about two or three weeks.

The reason why we are going on this journey was to find out who or what was out there, for we have been getting faint signals of intelligent codes, which we had deciphered as a very strange language for many years. Before we got too far into space, I wanted to start from the beginning of the story about planet Thrae and mankind.

Our planet is millions of years old, beginning as a ball of fire, until it was positioned in our solar system. God made the universe, which includes many galaxies. We live in one of them. We have a theory of evolution starting with the prehistoric age of large animals and birds, including different species in the water. Of course animal life took place many, many years after the planet was formed, with all types of vegetation and insects, and other species of the small world. With plants, insects, animals, sea, and land to give a well balanced environment, as we thought; it was believed that God made a number of planets with life on each of them. All were alike, with the same situations on each of them, just to see how animals and humans reacted as they lived together. It is believed that if life on each planet had failed the test, it was destroyed and had to start over again. Anyway, at one time the animals, both large and small, including land, sea, and air creatures, thrived on the environment to the fullest extent.

Our planet was made in eight days, according to our scriptures, and we accounted for a God somewhere in the universe, as it was witnessed in written history and stored in planet Thrae's archives. This planet was like a garden, peaceful in nature, and populated by a very few people who were supposed to be made in the image of God.

This population was started by created man; then woman from man. Also, aliens were sent from other planets of different races, which were believed to have been from another dimension out in the universe; different planets, in different galaxies, at different eras. These chosen few were of a different class of people, different skin and languages, but made up of the same features in body and mind. This planet was a complete paradise to live in, with everything a person would need and want. It was a clean environment, beautiful climate, all and anything you could eat. Everybody lived in harmony.

There was one stipulation that God instructed the people to obey, however. This command was to stay out of a certain area and not to enter or take anything out. In other words, "DO NOT TOUCH." This area was not a big place to begin with, but it was different from the rest of the planet. The plants were more exotic, and the food looked more pleasurable to eat. The people stayed out of this area of fruitfulness and minded their own business, because of the satisfaction of life that they had. Though there was always that temptation to find out what the forbidden area would bring them; maybe an even happier life than they had. This thinking, one would say, was greed.

In the forbidden isolated area, there was always a person hanging around who seemed to be congenial. The people talked to him sometimes. The conversation was always about how nice the planet was, and that the people all got along with each other. No one really wanted anything more than they already had. Then it was thought that this nice person was a demon in disguise for he was a smooth talker. He told the people how wonderful it was in the area that was forbidden to them. He said the food and the surroundings were much better than outside the area. Finally, the temptation got the better of the people. They strolled in and soon found themselves in a different atmosphere. It was very strange indeed. The food tasted better than theirs, and everything seemed much nicer. All of a sudden, they felt themselves trespassing; feeling very guilty. They started to feel strange things, like feeling ashamed because they were naked. They never felt this way before. Then a strange voice in the air said over and over again, "YOU HAVE SINNED, now leave this place! You will live in shame the rest of your days and so will all the people around the planet Thrae. They will share in your misfortune and so will all your generations to come. You will have to find out how to make your own peace on planet Thrae."

Planet Thrae, I would say, lasted in a state of turmoil

for about two thousand years. The people just could not get along with each other without hate, stealing, adultery, murder, and wars. There were few people that obeyed the law of God, who kept on repeating to the people of the planet that the end was near. The complete distruction of man would be inevitable. God instructed these few people to build an ark. It was to be such and so in length, width, and height. They were to gather all the animals in pairs, and load them into the ark.

They found a site to build this ark. All the material was at hand, so they did not have to travel too far for any of it. They laid down the keel and continued every day on its construction.

Most people that came by asked and wanted to know about this project. They were told that the planet was coming to an end, and all living things would perish. The people laughed and jeered, "Are you going to put big wheels on your boat and push it to the sea? Ha-ha-ha."

"Laugh if you will, but it will rain for fifty days and nights." They laughed all the more and went about their sinning ways.

It took a number of years for the ark to be completed. The time had come when all the animals from all over planet Thrae assembled and were ready to be loaded into the ark. The people outside the ark watched in awe, and thought they were going to open up a zoo somewhere, or was it some hallucination they were having. Remember, the planet was much smaller at this time and the land masses were more connected. Besides, the animals were also instructed by God with an instinct to leave for the ark. All the animals and fowl were loaded into the ark to their respective places. Then the ark was closed up tighter than a drum. Everyone waited patiently for it to start raining. They could hear at times people strolling by, calling them names, and even throwing stones against the side of the ark.

After a few weeks of frustration, they finally heard a few drops of rain falling on the roof and deck, until it was a drizzle. At first the people of the planet did not take it seriously, because eventually it only rained every now and then. They went about their daily, normal duties and talking among themselves of what crackpots the people on board the ark were, and continued to party and laugh as if it were a big joke. However, it rained even harder, and did not stop for a couple of weeks. Soon the planet started to tremble and shake. Volcanoes began to erupt and spew hot coals and ashes into the sky throughout the area. The outside people started to be a little more concerned about the strange things that were happening, and why. They were now saying to each other, "Maybe the ark people were not lying." Some of the people said these things sometimes happen and eventually would stop.

The water started to rise very slowly to the bottom of the ark. The people in the ark could hear a loud commotion outside. People yelling, crying, and screaming to let them in. Their pleas for help were getting very desperate and frantic. People in the ark could hear all kinds of begging like, "We will be good and obey the laws of God and help people who need help. PLEASE HELP US!" Instead, the planet got a little more rocky and the water kept on getting higher. It was raining harder than before. The people were pounding harder and harder on the side of the ark. The people in the ark could hear the commotion outside. It sounded like a crowd in a huge stadium. But the cries were not cheers. They were frantic cries for help. The people also prayed for mercy. There were some brave and erratic ones putting ladders against the side of the ark. The ark was too high. They had no ladders that long and there was no time to construct any. The ladders would fall away. It was very unsteady from all the tremors.

At the start of the third week, the rain came down so hard there were sheets of water. You could not see anything in front of your eyes. As the water rose, some of the outside people had boats small and large, but nothing like the ark. They were not prepared for what was to come. It was not long now that the massive structure of the ark started to creak and groan as it moved slowly off the ground with the rise of the swirling water into the abyss, putting them adrift. As the ark floated along in the rough waters, some of the craft tried to come alongside the ark, but they only crashed against the side of the huge structure and were destroyed. The deck was still too high for any smaller boat and no one could get aboard.

The waters started to look like a murky, dark, greenish black sewage from the volcanic ash that swirled around in the water. The skies were always dark. The waves were higher and rougher. The smaller craft sank quickly and everyone perished. The larger boats hoped it would be calm again. Instead it worsened. The land started to heave as hundreds of volcanoes erupted. People and animals, all in panic, tried to reach higher ground. All the people were screaming and there were abandoned children calling and crying out to their parents to save them. Everyone in the ark was praying for all the agonizing cries they were hearing to come to an end.

Imagine being in a boat, seeing what is happening around and beyond, watching the high waves big as a house, volcanoes spewing flames and ashes all over the surrounding areas and all over the uncontrollable boats. Thrae quake tremors, which split the land underneath the waters, caused tidal waves and mountains shooting out of the water in front of your eyes, putting you in a frantic situation. Your boat is rocking so much that you cannot hang on and it capsizes from the mountainous waves. Where there was high ground here and about, a few people and animals were gathered in bunches praying for forgiveness. Some never prayed before, and now it was a little late. Their lives flashed before their eyes and they thought of the wrong and evil they performed all their lives. Now it was time to pay the consequences. Soon these higher mountains would be covered with water and the people who were left, including the animals, would cling on hoping for a miracle that would not come. So they perished into the depths, right down to the last whimper.

The ark was alone on the great vastness of ocean, still being tossed around like a cork. I believe there was not too much boredom on the ark, because it must have taken every ounce of energy to take care of all the animals in every compartment.

After fifty days and nights of rain and tremors, and being tossed around, the wide vastness of water finally calmed down to a tranquil surrounding. The sun finally came out and the people got their first breath of fresh air, after being cooped up with all of the animals. They had been floating around for about six months and did not even see one mountain peak anywhere. The water had covered everything in sight. They assumed everything that was alive was now dead. After another two months, doves were sent out to find land. This went on for two more months. Finally, one dove returned from the east with a twig in its beak. They headed in that direction while the waters started to abate. Out in the distance they could distinguish vague mountain peaks. After seeing water day after day, this was a very welcome sight for a change. It would not be long before they would hit land. At this point, they would settle for land anywhere. After a few more days, the bottom of the ark was scraping land, until it came to rest on top of a mountain. The water was receding more and more each passing day, until enough land could be seen, with greenery throughout the whole area. We were on the move for one year and one month before coming to rest on a mountain. We named the mountain SALVATION.

We waited almost six months before letting all the animals out. When we did, they all seemed to know where they were going. When the people left the ark, it was not a pretty sight at first. There were bodies all over the land mixed with the carcasses of animals. But the land started to get its color back, and looked very beautiful. Now we had to start all over again, as new people.

After many, many generations with a large population, the same thing seemed to be happening all over again. Most people just liked to sin with their hate and wars. There was the ancient age, medieval age, and modern age. Our modern age took the cake. We had three Thrae wars. The third Thrae war was again the destruction of planet Thrae, this time by fire. It was the very last of the planet Thrae's wars.

From the years 1900 till about the 1980s, planet Thrae time, we had a few blissful years. There were a few hundred countries on our planet, and four planet leaders. Ours was the country of Sargarity. I would say we were the planet's main leader. We tried to keep the peace throughout. Most of the countries were peaceful nations. The other three main ones were Ucronmely, Larquonia, and Jarconi. Ucronmely and Larquonia were friendly countries, but Jarconi had demagogues, and wanted the whole planet for themselves. All the people were slaves, and obeyed one dictator. We tried to have peaceful meetings, but the representatives of the country of Jarconi would always threaten with war. So much for the political situation. We had other problems.

First, we had an outstanding economy. This economy throughout the years yielded all kinds of inventions in science and space, all kinds of transportation, travel, sports, and almost a decent way of life. They had tall buildings, stadiums, bridges with numerous metropolises throughout the planet. Also, there was much crime and corruption. The population of different nations were always trying to beat one another, to see who could earn or steal the most from one another, which led to little skirmishes. There was always one type of crime or another. In some places you could not walk down the street without getting mugged or murdered. People did not live in a harmonious way. It surely was no Utopia. The law enforcement agencies were always on their toes.

Let us go back a little, to after the 1850s. This was a time of inventions and discoveries, like moving vehicles on land and sea of things self-propelled; discoveries of oil, coal, and other minerals. There were enough raw materials to last thousands of years. We got around to the 1900s. Countries were not happy with what they had and fought for more that did not belong to them. There was bloodshed for greed. What was happening was war after war. Our country of Sargarity had to always intervene to get things calmed down back to normal. For many years the planet was at peace, financially, the economy did not look too good throughout the planet. Then another war started and took almost ten years to end. This time the other countries were more sophisticated and developed the same destructive weapons we had from the stolen secrets obtained from us. This was the nuclear age. Aircraft was invented earlier on. We were sending rockets into space.

In the meantime, we got ourselves into a polluted state because of all the toxic materials coming from industries and automotive vehicles. Our rain forests were being cut down all over the planet. I would say we had less than half of the rain forests left. This in time affected our environment all over the planet. The ozone was strongly affected, and was destroying the protective shield from the sun. The public was dying from different types of cancers and other diseases including many types of sexual viruses. People were dying by the thousands. Our religions had declined to the point where people had no morals and did not believe in anything. There were dope addicts, which led to stealing, rape and murder. The authorities had a hard time controlling the masses.

We had a well-developed space program, which started in the early seventies. We had men and women in space setting up satellites and space stations. In the late eighties, the voice had spoken again to a very few throughout the planet. It informed them to build a spacecity in outer space. The dimensions were to be as big as a small city to accommodate a few hundred chosen people, and to gather the animals in two-by-two fashion. This would take a period of about twenty years to complete. All the scientific equipment would be aboard to continue exploration, while the planet renewed itself from its destruction. This city was called the Ark in the Sky.

The spacecity was started in the early 1990s. Our scientific inventions and discoveries had bypassed the rocket fuel type to get to outer space. We had what you would call nuclear magnetic force, which was controlled by forwarding and reversing a magnetic field through the nucleus of an atom. Our computer system was so advanced you could store a whole library on the head of a pin. Our education was more of a robotic state, which could store any data at will when obtained. Of course all these things were tested and experimented on for many years, until everything was perfected. No matter how experimentation was performed to get everything just right, there would always be that tiny flaw that went unnoticed until found and corrected. We really had not had too many disasters throughout the years. In the years 1992 through to 1996, we had two unmanned remote-controlled craft crash into the ocean from computer malfunctions. We recovered the spacecraft and went over them thoroughly finding a small acceleration component that went bad, which caused the mishap. The secondary unit did not work, because the manufacturers did not wire it correctly. Why it did not show up on the test computer is still a mystery. That was the first spacecraft. The second spacecraft crashed from being overloaded. It got a few miles up, ready to make its second orbit around the planet, when the overweight panic light came on at the station. We were almost to the stratosphere and decided to bring it back down. It started to shudder and fall apart. It came down in pieces. It took months to gather all the pieces and data as to why it happened. The spacecraft was overloaded with the planet's dirt and rocks. When the air got thinner, the struts could not take the strain when the magnetic booster for more thrust was applied. It loosened the struts and everything started to fall apart and drop back to the planet. This did not happen again, because we used a different, stronger metal. They sent cargo craft after cargo craft into space for the last ten years.

In the meantime, planet Thrae was hardly in better shape than it was ten years ago. The people had been warned time and time again of the prophesies, but had ignored the warnings. They continued to live their sinful lives. A few good people continued to finish building the spacecity. Of course, they were jeered and laughed at, and they were told they were wasting their time and money. That sounded familiar, like before with the great flood and the ark.

Fifteen
Spacecity Orant

The Ark in the Sky was named Spacecity Orant, and had taken twenty years of architectural construction. All the material was transported from planet Thrae. Each time they transported material to outer space to build the spacecity, they had to send a few personnel also. They needed more and more to construct and maintain what already was constructed.

All personnel transported on this venture had to be trained in many fields, and had to be fairly educated beforehand. They had to be physically fit. Our architects on planet Thrae had spent many, many hours, days, and weeks preparing and drawing out all the specifications. They printed many copies of blueprints of the spacecity, down to the last detail. Everyone was thoroughly screened so the plans did not fall into the wrong hands, for that would be a disaster. It would also slow down our production to be completed at the scheduled time. It was almost like being drafted into the service, but on a volunteer basis. Each person sent out to the spacecity would serve about two years of service before being sent back to planet Thrae. If that person wanted to be reassigned, he or she would have to pass another physical and a simple aptitude test. After about a month furlough, they would take the trip again.

The framing of the spacecity was the most critical part of the construction and the most complicated. You had to start with the base of the structure, the longest length being about twenty feet. It was put together like an erector set. You could not use surveying instruments like you did on planet Thrae. It was all guided and perfected with the help of the stars. The stars were all in a fixed position so as to give an accurate measurement of each piece that went into place, especially the nuclear generators and power plant, to keep everything at a continuous pace. Once this power was installed, it made working conditions easier and quicker. The first section of framing was all erected after the nuclear generators and power plant were installed on its mounts of the floor frame. This section was about a quarter of a mile long and two stories high, with fittings for additional floors. The skin was being installed around the framing. Once this was done and sealed, it took about another four months with a work force of two hundred people.

Our spacecraft usually left planet Thrae about once a week at the beginning of construction. We had more spacecraft, and our trips were made every two or three days, depending on what was contained in the cargo. Some spacecraft had no personnel. We could get more material to our destination. Commander Sarlox from our country of Sargarity was going to make the trip. He knew what was going on first hand. This would be the first time the commander was to travel to outer space. Today, with our advanced technology in outer space it was like flying around our planet.

Of course this was to be top secret so there would not be any mishaps of any kind. This craft was more like a luxury liner. The commander would get a panoramic view of everything from when we left the country, the planet, the clouds, and the wide expanse of the universe with its millions of stars. We started out on the third calendar month of Jako 1993. It was a pleasant morning, the sun was shining.

At about seven A.M., there was a cool breeze with a couple of scattered clouds in the sky. It was a perfect day for a trip anywhere. We had one of our newest spacecraft made for just this occasion. Our most experienced pilot, copilot, and navigator were the crew to make the first flight to outer space to start construction on the spacecity. Commander Sarlox and his wife Tula arrived in their special aircraft, piloted by a veteran airpilot. A few inconspicuous bodyguards were always planted at various locations at all times.

Launch time was at nine A.M. The commander said good-bye to his wife, got on board, and made himself comfortable. It was not wise to take his wife on this first trip. When the spacecity was a little more complete with more facilities, there were more people who could travel for inspection. The commander was settled down in the spacecraft and a few of his aides also came along. At exactly nine A.M., they launched off, not like a rocket in the past but like a regular airliner at takeoff. Space rockets of the past had to be launched vertically and it took four stages to get into space. The rockets had to have enough thrust to get away from the planet's gravitational pull of about twenty-five thousand miles an hour, or it would fall back to the planet. Our new spacecraft had nuclear motors that used practically no fuel. They were controlled by electromagnetic forces to control the gravitation of the trip. We were far enough away for the cabin to be pressurized and the oxygen was put on. Everything was as comfortable as could be, and the commander seemed to be pleased. Since we were starting to leave the planet's atmosphere, we could feel a little weightlessness. At this time, the gravity neutralizer unit took over, which gave the spacecraft its man-made gravity. We were about to leave the atmosphere completely and start to touch outer space. Our speed started to increase at about a hundred miles per minute. In space around our planet, we will hit speeds of almost twenty thousand miles per hour. All other units are going about the same speed, but when you are in space, it seems like you are not moving at all. Our planet has an array of colors, which is awesome. We have a spectacular sunrise and sunset. The clouds look like you can walk on them.

We should reach the spacecity about three P.M. About halfway we watched a video on a large computer-sized screen of the progress made to the spacecity. We had a pleasant lunch and relaxed the rest of the journey before we landed. We have circled planet Thrae three times already, so we could be at the same distance level as the Spacecity Orant. That put us way out of the gravitational pull from the planet. We could now see our approach to the spacecity on the video screen in front of us. The signal had been given for our landing, which would happen in a few minutes. Actually, this was called docking. Everything was done systematically to make it a smooth and comfortable docking.

The first part of the protection shield was retracted. We got the second signal to reduce our speed to almost zero. To do this, we had to fire a couple of reverse jets, which slowed the ship down for touchdown to the platform. When the dashes of the red light came on it meant we made contact with the docking platform and all controls were shut down. This meant it automatically was overtaken by the space station's garage. The protection shield was once more slid into place. Before anyone or anything was moved from the spacecraft, everything was checked over for any contamination and destroyed so the inside of the spacecity would not get harmed in any way. The next step was to taxi the ship into its hangar after the hangar doors opened. Inside the hangar, we would taxi to our appointed stall. Between now and lunch time, everything was checked over. The hangar was big enough for six ships. As the Spacecity Orant grew in construction, there would be other hangars built to accommodate more spaceships. A four-man vehicle was waiting to take its leader to headquarters. Any vehicle that moved throughout the spacecity was powered by electromagnetic motors.

Our leader inspected all aspects of the construction going on. It took about four days to inspect all the major details, which was of the utmost importance; and of the best protection from aliens, asteroids, and moving objects from space or the planet. Everything was in satisfactory condition to the commander, and he and his advisors, after a meeting on the fifth day with the spacecity's authorities, were to step up production so Spacecity Orant could be finished ahead of schedule. We could then check out all operations. They were to start at once to construct two more landing stations. In all, there would be six landing stations, so as to accommodate more than one craft at a time and any possible accidents.

On the sixth day, the commander was ready to leave the spacecity and head back to planet Thrae. We would lift off at nine A.M. Everyone was now on board, waiting for the green light to lift off. The green light finally came on and we lifted slowly up with a little help from the jets on the bottom of the craft. We had to clear the spacecity so the spacecraft could speed by the city.

Once past the spacecity, we could start our descent toward planet Thrae. We had to circle planet Thrae three times as we descended through the ionsphere, stratosphere to the atmosphere. If you go down too fast, there would be too much air friction and the spacecraft would burn up and disintegrate. Warning lights and a horn would blow if you were descending too fast. It took two hours to complete the journey back to Thrae, without any incidents. When we got back to Thrae, the commander's special aircraft was waiting to take him back to headquarters, which was like a palace.

The next day, some of the planet's leaders had a special meeting. They discussed having more protection around the spacecity. You do not know what kind of space program the alien countries have. The spacecity is still vulnerable and would be until completion, with its protection shield around the whole spacecity and surrounding satellites. This spacecity is like a large disc, with a hub in the middle. It is about ten miles in diameter, and a quarter of a mile high. In time, there would be additions built onto the city, probably extending for fifty miles. The hub was built with the main nuclear generator to control the centrifugal and centripetal force. Also, there are special water compartments at certain points of the spacecity, so it can maintain a well-balanced position. The spacecity has to rotate at a certain speed so it can stay in the right gravitational position. In other words, it could get out of control and be lost in space.

Water was no problem in the spacecity, because inside there would be enough condensation where we would never run out of water. This would fill up our space tanks for the spacecity's balance, including purified drinking and bathing water which has to dissipate into outer space. Oxygen was brought up from planet Thrae in great quantities and stored through the spacecity. Oxygen was a must when we started construction; and since the city is almost completed with its own artificial air, which is produced from the miniature forests in different parts of the spacecity. These forests were transported from planet Thrae as an experiment, and it works. Tons of earth were brought up, including seedlings of all kinds, and vegetable plants and fruit trees. We have enough water to irrigate these forests, and light, which is filtered through the glass-like skydomes of the spacecity. It is almost like being on planet Thrae. This spacecity has about the same facilities as you have back home. The family living quarters is like a large condominium community.

There are stores and entertainment of all sorts. Travel throughout the spacecity is done by electronic robot vehicles, which can accommodate four people. Almost completed is a monorail train to accommodate a larger number of people that will travel from one end of the city to the other. Each living quarter has a picture phone for communication. Also there are emergency codes. There is always an emergency unit ready for any and all calls that may come in. There is the infirmary, very well equipped to cope with any type of emergency. All doctors and aides are very well educated to the highest degree.

The year was 2008. The Spacecity Orant was now complete with every possible means of supplies, machinery, and all the advanced technology that could be acquired. The task was at hand to gather all the animals, two by two, at the departure area for liftoff. This took almost two years of shuttling back and forth. Finally everything was in order, with all the animal stalls dispersed evenly throughout the spacecity to keep everything balanced. Now that this was done, it was time to notify the rest of the chosen people to gather at the meeting point for liftoff, and to take their last look at humanity. The last spacecraft lifted off one month before the end of the year 2009. The last spacecraft reached the spacecity in about twenty hours. Everyone was now on board the spacecity. Incidentally, all the crews, laborers, and anyone that was connected with this project, were indoctrinated to obey the laws of the Lord. These teachings were issued throughout the twenty years while the Spacecity

Orant was being constructed. Everyone had a clean spirit, mind, and being. If these laws were broken during that time, the person or persons were transported back to planet Thrae to stay. In other words, they signed their own death sentence.

We accumulated about five thousand men, women, and children. Way more than we anticipated, but there is still enough room. A few people were concerned and a little frightened in taking this permanent voyage. They were consoled and reminded of a better life in the future. After a few weeks in space, everyone was getting used to the idea of their new life and did not seem to mind so much. In the meantime, the messages were coming through to us of hostility from the country of Jarconi, and a few of their crony countries. We sent message after message to tell all the countries that the planet was going to be destroyed by their own hand and finished by God Almighty. Every warning was completely ignored. The leaders of Jarconi figured this was their chance to take over the planet. It was not that simple. So it finally started Nuclear Warfare.

Sixteen
Year of Destruction on Planet Thrae

The year 2010 was a year of destruction. The year beginning 2009 was the last meeting held with all the planet
leaders, trying to avoid a planet catastrophe. But this was to
no avail. The country of Jarconi and a few other small countries, siding with the country of Jarconi, wanted to rule the
planet as dictators. We were now heading toward a nuclear
war. Many countries had nuclear weapons. If this war
started, it would be the end of mankind on planet Thrae for
the second time.

Incidentally, all the prophets pointed out that the end
of the planet would be at the end of the twentieth century.
Most people said they were a bunch of liars and screwballs,
because here we are nine years into the twenty-first century, and laughed it off. They assumed the planet was too
modern and advanced with all the technology, industry,
and so forth. They forgot there were always some that want
it all, because they were dictators with a gift of gab and
greed. People would believe in their lies.

We were now approaching the middle of the year 2009.
Already some of the smaller, unprotected countries had
been notified to leave the planet at once to go to the
Spacecity Orant. This being done, the few that stayed
behind trying in vain to avert danger to the planet had
failed.

The country of Jarconi had dropped its first nuclear

bomb, and destroyed part of one of our cities in the north. Many people were killed or injured. They told us that was just a warning, if we did not comply with their demands. In a month it would be the year 2010. The rest of the chosen ones left three moths ago to go to the Spacecity Orant. We send out messages and told the leaders that they were insane not only causing their own destruction but the destruction of mankind. As soon as they sent over a few more nuclear bombs it was the beginning of the end. From our space station, we could observe the whole matter to the minutest detail. All our armed forces were controlled from the military part of the space station. By the third month of the year 2010 a quarter of the planet's population had been destroyed. Nobody could stop their insanity.

All the centuries it took to build up the planet, with beautiful buildings and all its wonders, for example, art, culture, technology, and education—all was destroyed because of greed. All the nuclear war bombs and what have you, caused a chain reaction, because half of the ozone was gone. This meant there was less protection from the sun. The sun gave out too much radiation that mixed with all the nuclear activity. The planet was now at the stage of burning up with atoms and lightning mixed with flames, that would burn anything, melt any kind of metal, and pulverize all stone and cement to powder. The chain reaction was so powerful and swift, it went with lightning speed around the planet, like a huge flame thrower. There were also balls of fire that were hundreds of feet high, rolling around the planet. Everything they passed was disintegrated into thin air. Everything burned that would burn. Even the ashes disappeared. The water boiled to nothing and the steam evaporated to nothing. This lasted for three months. The lightning and atoms just kept going around the planet continuously. The planet looked like one big fireball. At the same time, there was volcanic activity and planet quakes. The ground shook and shuddered, and the appearance of the planet changed.

All of this devastation on the planet was being observed from the spacecity. It was also being recorded on our computers. We have sophisticated equipment in the form of telescopes, and such apparatuses to record every detail. For future life this would remind everyone of the consequences that were realized.

In the meantime, some of the enemy nations went into space for a small duration. Our space station was well-equipped like the planet was, but on a very much smaller scale; enough to last about twenty years. This was so because of the specifications God had given to us. Like the mentality to find the unknown materials to make metals for our products and the like.

The enemy countries figured that the planet would soon get back to normal. They were dead wrong. As soon as all the fires of hell died down, they thought they could just go back and continue where they left off. Some tried, and when they got close enough, they found there was absolutely nothing. At this point, their ships started to falter because of the deadly atmosphere and pressure of sulphuric fumes and other deadly gases. It made their ships disintegrate before they could get the slightest chance to get back to outer space. We did not try because God instructed us chosen few to stay put. We were supposed to prepare ourselves on our spacecity with all the knowledge we had acquired throughout the years. We were to experiment with everything possible to make sure everything fell into place, when the time came to go back. We were also instructed, which was also God's decree, to keep the doors to the spacecity shut to all outsiders who managed to escape from the planet Thrae. These people were the smarter ones, but not smart enough. In time, they would perish. No one would be bothered with their nuisance. We were not to communicate with them, no matter what their plans were. Believe me, there were enough cries for help. It took this agonizing situation nearly a year before the last enemy spacecraft came to an end, for they had all died. They died because they lacked the necessities such as food, water, oxygen, and so forth. In desperation, they tried to land their spaceships onto our spacecity. To their disappointment the spacecity was protected with an almost invisible shield, so we could be protected from asteroids and any other foreign bodies. They even tried crashing through. Now finally, it was over. No more life on any of the enemy spaceships. Space just outside the planet looked like one big junkyard, with thousands of tons of debris floating around aimlessly in space.

Another year went by without any activity outside the spacecity and the planet. Through our observation, the planet seemed to have calmed down and started the beginning of an upward swing. God said not to worry about the planet at this time. Things would take care of themselves. Everything would grow with a rapid pace because of the atomic radiation. After about twenty years the forests, seas, and ocean would reappear. Everything would begin to get back to normal. The word would be given to go back and disperse the birds and animals and then the people. By that time we would be running out of a few of the resources on the spacecity. For now, we were told to step out of the spacecity and collect all the junk and debris that was floating around, so it could be recycled. Also, we were told to mend the ozone so the planet would be protected from the sun. This will be done through scientific instructions. They cleaned up most of the debris that was floating around in space. Most of the spaceships we towed in had a few corpses in each. They probably died from lack of oxygen. We also had about a dozen crews with their repair ships to work on the ozone. The accomplishment was wonderfully done. The ozone was at first hard to detect, but then we started to use infrared light, which made the ozone gases show up. We gathered these gases in huge vats like big milk bottles. We used the same method to find where the ozone ended and started. This took about five years to accomplish.

While living on Spacecity Orant, we had a number of astronomers who studied the galaxy. They knew about the nine planets that revolved around their sun. These were called Arba, Bica, Cirac, and the fourth planet, Thrae, which was their planet. There was Darfi, Horto, Jarmax, Komo and Mirni. Since we were this far out in space, they had the opportunity to study even further out into our galaxy. They discovered three more planets, which were named Otamu, Terquam, and Zumi. There was one hitch about these three planets. Our first nine planets revolved around our sun one way, and these three new planets seemed to revolve in the opposite direction. We were beginning to believe this might be the beginning of another solar system. They would find out someday when they got more advanced in the space program. They still had a lot to learn.

They knew there was a strange phenomenon in certain places in the universe, like the spots and small areas. We sent out unmanned probes to one particular area, which took about two weeks. The probes were sent out from our spacecity having all the latest data equipment. Their technicians kept tabs on one probe that was headed for an empty cylinder. After about ten days of travel at the same constant speed, it seemed to increase its speed. By the thirteenth day, the speed was about threefold, which we could not control and also started to change direction on a downward curvature. The fourteenth day, we started to get fainter and fainter signals, until there were none. We never heard from that probe again. They analyzed every possibility of what might have happened. They came to the conclusion that this was a large magnetic black hole. If close enough, it would draw you right into the unknown to anyone. There just was not any scientific explanation of this phenomenon. They must know all the facts of black holes, comets, cosmic dust or any other unexplained matter that was in space before they could begin any journey to find out if there was any other life in the universe and our galaxy.

They had an exploration planned that would take at least a year, according to the out signals being received. It also took us in one straight line past all our planets. With all the modern technology, the space program was more advanced and would be ready to go any year. Their personnel had already started to be picked. Their aptitude test was, I would say, out of this planet. In fact, you had to be practically a genius! You had to know weather, astronomy, and math galore. If the student could not come up with the answers right away, forget it. On this kind of a trip you had to be quick, smart, and healthy, and have nerves of steel so you could get through any crisis. The tests were crucial and supposed to simulate the same conditions you would encounter. Again, you don't know what to expect when you're that far away from your own planet.

Out of every hundred cadets who took these tests, only two or three made the grade. These were the chosen ones, who also had religious backgrounds. They were not trying to be discriminatory in this process and were not trying to form any Utopia. All were striving for a nice, clean and honest race. We already had two destructable ends of planet Thrae. One by water and one by fire. The latter one really cleaned up the planet. When things were back to normal, we shall continue to build the cities in a unique and conservative way. It would take time, a lot of time. It still took nine months to have a child, and it would take many generations to multiply to again have a large population.

The belief was through the scriptures and other means, that we would also be populated by other beings, from other places, that were in our universe. If one believed in such a being, it would be interesting to know if there really was life on another planet.

As time went by on Spacecity Orant, one became used to living in space. They had the same facilities as on planet Thrae. They have been taking care of all the animals, which were in a special area on the spacecity, like in a big zoo. They had to control the population of the animals, or deal with being overcrowded. That also held true for the humans, until the spacecity was enlarged in the near future. They learned newer medical technology toward the cure for sickness and diseases. They have more time to do these things and have no time for such things as wars and the like. Of course, there were always a few people that thought they were above the law. They thought they could get away with any wrongdoing. You had to remember though, we numbered a few thousand, but in time in a city this size, you get to know just about everyone at one time or another.

Punishment was dealt with very swiftly. The culprits all got a fair trail. If found guilty, the consequences were very seriously taken care of. We had no jails on Spacecity Orant. A jail had been constructed outside the spacecity, a few miles' distance in space. The prisoner would have enough time to think of his wrongdoings. We had a few guards that worked in jail in intervals, to make sure the prisoners were well taken care of. This was considered a penal colony. Their quarters were much smaller, the recreation was not too hip, and they had to work on projects that concerned the spacecity. There was virtually no escape from the space jail, so you had to make the best of it. The length of time one stayed in jail depended on the crime committed. Once the time was served and the person was back on Spacecity Orant, they were almost like an angel, never trying anything out of the ordinary. You are watched like a hawk and you are never done with extra-community service hours. All in all, when you are back, it is a lot better than in jail, away from the city. You at least have your freedom back.

A few more years went by and it was now the year 2017. All the activity that had been going on with inventions for space travel, and for the spacecity was growing larger and larger. We have been getting our raw materials from our moon, which was closer to our planet and even closer to Spacecity Orant. Our moon had about the same type of minerals as the planet Thrae. We also found a few other minerals that planet Thrae did not have. It was also a better quality for building projects.

We had been observing planet Thrae throughout the years. It seemed to be getting back to normal with oceans, lakes, and forests. We figured in about three years most of the people would be heading back to colonize in all parts of the planet. It had all been planned out for the cities that would be built. With the technology, skill, and the raw materials, it should not take long to populate and continue to have a decent living. The new leaders, with the new laws, would make things a lot better and easier to live with; which was far better than the old planet. Besides, it was starting to get a little crowded on Spacecity Orant.

In the middle of the year 2018, we had been studying all the planets in our galaxy with the aid of our advanced probes, traveling across space to photograph each planet. We wanted to get some type of data as to why they are out there, and for what purpose. We also sent out messages in code as far away as a signal could travel. It had taken about a year or so when we finally received very faint messages. We could not make any sense of it. The messages or codes were not strong enough. Maybe this was so because it was in a strange language, or they did not have a strong enough transmitter.

We had small colonies on the moon and also on planet Darfi. Since the signals were coming from that direction, we decided to build a transmitter and receiver on planet Darfi so we could decipher any future messages that might come in. In the meantime, we started to manufacture all the necessary materials for the towers, and the equipment needed to operate a proper station farther out in space.

We still had not come to any conclusion as to why the last three planets, Otamu, Tarquam, and Zumi, orbited in the opposite way from our original nine planets. The only way to find out was to take a trip out there and find the answer. We spent two years on spaceship plans for a long distance and long period of travel time that would withhold any problem it might encounter. By the time this spaceship was ready, it would be time to migrate back to planet Thrae.

They did not know if everyone wanted to go back to planet Thrae. They thought they got a little spoiled on this spacecity. The living was easy with theaters, sports, good schools, markets, amusement parks; and especially how everyone lived in harmony with hardly any crime. There was no pollution in Spacecity Orant, because everything was run on electric magnetics, which was mostly powered by the sun. We stored the radiation from the sun for now and for future use, that operated everything that was on Spacecity Orant.

But once back on planet Thrae, and things became established, it would be a lot better with a lot of room and a lot of things to see and do. One sure would be kept busy. All the plans, blueprints, and photos of all past events of life on planet Thrae, were all on microchips, stored away in the archives for future use, when we would populate the planet again. We also have been working on more modern plans for a better, safer planet to live on.

The people that had been chosen to go back to planet Thrae were some of the original group and their families, who were the young that were first born on Spacecity Orant. Most of them were anticipating what lay ahead for their futures. But before they went to live there, we shall see the architects, engineers and all the skilled labor to different parts of the planet to start construction. They would build cities and farms, and populate a few at the same time. It would take about three or four years just to get started. In the next two years there were meetings, seminars, and preparation for travel back to planet Thrae. We also built a large warehouse next to the spacecity, in which had been stored all the needs to be taken back to planet Thrae. There was prefabrication of housing materials and transportation, quantities of food, hospital units, and everything needed on planet Thrae.

In the year 2030 the time had finally come to migrate the majority back to the planet with more work crews included. We picked the right locations for the living quarters, then we worked from there. We started with five spaceships for the trip, loaded with the crew, bosses, and workers with about fifty personnel to a spaceship.

Before any trip was to be made, we sent out about one hundred probes to circle the planet for about a month so they could send back all the data to make sure everything was safe. So far, the air was clean, the water was safe, and everything was growing as before. Now everything was ready. They started to leave the spacecity one by one. When they landed and started on their way out of the spaceships, everything was very strange and desolate.

Almost all the pilots were veteran pilots from planet Thrae in the first place. So they were more experienced. They were only twenty years older and still in good shape for space travel. They were glad to go through the atmosphere and clouds, and see the beauty of soaring through clean air for the first time in over twenty years.

A ship loaded about every six hours. The first ship landed and everyone got out to unload everything; including the communication equipment, so as to get their orders direct. The communication equipment was a more advanced invention called a vision phone. With this equipment you could see who you were talking to. The conversations were recorded on a microdisc within the unit for future analysis. It was dated and timed. If there were any errors, it would be rectified. Each unit was coded for one user only. That person was responsible for it. All six ships had landed safely. They unloaded and were sent back for more people and cargo. The go-ahead was also given to start sending the unmanned remote controlled ships with all the different building material, plus the machinery that was needed for any construction. All the machinery had to be put together, especially the bigger pieces. The remote spaceships were flown and landed with precision from computers on the spacecity. As Spacecity Orant had been orbiting the planet Thrae, it had been monitoring, recording, and filing everything that was happening.

After a year of building and expanding, it was time to disperse all the animals to all parts of planet Thrae. This had taken about ten months to deliver all of the animals to the planet. There were a number of domesticated animals and birds that were kept in the spacecity's zoos. Initially, every available spaceship had to be converted for the different types of animals to be transported safely down without any mishaps, which could endanger the ship or the animals. It was a miracle, I would say. We did not lose one animal through all of the trips that we made. When all the animal transporting was complete, we continued at full blast bringing more equipment down. We were building much more and faster. The only incident involved one of the remote cargo ships, which malfunctioned on re-entry through the atmosphere. There was too much descending speed and it just burned up and disintegrated. These vehicles had made a great number of trips back and forth without any serious accidents. We have to be extra carful. We were about to send most of the population back to the planet and would have a brand new beginning.

It has been three years since we landed back on planet Thrae. Everything was going along just fine. A few mishaps, a few deaths to be expected, and more people working on all different phases of business and industry, and just plain living. Spacecity Orant still had about twelve thousand people, including leaders and planners. We were starting to transport about seven thousand more people back to planet Thrae so we could continue building up the population. Most of the housing and businesses, including farms, were all waiting to be occupied. The seven thousand would take six to eight months of moving, with all their belongings and kin folk.

We had elected a few desirable people to take over the government and religious sect of the new planet. They would be the directors of law and order of and for the people of the new land. They would assume their positions first thing as they arrived, and then the rest of the population would follow.

As time went by, the people on planet Thrae had been building and expanding with an enormous growth in population. There were now tenfold the amount of people on the planet. When the thousands of people from the spacecity landed, they were scattered all over the planet, with a few hundred people in each colony. The growth had been progressing for about fifty years.

Seventeen
Disaster on Orant

Deton was one of the captains and a pilot who also helped in organizing the beginning of the spacecity's construction. Now retired from active duty for the government of planet Thrae for about five years, he was on vacation with his wife Tarla. They went from planet Thrae to Spacecity Orant. Tarla was shopping with a friend, while Deton was visiting an old friend, Doctor Adin. Deton had not seen Doctor Adin in a couple of years due to Doctor Adin being on furlough on planet Thrae.

While Deton and Doctor Adin were having lunch in the break room, Doctor Adin's assistant popped in for him to come quickly to witness what was happening. The computer was registering a pre-collision or hoping a near miss of a meteor shower heading for the spacecity. They were a little late detecting this meteor shower for an emergency movement of a spacecity this large. They tried anyway, with all the power they had. The meteor shower did not last long, but did enough damage to the east end of the city, where one of the observatories and lookout stations was located.

Everyone was alerted and they strapped themselves in. Most of the meteor shower was in small particles, the sizes of one- to five-inch rocks. You could hear the stones bounce off the protective shield throughout the city. The part that was damaged the most was caused by a projectile of about forty to sixty feet in diameter. It went right through the protective shield and destroyed most of the new telescope and other important instruments. It also cut communication lines and the water system that balanced the city.

Emergency crews were assigned to the area immediately to shut off those lines that were severed so they would not lose too much water. About a mile in all directions, at the east end of the city, the power was cut off. The meteor hit with such force that it shook the east end to a pile of rubble. The tremor was felt throughout the whole city for miles, right to the other end. They did not know how many people were lost until they analyzed the whole situation. When the haze, sparks and water settled down, then they could see a huge gaping hole. It extended from the top right through the bottom of the spacecity.

Spacecity Orant started to list to about seven degrees to port and drift outwards farther into space at about a half a mile an hour. They started the several hundred electro-magnetic jets, which were situated across the entire length of the spacecity. We had to activate about fifty jets to bring the city back to its normal position. These jets were usable for only about two weeks before they were replaced.

In the meantime, they had an emergency meeting with the leaders, including the four main architects and builders. They looked over the situation, which did not look good. The one spaceport was out of commission for lack of power that controlled the opening and closing of the protection shields in that area, and also the servicing of the spaceships. By the way, they had to wear their spacesuits so they would not be exposed to any radiation coming through the damaged hole. Their lifelines were on with oxygen. Captain Jarox of the emergency repair crew almost threw up inside his spacesuit when he discovered all the blood and human remains throughout the damaged area. "Man, that big stone went right through all three levels. What a mess!" They hiked back the way they came, through a series of doors they had to work manually on account of power failure for almost a mile. When they got through the first door and shut it, they unhooked the main lifelines. They left their suits on just in case, and switched to portable oxygen masks because the artificial atmosphere was also destroyed in the area.

When they got back to the conference room, they discussed how to repair all that was damaged, and how long it might take. They checked the stock on the spacecity, and what had to be ordered from planet Thrae. The meeting ended and they got started at once.

The first thing that had to be done was to repair the ballast. We had a few ballast pipes on board at the northeast end, but we could not get to them on account of damaged doors to where they were stored. We called planet Thrae at the main supply depot and explained what happened. They already knew what happened through the news media. We ordered so many lengths of ballast tubes and a few thousand gallons of water, with the chemical so the water would not freeze. In two days the first cargo spaceship arrived at the dysfunctional spaceport. It was put back in commission the first day of the accident. Emergency lines were run almost a mile to the spaceport, until the malfunctions were located. They had portable-generated vehicles, but not enough power for this type of situation to open and close the protection shield and doors, and to service the spaceships. Everything is working now due to the temporary energy supply. All spaceships were evacuated so all the supplies could be unloaded without any interruptions. The supplies kept coming in twenty-six hours a day, (which is planet Thrae's day length) until we had everything we needed.

While the first few loads of supplies were coming in, there were a number of crews cleaning up the damaged area, and non-working parts just in case they did not work when everything was assembled. As soon as a few pieces were dismantled and taken away, and the area cleaned up, a crew was there to prepare the area with a new floor, walls and ceiling. They gave the area a fresh coat of a very fast drying magnetic paint. As soon as that was done, another crew was ready to install the pipes and different valves that were needed. Then the electricians went in and connected practically all new lines to the area. Everything was modified, so if anything ever happened like this again, there would not be such a large area that would go out of commission.

The large hole, which was about seventy-five feet in diameter, was larger than the meteor because it came in at an angle. The three floors were repaired and sealed with all the hardware that was needed. For now, only the top and bottom of the spacecity, which took four days and nights to complete, could get the spacecity's air back in circulation. We could take off the spacesuits and breathing apparatuses. It was a little awkward working while wearing all that paraphernalia. The floor with the spaceport was put back into operation first to keep the spaceships on the move. The other two floors would have to wait for installation of equipment, so that the architects could design a better plan for a modern observatory. It would take a good two months before everything was operational with a new crew, to replace what we lost in personnel.

The medics had a gruesome job, picking up bodies and parts of bodies and transporting them to the morgue. It was attached to the prison a few miles away from the spacecity. There were twenty-two killed, including Doctor Adin, who was the astronomer, his assistant, and Captain

Deton, who used to work with Doctor Adin at one time before he retired. As fate had it, he was just visiting his friend. There were fourteen bodies plus parts recovered, and eight were missing and presumed dead.

Captain Deton's wife was told of her husband's death. She went into hysteria and had to be given a sedative. Later on she went back home to planet Thrae and lived with one of her children. Two months later, there was a memorial service held on Spacecity Orant. A commemorative plaque was installed on the new east end wall where the accident occurred. Also, a new telescope was named to commemorate Doctor Adin and Captain Deton.

It was now the year 2085 on Spacecity Orant. With the two thousand or so people that were still on the spacecity, it had grown to a population of about 55,000 people. The spacecity had been constructed in size to about triple its original size. Colonies were also built on the moon and their two nearest planets, Darfi and Horto. It took all of three years of new technology and the finest equipment made. The new station on planet Horto gave us a great deal more information and new discoveries in outer space. They also got a newer and better idea, and a closer look at the black hole. They discovered that the magnetic field within a star became inverted and sucked the whole star with such great force it left a great hole. Anything that was near it would also disappear. We already found this out with our first probe. We would have to send out a few more unmanned probes so we could calculate the speed that was needed to stay away from the hole. That would be the direction we would travel to find out if there was life elsewhere. The black hole was located between the eighth planet Komo and the Nubulea Paranta. They also discovered that our ninth planet, Mirna, was much farther away than originally figured from the opposite three planets.

266

They also believed they discovered a new planet that was past the twelfth planet Zumi. It traveled in the opposite direction, which brought this discovery to a simple conclusion. These last four planets belonged to another solar system. How many more other planets were there still to be discovered? Was there life on any of them? They would find this out in the near future.

2087 was the year of communication with other beings way out somewhere in space. All year it had been touch and go with codes that had been coming in almost every day. Years ago they were getting bits of static codes and could not make out any of it, but we knew there were some kind of messages from intelligent beings. They believed they were trying to answer the signals that were sent, but they did not have the sophisticated equipment that planet Thrae had. Either they were trying to send an answer to planet Thrae's messages or just to find out if there was really life anywhere else in the universe.

Every time a message came in, it automatically went through the decoding machine, which was actually a computer that was devised for such communications. This type of computer had been used to break all of the ancient language barriers on planet Thrae. So they do not see why there should be any different reason for it not breaking the language barrier anywhere else, including out in space. If the message was sent right, we would make it out sooner or later.

Planet Thrae had a colony of about two hundred people on planet Horto. They had been stationed there for almost two years, and had been building an observatory and a communication station, which now would be closer to whatever we would find at the other end of the galaxy. It should be complete in about six months. All this took time. They had to transport everything a little at a time, and be very careful of their calculations to avoid errors. When this project was completed and working properly, any information obtained was automatically computerized back to headquarters on Spacecity Orant, and to the central command headquarters on planet Thrae. In this way, they could get their orders more quickly from the commanders.

It was now the early part of the year 2088. Messages had been sent to outer space constantly. For some reason, the messages were not getting through, because they were not getting any more messages from the other end. They also had not received any information from any of their other satellites that were sent out in that direction. So they sent out one of the newest probes, called Eye. It would probably take two weeks or so before any answers are received. Most of their satellites and probes were usually sent from Spacecity Orant. It was much easier and safer for these spaceships to be launched from Spacecity Orant because there was not any atmosphere to go through like on planet Thrae. Also, they were out of the gravitational pull so the spaceship did not need too much thrust and hardly any fuel at all.

It had been exactly two weeks since they sent the probe Eye. They were getting a response to what the communication problem was. The photos that were sent back showed that there was a high-powered dust storm of cosmos particles so thick it would be impossible for anything to get through. That included transmitting messages or probes or any other craft. These kinds of storms sometimes took weeks, months, and sometimes even years. They were lucky on this one. The scanning from the probe Eye had now caught the tail end of the storm. In a couple of weeks it should pass. The planet that was sending and receiving messages was probably wondering what was happening with the communication. If they did not find out why, we would have to tell them what happened. This meant whatever they sent out in the last couple of months must have been absorbed into the dust storm. So you could kiss those probes and messages good-bye. Since it was the tail end of the storm, they were going to send the newest communication probe. By the time it reached the area of the storm, it should be cleared up. It was explained to the planet that the storm in outer space must have absorbed anything in its path, including all signals that were sent.

Commander Siro stated, "That is why we had no communications for a few weeks, on account of the cosmic dust storm. It brought us up-to-date on the trip to planet Earth to this day. Now that you know the story and history of planet Thrae and Spacecity Orant, it is time to get going back to the Spaceship Ventara."

Eighteen
Inconspicuous Time on Earth

It was dark enough for an inconspicuous takeoff. George could not believe the speed and how fast they arrived to the mothership. Everyone welcomed back the commander.

The next couple of days everything was discussed about the dispersion of the seven probes, covering all aspects of planet Earth and its future survival. All the items were distributed among the crews of each probe. All else that could be needed would have to be obtained on their own. The seven crews of the probes were wished safe journeys and would keep in touch weekly, sooner if there was an emergency that might occur. The next morning, the seven probes took off on their separate assignments. One probe was to stay with the mothership until its repairs were begun.

After everything was settled, and the seven probes left, the commander talked to the remainder of the roughly 100 personnel. They would get their chance to see the world when it was time for relief of the probes' crews. In the meantime, there would be enough information to learn all about the planet through the spaceship's computer; hooked up into the world's internet and website. The communication system of the spaceship could copy and make up any identification for all the crews.

The commander and his guests were all set to return to the Chesterland station. First they needed a sample of the spaceship's outer shell to see if any of that type material could be found. It did not take long to get back to Ohio. They landed in about the same spot without being noticed, since it was dark anyway. The spaceship's technician, Mali, came along so he could revamp the communication system at the Chesterland station.

The commander had a new identification, alias Jimmy Farnack. When the company Cessna came back, Bart was at the controls calling in for landing instructions with assumed passengers on board, listing Al, George, Joe, and Jimmy Farnack. Walking to the office, the commander remarked that he would not mind having some more coffee. Joe said, "We always have coffee on the burners."

It was already getting late, going on ten P.M. After a brief group talk, they could plan the next day's events. Al said, "Let us call it a night," and asked the commander to be his guest at his home.

The commander was delighted, and told technician Mali to resume the next day. "Yes, Sir," said Mali. "Five more minutes I will have everything locked up in my brain."

Commander: "Okay, then we will walk you back to the probe. I have to get a couple of things anyway."

From the probe they went to the parking lot and everyone went their separate ways. The commander went to Al's home. Al introduced Jimmy to his wife as a business associate from California. "He will stay here until he gets situated and then he will find his own place to stay."

Early next morning, the commander was already up. The grandkids were off to school. Rose made breakfast while Al was getting ready in the bathroom. It was almost seven o'clock when they left. The commander thanked Rose for the wonderful breakfast. Al kissed his wife goodbye and said, "See you later." They headed for the Chesterland station. When they got to the communication room, Mali was already modifying the equipment. Al asked how he got in without being stopped. Commander said, "We have our ways of almost being invisible at opportune times." Mali told Al he added a couple of components to the receiver and transmitter, and readjusted the frequencies for clarity. Al and the commander were discussing where to obtain material to repair the mothership.

Al said, "We should find a geologist company or one of the Cleveland colleges. We will try them this afternoon."

Mali interrupted the two. "I think there is a coded message coming in."

Al asked, "Is the recording disc on?"

Mali said, "Yes." After a few minutes the coded message stopped.

The three looked at each other. Then Al remarked, "We had not had a message since we contacted you on your landing." Al walked over to the unit to look it over. It was on a different frequency.

"I tried out a few frequencies to see if the set was working until this one," Mali commented. Al checked out the records for that frequency, and came across the messages that were recorded while investigating Father Carl. Al explained to the commander that Father Carl was an undercover agent whose real name was Komrade Kroski. He was from another country named Russia. At that time, he was obtaining data through our system to their counterpart who was stationed on planet Uranus. They supposedly are building up troops who are from planet Koton. I believe their intention is to invade and take over planet Earth. The commander in disbelief said, "Very interesting. I believe they are the same enemy we encountered on our trip to Earth. We destroyed their station and spacecraft, which probably set them back a year."

Al remarked, "How do you know that?"

The commander said, "The prisoners we have are from that group. They were programmed like robots to fight to the end. The implant discs in the brain malfunctioned and they surrendered to us. The main ship and more equipment will be back within a year. I sent a message back to planet Thrae to send help, and hope to be there waiting for the enemy to stop any invasion that might occur."

George looked at the message, and said, "We will have to get this latest message interpreted."

The commander said, "Yes indeed, we will take a trip back to the spaceship for our interpreter to look it over."

"Can't you just send the message?" Joe commented. The commander said it would be too risky in case someone was listening in.

Mali interrupted again, "Sir, I believe we have more messages coming in on another frequency from the Spaceship Cosmic, which they say they are stationed on planet Zumi (Uranus) and their home base is planet Thrae. They claim they were in a star wars battle with the enemy, who had a very powerful buildup; and had the intentions of an invasion of any planet with life on it. Their army would be well supplied to stay in existence in the galaxy. We would keep in touch, Commander Muzet, Spaceship Cosmic. Twenty-one of Zon year 2214." After Mali read off the messages to the commander, he said, since it was in planet Thrae's language, "Interesting, see if you can contact them and get more information out of them? Tell them they made a mistake on the date when they signed off. It is 2114 not 2214. Who is Commander Muzet anyway?"

It did not take Mali long to get in contact with Commander Muzet. Mali read off the continuing message, saying that the enemy on planet Zumi had been destroyed completely, and that Emperor Daka would be pleased when the news reached him. He signed off again as before, 2214. Commander Siro was a little stupefied for a minute. "Are you sure they said they were from planet Thrae? Who the hell is Emperor Daka and the year 2214? There is something very strange going on."

Mali stated, "It is all recorded on a disc, we also have written transcripts of it, sir."

The commander said, "We will take up this matter at a later date. There must be an error somewhere, which eventually will be corrected. But right now, we have more important matters to attend to." The commander told Mali, "When we get back this evening, we will take a trip back to the Spaceship Ventara. We will have our history and science professors check out the data we received."

Joe, Al, George, and the commander drove off from the station to a college in Cleveland. We parked in the visitors' parking lot and walked over to the science building inside and found the office. We talked to the clerk and were directed to Doctor Wilton's room. They introduced each other, then showed the spaceship's outer skin sample. Doctor Wilton called over his assistant, giving him the sample, and told him to run a few tests to find out where it came from. "In the meantime, I will show our guests around." The four of them were taken to different buildings, and to the Advancement of Technology on Earth and Space. They were also taken to the Lowercase Observatory. The commander was impressed. He said it looked like a copy of what he had seen before. "You know what I mean, Al?"

About two hours later, Doctor Wilton's beeper went off, Doctor Wilton said, "I guess we're ready to go back." The five of them got back to Doctor Wilton's laboratory. His assistant explained that there was not any type of metal like this anywhere. But there was one option. "I do not know where they obtained this alloy, but the molecules seem to look the same as the molecules in the moon rocks at the Smithsonian Museum in Washington, D.C."

George, "Really? I guess we will have to take a ride after lunch to Washington, D.C."

After lunch, they drove back to the television station, checked in to see if anything new occurred, then drove to the Cuyahoga Airport. The four got in the plane, which was cleared for takeoff, and away they went to Washington, D.C. It was about four P.M. when they got to the Smithsonian Museum. They had the curator remove a sample of moon rock to compare for molecules in the metal and rock, which were the same. The commander said, "I guess we will have to summon a number of our probes for a trip to the moon, so we can obtain the ore, bring it back to be smelted, until we have enough to repair the spaceship."

They headed back to Chesterland in time for supper. Then the commander, Al, Joe, and George boarded the probe and flew down to Peru. They arrived, zeroing in by instruments since the spaceship was camouflaged to match the terrain. They guided the probe quite easily through the hatch of the spaceship. After docking, the four of them got out heading for the commander's quarters. The commander called in the interpreter. He gave him the messages from the Chesterland station to decode at once. Some refreshments were brought in. Then they relaxed for a while. The commander finally spoke up, "It has been a long day, and it is going on ten o'clock P.M. Earth time. We should call it a day and discuss the present problems tomorrow with fresh minds, to see where we stand. You guys know where the guest rooms are, so I will say goodnight."

The next morning, after everyone had a good night's rest, the commander and the Earthlings got together for breakfast, which, of course, was very unusually delicious. Finishing breakfast, they headed for the spaceship's planning room to discuss the day's events. Commander Siro had all the leaders in for a meeting. He told the communicator to summon one of the probes back to the mothership, and set him up for a trip to the Earth's moon for samples of minerals to match the alloy that was on the spaceship. As soon as the ore is located, we will send the other probes to fetch enough ore for repairs. In the meantime, the other probes will investigate the Earth until they are recalled.

The messages from planet Uranus were decoded and presented to Commander Siro. They had been sent to Komrad Kroski, alias Father Carl. They stated that their stations have been destroyed, including the mothercraft and all the fighters. The whole plan was called off until further plans and communications. Leader Marder from planet Koton.

The interpreter, with a worried look on his face, said to Commander Siro, "I do not think you want to hear this."

Commander said, "Well, spill it out anyway. I am going to hear about it sooner or later."

The interpreter choked it out. "Well, here goes. This pertains to Commander Muzet, Emperor Daka, and the year 2214 in connection with the vortex, when we were caught in between solar systems. Most of the foreign voices that we heard in the vortex were interpreted as saying over and over again, 'Your time is eternity. You will be at a standstill forever and ever. One minute will equal one day, one day will equal a month, a month will equal a year, and a year will equal forever.' Then repeating it again and again. In other words, Commander, the twenty days being trapped in that vortex gained us at least a hundred years. One month equals almost a hundred years, and we never age."

The commander said, "Now let's be realistic. That means when and if we get back to planet Thrae, we will not know anyone."

Interpreter said, "That is right, sir, sooner or later, we will have to tell the rest of the crew and personnel what kind of a dilemma we are in."

The commander told the interpreter, "Right now, let's concentrate on our present mission and get our spaceship repaired. Then we will have a meeting on what we are going to do for the future."

Probe number four with Captain Zell, the geologist, was summoned back to the mothership for its mission to the Earth's moon for samples. Commander Siro wished Captain Zell of probe four luck.

Commander Siro asked Al, Joe, and George if they wanted to tour their planet for a few days. "We will stop by the Chesterland station so you can tell your families and get a few things you might need."

They all answered at the same time. "It is all right with us."

"Fine, let us get started," said the commander. They were back to the station in no time. They told their families they were going on a business trip for a few days.

The probe was supplied with all the necessities that may be needed. It was about one P.M. when the probe took off, at the same low altitude and speed so the probe could not be detected. George asked Commander Siro how long the probe could stay flying without refueling or recharging. The commander answered, "In outer space, almost indefinitely. In planet's atmosphere and gravity, about three months, because we have to switch over to a different type of power source."

Commander asked where they thought they ought to start. Joe spoke up, saying they ought to tour the United States first. "All right," said the commander. He told his pilot to climb the highest altitude without getting into space. The scanner was set to the highest degree for enlargement and clarity. Sections of the United States could be focused, making you feel like you were there. A close-up view of all the important places were recorded, while Al, Joe, and George explained what they were. The probe crisscrossed the country all day, until enough data was compiled. They stopped the first night at one of the ghost towns near Tombstone, Arizona, for supper and resting. The next day they crisscrossed Europe and Asia. They traveled the troubled countries, and the ones that cause trouble. Commander Siro remarked, "Your planet actually is not much different than planet Thrae. The only difference is planet Earth is a little smaller in size and not as advanced as planet Thrae." The commander asked if there was anywhere they wanted to have supper. Al said, "You mean anywhere?"

"Yes," replied the commander.

Al suggested, "How about Rome, Italy, for some Dago food?" The commander wanted to know what Dago food was. Joe said it was slang for Italians, in other words Italian food. The commander said it sounded good. He would try it.

George asked, "How do we manage to get from the probe to the city?" The commander said, "Each probe has two main scoots powered by gyro jets. They were very handy vehicles to get around, and supposed to be used only for emergencies. We are using them now just to be inconspicuous with the probe. The scoots were very simple to operate. I will show you when we land."

They reached the outskirts of Rome in about twenty minutes. Commander Siro showed them the simple controls. It was like driving a golf cart. Joe asked, "Where are the wheels?" The commander laughed, and explained, "The bottom of the vehicle is cushioned and the jets have a little thrust to raise it off the ground and to clear any obstacles in its path, and the rear jets push forward, but you have to be careful because it is a powerful little machine."

They got to the heart of the city and were directed to one of the finest cafés. It was already eight P.M. and they were starving. When parking the scoots, someone asked, at the first in Italian and then in broken up English, what kind of motor bikes were those. Al said, "That is an innovation from the United States we were trying out." While they were eating spaghetti and other delicious Italian food and wine, the commander remarked, "A little spicy, but very good."

George said, "Easy on the wine or it will give you a kick later on."

Joe asked the commander, "Are the scoots safe outside? Suppose someone might steal them?"

"Not a chance. I activated the protective shield. If you touch the scoots it will give you a shock, even if you throw rocks at it, it would not hurt the scoots."

After supper they went sightseeing all through Rome. After a couple of hours, they headed back to the probe so they could get a good night's sleep. The probe pilot greeted the group as they entered, asking how everything went. The next morning everyone was up before Commander Siro. When he showed up, he looked kind of miserable with a hangover. He asked what the hell was in that wine. George laughed, "We told you to watch the wine. We call that wine dago red, and it is potent. Tastes good to drink, but the effect later is miserable if you drink too much of it. You are not used to that Italian drink, that is why."

The pilot said, "A message came in from the mother-ship that the ore had been located." The commander had the pilot send a message. "We are on our way back. I guess we will have a breakfast on the mothership when we arrive." It did not take long to get back, and breakfast was on the table waiting for them. They all had a good break-fast, then relaxed for awhile. They were then given the order to get all the probes back and fitted for the trip to the Earth's moon to bring back as much ore as was needed. While most of the probes were sent out to retrieve the ore from the moon, a smelting plant was set up near the moth-ership.

Commander Siro asked how long all this was going to take. Scientist Carta said, "It depends on how the grade of ore is, and how much material we need for the oven. It was figured out, if everything goes right, it should not take any more than eight or nine months."

Commander Siro remarked, "It really does not make any difference. We probably have no place to go. When we get back to the Chesterland station, get in contact with the Spaceship Cosmic. I would like to know what their orders are concerning their trip back to planet Uranus. We will leave here tomorrow afternoon, so we can land under the cover of darkness."

The next day, when everything was situated and the orders were given out, the four of them and the probe's pilot took off for the Chesterland station. When the probe arrived Al, Joe, and George took off for their homes, telling the commander they would be back in the morning to dis-cuss any further plans. They all said good night and left. The commander and the communicator stayed at the sta-tion, trying to get ahold of Spaceship Cosmic that was sta-tioned on planet Zumi (Uranus). They both stayed a couple of hours drinking coffee and talking up a storm about the trip getting to planet Earth, and what was to become of them if they decided to travel back to planet Thrae.

Another hour went by. It was going on eleven o'clock, and they decided to leave and go back to their probe for a good night's sleep. They turned out the lights and just opened the door. A signal came in on the receiver. The communicator rushed over, copying the message. He read the message to the commander. They communicated with headquarters on Spacecity Orant, getting permission for a trip to planet Earth. Headquarters would give an okay only if they were supplied with enough material to get back to planet Thrae. Commander Siro gave his message to his communicator, which he transmitted, saying, "Planet Earth is similar to planet Thrae, and should have no problems supplying your spaceship for the return trip. It took our craft about four months from planet Zumi (planet Uranus) to reach planet Earth. That was a hundred years ago. It should be faster for your ship, assuming it is more advanced than ours. I will explain the hundred years difference when you get here. Over. Commander Siro of Spaceship Ventara.

"It is getting late, so let's get back to the probe for some sleep. We will check on the receiver in the morning for any message." After a good night's rest, the commander and communicator arrived at the communications office about fifteen minutes before the others.

There was a message already from Spaceship Cosmic. The others arrived. All eight of the club members were informed of another spaceship that would arrive in about three months. "Really?" George said. "Well, it better be kept a secret from the world for awhile."

"Why?" asked the commander.

"Because there was a fellow waiting outside the gate and each one of us was subpoenaed to appear in court for a hearing on activity against the government of the United States. Furthermore, you better stay incognito for awhile."

Commander Siro, being a little perplexed asked, "Why, and what is a subpoena?"

George explained what a subpoena was, and that fellow giving out the subpoenaes asked where he could find a Jimmy Farnack. "As long as you do not receive a piece of paper from him, you do not have to appear. He had to give it to you personally."

The dates on the subpoenaes were for March 18, 1998 at Washington District Court at nine o'clock A.M. We got in contact with our lawyer, Phillip Lorance, to discuss what situation we were in against the government of the United States. The only thing we could come up with was Father Carl being a Russian undercover agent that infiltrated our club.

Commander Siro said, "I will stay in hiding until Spaceship Ventara is repaired; or if it is really necessary to appear for the hearing, I will be there. We will have to contact Spaceship Cosmic with one more message in code in the Thrae language. We are setting the transmitting and receiving equipment in a different location, so as not to be detected."

"And where might that be?" asked Al.

The commander explained, "We will transport the necessary equipment onto the probe and rebuild it with the material from the Ventara's storeroom down in Peru. We'd better start now in case your government should want to seize it for evidence."

"Good idea," said George.

They started to dismantle the equipment as soon as they were done with their last messages. Miss Choa went to the studio for her program, "Helping the Poor Children of the World," and later on she would go to Lakeland College to teach her class, as if nothing happened. It took about a week to transport all of the equipment to Spaceship Ventara in Peru, and to set up the communication system so Spaceship Cosmic could be in contact regularly for their landing.

In the meantime, all of the other probes were traveling back and forth to and from the moon with the special ore that would be needed for smelting to make the metal covering for Spaceship Ventara. That would take at least another seven months.

The time came for the hearing and all were present. The mediator started with, "You are not on trial. We are here to find out what is going on with the Thorme Club, which is believed to be used by the Television Station, Future Vision, as a front to hide anti-government activities against the United States Government."

Lawyer Phillip Lorance said, "There is no activity against the United States Government. They are all honest people."

The hearing lasted for three days, and the Thorme Club members could not convince the mediator of their innocence, which pushed this hearing for a trial date.

Nineteen
Trial Continuation

Al, drifting from his flashback to the courtroom, was startled by the prosecutor's voice. "They sure are," said the prosecutor, naming Al, George, Joe, Mike, Roosevelt, Tom and Bart. "Are these who you call your colleagues, Miss Choa Mio?"

Miss Mio: "Yes they are," she answered.

Prosecutor: "Now Miss Mio, are you not an alien, and I do not mean from another planet?" (The audience laughed.) "I mean you were born in China."

Miss Mio: "No I was born in Hong Kong where I grew up." (Thinking to herself, *How I wish I was back home in Hong Kong with my parents.*)

Prosecutor: "Is not that still considered a part of China?"

Miss Mio: "To some people yes, but it was a colony under British rule until Hong Kong got their independence."

Prosecutor: "I see, now Miss Mio, how did you get to join the Thorme group, and why did you join?"

Miss Mio: "I read an article in a magazine about reincarnation, which was very interesting. That kind of related to me. So I wrote back, and I received a call asking if I wanted to come to a meeting, which I agreed. Then I joined a couple of weeks later, and they even set up a children's program called Saving the Children of the World."

Prosecutor: "Miss Mio, is it true that you lived in Russia for at least two years, and belonged to the Communist Party as an active member? When you came to the United States that you did not report that you were a Communist when you obtained your citizenship?"

Miss Mio: "Yes, it is true, I lived in Russia for two years. That is because I went to college to learn the Russian language and a couple of other curriculums."

Prosecutor: "What about you joining the Communist Party?"

Miss Mio: "I hate Communism. They made me join or they would kick me out of college."

Prosecutor: "Who are they?"

Miss Mio: "Mostly the teachers, and some students, especially the teachers. All the teachers are Communists or they would not be teachers in Russia."

Prosecutor: "How did you manage to come to the United States?"

Miss Mio: "I was an exchange student. While I was going to college I worked as an interpreter, and my boss helped me obtain my citizenship papers."

Prosecutor: "Miss Mio, you now reside in Mentor, Ohio, and teach classes at Lakeland College. Am I right? You could then be closer to the television station in Chesterland."

Miss Mio: "It is true, I am closer to the station, but that was a coincidence, because they asked me at Lakeland College if I wanted a position there. It also made it easier and closer to get my children's program, which keeps me pretty busy."

Prosecutor: "How well were you acquainted with Father Carl?"

Miss Mio: "I saw him at the Thorme meetings, which was rare, and talked to him a few times about matters at hand."

Prosecutor: "About what matters, be more specific please?"

Miss Mio: "Things about how his church was getting along. He asked me how my teaching was getting along at Lakeland College. You know things like that."

Prosecutor: "Miss Mio, when you started receiving messages from Father Carl, what did you do with them?"

Defense Attorney, Phillip Lorance: "Objection. Prosecutor is leading the witness."

Judge: "Overruled."

Prosecutor: "I will rephrase my question. Did you obtain any information about Father Carl and his future activities?"

Miss Mio: "Yes."

Prosecutor: "How and what were the messages?"

Miss Mio: (Looking at Al for his approval as he nodded) "The information was on tape between Father Carl, whose real name is Comrade Krocha, who was conversing to his Russian counterpart Comrade Troski. The message was about leaving the United States, sneaking back to Russia as soon as they compiled enough information about the Chesterland Television Station, and some other counterparts in outerspace who were supposed to take over our World." (The courtroom crowd took another gasp and started to get a little loud. The judge pounded his gavel, hollering for order in the court.)

Prosecutor: As soon as the courtroom was back to normal, the prosecutor resumed, asking Miss Mio, "Since you belong to the Communist Party, you must have known what was going on, if there was a takeover of the world by aliens affiliated with Russia."

Attorney Lorance: "Objection, Your Honor. The prosecutor is speculating. Besides, Your Honor, Miss Mio already answered that question that she had to join the Communist

Party to stay in college. She has not had any dealings with the Communists in over ten years, after leaving Russia."

Judge: "Overruled. Any more questions?"

Prosecutor: "No, Your Honor."

Defense: "No, Your Honor, not at this time."

Judge: "You may step down Miss Mio."

Bailiff: "May the court call Captain Allen Gray to the stand."

Captain Allen Gray got up, walked to the stand in his professional navy way, as the onlookers wondered why a naval officer was involved in this situation. The captain put his hand on the Bible, took the oath, then sat down in the witness box.

Prosecutor: "Name please."

Captain Gray: "I am Captain Gray of the United States Coast Guard, stationed at Wates, Alaska, off the Bering Strait."

Prosecutor: "Now! What are your duties as an officer stationed in Alaska?"

Captain Gray: "My duties are to control the waters up and down the coast of Alaska, and across the Bering Strait up to the international borderline that divides Russia and the United States.

Al took one look at Joe and slightly nodded a couple of times, both thinking the same thing. After all this time, it is finally going to come out.

Prosecutor: "Is it a fact, at one time or another you caught smugglers and spies trying to cross the straits to and from Russia?"

Captain Gray: "That is correct."

Prosecutor: "Tell the court what happened on September the twenty-first 1999 at the crack of dawn."

Captain Gray: "First of all, we received an anonymous phone call about a seaplane that was to fly across the

Bering Strait to Russia smuggling two Russian spies. When the plane was to return to Alaska, it was set to blow up when the pilot got halfway across, so the pilot could not answer any questions if caught. The call was made at the same time while getting another call, east up the Alaska coast from Captain Trax fishing in that area, telling us that a plane exploded a few miles away near the Diomede Islands. A Coast Guard cutter proceeded to the area near the Diomede Islands where the assumed crash took place. The sea happened to be calmer than usual with two to three foot waves or swells. When we arrived, there was debris all over the area from the crash, including parts of bodies. The crew started to retrieve as much debris and body parts as possible, until a Russian patrol boat arrived asking what happened. I told them a seaplane went down. Then the Russian captain told us to leave everything alone, because we were in Russian waters. I told them to check their charts and compass, and if they did not go back to their side they would be arrested and taken prisoners for being in the jurisdiction of the United States."

Prosecutor: "Then what happened?"

Captain Gray: "The Russian patrol boat left and we continued to pick up the rest of the debris, which took up most of the day."

Prosecutor: "Were there any other witnesses to this event?"

Captain Gray: "Yes there were."

Prosecutor: "Are they in this room?"

Captain Gray: "Yes, the two who are sitting in the front row. Actually, there was a third person with them."

Prosecutor: "What were they doing?"

Captain Gray: "They were flying and circling around the area of the wreckage while we were picking up the debris."

Prosecutor: "Then what?"

Captain Gray: "I called them by radio and asked them what they were looking for. They said, just curiosity. I got their number and told the pilot to report to the Coast Guard station and to wait until we got back. We continued to pick up the rest of the wreckage and headed back to the station. After lunch, the pilot and his two companions came to the station. They were asked a few questions, then they left."

Prosecutor: "Is it true in picking up debris and body parts, you also retrieved an attaché case in the process, and what did you do with it?"

Captain Gray: "Yes, we picked up such an item, and took it back to headquarters. We did not really open it for two days. We had to get it analyzed and x-rayed just in case it was another bomb."

Prosecutor: "Go on, Captain."

Captain Gray: "When it was finally opened, we found maps, diagrams, some kind of code, and numerous sheets of information in Russian and some other unknown language. Then we turned it over to the CIA for interpretation and to be investigated. That was the extent of the Coast Guard investigation. I also informed the pilot of the circling plane that he might be questioned again sometime in the future."

Prosecutor: "That is all for now, Your Honor."

Judge: "Mister Lorance, do you have any questions?"

Attorney Lorance: "Yes, Your Honor." Lorance got up, walking slowly toward the captain thinking of exactly how to word his questions. "Captain, did you think or have any idea that the persons in the circling plane might have had any connection with the deceased in question, and who might have made the anonymous phone call?"

Captain Gray: "I really had no idea if there was a connection outside of what I asked and what they told me."

Attorney Lorance: "Or do you think the information in the attaché case had anything concerning any of the persons of the circling seaplane? Also, why did all three persons blow up instead of just the pilot on his return?"

Captain Gray: "Not to my knowledge, that is being investigated by the C.I.A."

Attorney Lorance: "That will be all, Your Honor."

Judge: "You may step down, thank you, Captain. Bailiff, call the next witness please."

Bailiff: "Will George Karnes take the stand please?"

George got up and walked to the stand, kind of reluctantly thinking to himself, *This is a bunch of bullcrap*. He took the oath, and sat down in the witness box, and all the questioning started.

Prosecutor: "You are also a member of the Thorme Club?"

George: "Yes I am."

Prosecutor: "Also, vice president of the Future Vision Cable Company. The Thorme club is located in the same building complex?"

George: "Yes."

Prosecutor: "What is the connection between the cable company and the Thorme Club? Why is it fenced in with security guards?"

George: "First of all, the club and cable company have nothing to do with each other. Future Vision Cable Company sells cable to customers and televises channels for entertainment. This is our revenue to pay for the needs for the company and pay all the employees that work there. The additional part of the building is our observatory and communication center that belongs solely to the Thorme Club."

Prosecutor: "But why all the security?"

George: "I thought you people already knew that answer."

Prosecutor: "Well, we went to hear it again."

George: "The building was broken into and some information was taken, so we have taken precautionary measures."

Prosecutor: "What was taken that was so important that you fenced the property in and with guards?"

George: "The information was important to the club members only. It had no meaning to persons outside the club."

Prosecutor: "Were there any other break-ins since then?"

George: "No, we found out later it was a ploy, so the FBI could install a bug to listen in on what was happening."

Prosecutor: "What makes you think your place was bugged?"

George: "Because we found the bug."

Prosecutor: "Now, I am going to ask you a simple question, and all I want is a yes or no. Remember you are under oath. Have you or any of your group communicated with any aliens from outerspace? Yes or no?"

George: George thinking to himself. *If I say no, it is perjury. If I say yes, the questions will keep coming. I am screwed either way.* George was looking at the room packed with spectators. He could see Commander Siro from the spaceship standing in the back, and in George's mind, still thanking him for curing him from the ordeals he had when the weather would get bad. The commander was looking at George with a little smile, nodding to answer. Then George looked at the prosecutor and said with a loud "Yes." At the same time, there was a loud murmur in the courtroom. The commander also left. The judge pounded his gavel for silence.

Prosecutor: "How many times would you say you have communicated with these so-called aliens?"

George: "A number of times."

Prosecutor: "Now let us be precise on this matter of communication. Was it two, three, twenty, or maybe fifty times?"

George: George thought for a moment so he would give the right answer. Then slowly answered, "About three and one half years ago, we sent messages out to see if we could communicate with any being in outerspace. The first few months were hopeless, because we did not get anything on our receiver. We thought we were wasting our time. Then we invested in a more powerful set with a better receiving disc. We tried for about a month and thinking we were still wasting our time, we quit trying for awhile. However, we left the receiver on. At that time, we had started the Future Vision Cable Company, We spent most of our time on the construction and getting things in order. One day Al went to the club office for some paperwork. He noticed on the computer printout there were a few lines of type. Al came back to get me. We checked out the message. We noticed the messages were sent on two different dates about a week apart, four days before we discovered it."

Prosecutor: "What makes you think these messages came from outerspace and not from some practical joker here on Earth. Or maybe you could have made it up."

Attorney Lorance: "I object! The prosecutor is speculating, besides, my client has not finished answering the question."

Judge: "Strike the prosecutor's last remarks. Please continue Mr. Karnes."

George: "That was the beginning of communications with the aliens. We have received hundreds of messages from around 1995 until ten months ago."

Prosecutor: "Where are all these messages?"

George: "Our whole system of messages was turned over to the aliens at their request, for safekeeping."

Prosecutor: "Why would you turn over the messages to the aliens, like you already met them? Please tell the court where exactly are your so-called aliens? Are they in this courtroom?"

George: "They are not in the courtroom. I do not know where they are anymore than you know."

Prosecutor: "Have you ever met the aliens in person? If you have, tell the court where and when."

George: "We first got in contact ten months ago in the state of New Mexico for a few minutes when the spaceship arrived. They wanted to know what the vehicles were with the flashing red lights, speeding towards us. I replied, 'It is probably the authorities coming to investigate on our activities.' So we all boarded the spaceship and headed for Peru."

Prosecutor: "How did you get to the first landing site, and why all the way down to Peru? And who are we?"

George: "The three of us are club members, Al, Joe, and I. We flew down to New Mexico in our twin jet Cessna, owned by the Future Vision Company, waiting for the arrival of the spaceship. When it did arrive we had to leave in a hurry, because the aliens did not want to confront the authorities at that time. Therefore, we left for a more secluded place down in Peru, close to Lima."

Prosecutor: "In other words, you took off, evading the authorities. How did you cross the border without being detected? You had to stop on the way to refuel. What happened to the spaceship?"

George: "Al, Joe, and I did not evade the authorities. They did not even know we were there. They were probably following the spaceship. Our jet plane was hoisted into the spaceship when we also boarded. Then we sped off watching the authority vehicles come to a stop."

Prosecutor: "How long did the spaceship take to get to Peru? Besides, how large was this ship, when it had room to board you and your jet?"

George: "I would estimate it took us a little less than an hour to reach Peru." There was a low murmur in the courtroom. George continued. "As for the spaceship, I would say it is about half the size of a football field, maybe larger." The courtroom really got noisy, with remarks, "The Earth has been invaded by aliens," and so forth.

Prosecutor; "How long were you down in Peru?"

George; "We were in Peru for about a week. Then we were dropped back off at the Chesterland station, by one of the spaceship's probes, after the jet plane was dropped off where it was picked up in New Mexico."

Prosecutor: "After you have been taken to your station, how long did you stay in contact with each other?'

George: "We have been in touch ever since we met."

Prosecutor; "Why don't they come forward and be known."

George; "They are not ready at this time. In the near future they will make their public appearance."

Prosecutor: "What connection did the deceased Father Carl, and the Russian, have with the aliens in the takeover of the world?"

George: "They have no connection at all. The aliens that landed are friendly people. They did not come here to take over the world. They came to help us."

Prosecutor: "Then why did Father Carl try to make contact with aliens in outerspace?"

George: "Against our knowledge, Father Carl was contacting unfriendly aliens that were from a different planet. I cannot give you full answers. You will have to wait until the commander shows up. He will give you a full report."

Prosecutor: "Why didn't you notify the authorities when you first suspected Father Carl of being a Russian spy?"

George: "We wanted to be sure of what was going on between Father Carl and his Russian counterpart. When we found out that they left ahead of time for Russia, we contacted Joe's Uncle Charles and the Coast Guard up in Alaska. By that time it was too late."

Prosecutor: "That will be all for now. Thank you." Turning to Phillip Lorance. "Your witness."

Attorney Lorance: "Nothing at this time."

Judge: "The witness may step down. The court will adjourn for the holidays, and continue Tuesday morning at nine o'clock, January 4, 2001. Thank you and have a nice holiday."

Thursday, December 23 of year 2000. It was three o'clock in the afternoon when the Thorme Club members left the courthouse in Washington, D.C., heading for the Dulles Airport to board the company's twin Cessna.

There was not much said between the group on the way back to the Chesterland station. It looked like it snowed a little when we hit Ohio. Everything was white and so beautiful. We decided to land at the Cuyahoga Airport so the plane could be checked over and have its periodic maintenance. Joe was at the controls and got instructions to land. We landed without any trouble, then taxied to our hangar. The shuttle bus was waiting to take us to the Chesterland station.

It was already eight P.M. when we arrived. It was snowing lightly, with the flakes glistening in the dark against the soft lights from the station. We walked to the station office, listening to the soft music over the parking lot speakers. "It Came Upon A Midnight Clear." No one said a word, and just listened to the music, which made it mystical, as we walked through the powdery snow. Finally inside, we all sat down around the meeting table while the coffee was brewing. It was George who spoke up. "It is sure good to get back home and relax our brains." Joe, clearing his throat, said, "I think we should not discuss, or even mention, the trial or anything connected to the trial, until after the holidays. Have a meeting Sunday before the trial at two P.M."

They all agreed and wished each other happy holidays. Commander Siro (alias Jim Farnack) and Choa Mio were invited two weeks ago to come to Al's house for the holidays. Choa told Al she was thrilled to come. Choa remarked, "What about the commander? We have not heard from him since he left the courtroom a few days ago."

Al said with confidence, "He will show up. I know he is a man of his word. We will wait and see."

It was seven o'clock P.M. Christmas Eve when the door bell rang at Al's house. His wife answered the door, greeting the commander. Rose was delighted with a big smile saying, "Merry Christmas Mr. Farnack. Come on in."

Rose led the commander into the livingroom where Al and Choa were chatting. The grandkids were in the den watching television.

Al and Choa at the same time said, "Merry Christmas, Jim."

"Merry Christmas to you," said the commander, not really knowing what it meant. The commander sat down in one of the sofa chairs, saying, "Umm nice and comfortable." Rose went back to the kitchen to finish preparing supper. The commander asked Al to clue him in about Christmas. He was told the whole story before supper was on the table, or a quick version of it. Commander, thinking out loud, "The savior of the world, huh! He has a lot of work cut our for himself."

Choa stayed a couple of days at Al's, then went to her place so she could get ready to go back to the television show at the station, showing, "Save the Children of the World." The commander stayed until the meeting on the second of January. He thanked Al and his wife for the wonderful hospitality and said that he had a good time. Al and the commander drove down to the station where the rest of the group was waiting for them.

The Happy New Year's greetings were said and the meeting was underway. The commander said, "Before we get into any discussion about the trial, I gave George a unit that was to record the whole trial." George gave the recorder to the commander. The commander explained, "A certain code has to be pressed in before you get it to record. I have to know everything that is going on, so when I take the stand I will be prepared with the right answers. We are the only ones who know about this recording and future recordings of the trial. This little unit is detector proof, and no one will ever know it is a recorder." The meeting went on for a few hours before it was over. The next day, everyone met at the Cuyahoga airport, except the commander. The commander used a different disguise and name attending the trial, to avoid being detected.

The plane arrived at Dulles Airport about five P.M. and we were transported by the airport limousine to the hotel near the courthouse. They ate at the hotel restaurant, then sat in the lounge for the evening before going to their rooms. Lorance, the attorney, showed up about the same time. He spent the evening with them having a good time. Then Lorance remarked, "We might as well enjoy tonight. We do not know what tomorrow will bring."

The next morning, January 4, 2001, they arrived at the courthouse, being seated in front of the spectators that crowded the room. The news media was there, but did not get any information out of any of the group.

Nine o'clock sharp and the sound of the bailiff, "All rise, Honorable Judge Eugene Cornell. Be seated." After a few words the first witness was called.

Bailiff: "Will Albert Di Fiare please stand?"

Al got up, walked to the witness stand with a serene look on his face. He took the oath, sat down and waited for the prosecutor to ask his questions.

Prosecutor: "Are you the president and founder of this Thorme Club? About when did this club start and why?"

Al: "Yes, I am the president of the club. Actually the club started quite by accident, about seven years ago."

Prosecutor: "How do you mean by accident?"

Al: "All my life I have had these strange visions, and things I would do, or places I would go to. It felt like I had done these things before, like déjà vu."

Prosecutor: "But where does the start of the club come in?"

Al: "I am coming to that. I wrote some articles about reincarnation and having a second life on another planet. Not to find members of a club or anything like that. There was no club. But to my surprise, I received a few letters from other persons who were in the same situation that I was in. So we decided to have a meeting to discuss this matter. Then we picked Chesterland, Ohio, for a permanent meeting place. Some of the group moved to Ohio and we started the Future Vision Cable Company, after we pooled our money and were lucky enough to win some on the Ohio lotto. At the same time we started the Thorme Club."

Prosecutor: "Mr. Di Fiare, at the time this Thorme Club started weren't you working for NASA on space projects? Also, you were using an alias name, Joe Santini."

Al: "Yes, I worked for NASA for a few years, right up until I retired and received a pension."

Prosecutor: "But why the alias name Joe Santini?"

Al: "Because I did not want to jeopardize my job at NASA. People would think I was a crackpot to think I might be from another planet."

Prosecutor: "You must have compiled quite a bit of information while working for NASA. Is that what you really discussed at your meetings, setting up the takeover of the world with the help of Russia and the assumed aliens from other planets?"

Attorney Lorance: Again getting up from his chair, objecting. "The prosecutor was speculating with his line of questioning. And has really no proof that they were involved in any conspiracy against the governments of the world."

Judge: "Overruled. There is also not much evidence that they are not conspiring against the governments."

Prosecutor: "May I continue?" After calming down the courtroom. "It looks to me, and probably the jury also, that everything your club was doing was a secret. Each one of your members seemed to have a part in getting things organized for a takeover, especially you and Joe Malita."

Al: "That is not true at all. We run a legitimate club and we like what we do."

Prosecutor: "Then why all the secrecy and hiding of evidence from the FBI?"

Al: "We did not know anything was being hidden from the FBI."

Prosecutor: "Now let us get back to Father Carl, whom you say was a member of the Thorme Club, but really a Russian spy. Why wasn't the FBI notified when you first suspected Father Carl was snooping around the observatory at the Chesterland station?"

Al: "We did not suspect anything because Father Carl was a member of the Thorme Club and assumed he was improving on the equipment. Not knowing he was getting data and using the equipment and contacting unfriendly aliens instead."

Prosecutor: "How did you find out he was a spy?"

Al: "It was by accident."

Prosecutor: "Explain this so-called accident."

Al: "Father Carl would stay late at the station, pretending he had things to repair or check out. One evening I stayed late also, because there were a few things to catch up on. The weather was bad that night with lightning and thunder. I noticed something unusual."

Prosecutor: "And what might that be?"

Al: "The room Father Carl was in with the transmitting and receiving equipment is a soundproof room with no windows."

Prosecutor: "What does that have to do with anything?"

Al: "That is the point, every time it thundered you can hear it in his room and mine."

Prosecutor: "I still do not know where you are getting with this."

Al: "Here is the catch, when it lightninged, I could see the lightning flashes in my room, but I was also seeing flashes under the door of Father Carl's room, which has no windows."

Prosecutor: "So how does that make Father Carl a suspect?"

Al: "I walked into the room and noticed a camera case, half hidden under his coat that was on the chair. I pretended there were papers I needed and went in. A few minutes later, I walked in again to say I forgot something. When I looked at his coat again, on the chair the camera case was gone. I told him that was sure some lightning. He said, 'It sure was.' "

Prosecutor: "So that makes him a criminal because he took pictures of the equipment he was to modify? What makes you think he was a Russian spy and not an American priest? He was a priest and was born in Montana. He also graduated from Saint John's Seminary down in Ohio. And that makes you think that the other assumed passenger was another Russian spy and not just a tourist going fishing. There was no evidence that he ever was a Russian. I believe the story is a concoction just to cover up for you and your counterparts, so to put the government of the United States in jeopardy."

Attorney Lorance: He slid his chair back as he got up, objecting to the last remarks. "How can the prosecutor make a remark like that without any proof of what really happened? My clients were there most of the time."

Judge: "Sustained, will the prosecutor please continue?"

Prosecutor: "That will be all for now! Thank you."

Judge: "Mr. Lorance, any questions?"

Attorney Lorance: "Not at this time."

Judge: "You may step down."

The commander at this time made himself known to the authorities as Jimmy Farnack, and was to be the next witness on the stand.

Twenty
Commander Siro As Witness
Plus Doomsday

Bailiff: "Will Mister Jimmy Farnack take the stand please?"

Commander Siro got up, walked to the stand and took the oath before being seated.

Prosecutor: "Are you a member of the Thorme Club?"

Alias Farnack: "No, I am not."

Prosecutor: "Do you know any of the Thorme members?"

Alias Farnack: "Yes."

Prosecutor: "Mister Farnack, what is your purpose as a member of this so-called Thorme Club?"

Alias Farnack: "I repeat, I am not a member of the Thorme Club. My function is as the club's friend, to give advice and to analyze any situation that might arise."

Prosecutor: "Very interesting. Like the situation the members of the Thorme Club are in now, trying to over-throw the United States government?"

Attorney Lorance: Pushing his chair back, standing up, he objected with a loud voice to the judge, that the prosecutor was again speculating, and had not any concrete evidence to back him up.

Prosecutor: "Oh, but we do have the evidence to back us up, Your Honor."

Judge: "Then show the evidence."

Prosecutor: He opened the attaché case that was

retrieved by the Coast Guard in the Bering Strait, Alaska, of the plane crash, and took out all the information about the contacts with aliens from their station on planet Uranus. "They were planning an invasion to take over planet Earth with the help of Russia and some Eastern countries. Other pages indicating to help win the presidential election with a Jewish vice president, and then assassinate the president so the Jewish vice president would become president. He could then be in good with the Arab countries and help the aliens and Russia take over the world. It sounds pretty ridiculous, but it was all here in writing."

Attorney Lorance: "If that is the case, then who blew up the plane over the Bering Straits in Alaska?"

Prosecutor: "That is being investigated."

Judge: "We will continue that evidence later. Prosecutor, please continue your questioning with Mister Farnack."

Prosecutor: "Mister Farnack, how long have you been acquainted with the members of this so-called Thorme Club, and what kind of advice have you offered that may have helped?"

Alias Farnack: "I have known them for a number of years, and my advice was to analyze any situation carefully and slowly, so you come up with the right solution or answer. Mistakes can be costly."

Prosecutor: "You claim that you are from Windgap, Pennsylvania, right?"

Alias Farnack: "Sorry, but I did not say I was from Pennsylvania. You asked for my name and address. I gave my name, but I said I have an address from Pennsylvania, I never said I was from there."

Prosecutor: "Then exactly where are you from?"

Al whispered to George, "I think the shit is going to hit the fan any minute now."

Alias Farnack: "Before I tell you where I am from, I

have to tell you this story of the end of your government plus all of the governments." The spectators were stirring with uneasiness and could not believe what they were hearing, and about to hear.

"The Thorme Club has nothing to do with the demise of the government. You do not need aliens from outerspace to take over the world and destroy it. The people of the world are doing it themselves, with the help of God and Mother Nature. It started many, many years ago. The world was once a balanced natural habitat, until the greed of man came into existence and destroyed everything they touched. They learned how to cut down most of the forests, especially the rain forests. Without the rain forests, the ingredients from the forests would not spread throughout the world. Which in turn, destroyed and made extinct, thousands of creatures that depend on all those ingredients. Also many medicines are derived from rain forests, to cure the sick. You do not need wars to kill people. There is enough pollution in the air that causes all these cancers and other diseases. Now you have more hospitals, clinics, asylums, and doctors, which is ridiculous. You do not have to be old to get sick and die, the young are catching up. All the modern medicines that have been invented do is prolong life so you can suffer a few more years longer.

"You also have many countries fighting each other. Looking at the world's history, there have been wars since the beginning of time, and there is no end. What is worse than all these things are terrorists, the unknown enemy, who strike anywhere anytime. But that is only the beginning of the end. The testing of nuclear arms is doing more damage than using them on each other. Especially underground testing, which in turn is destroying the Earth internally. The Earth is so unbalanced, from all that testing, it is no wonder you have so many earthquakes and other unnatural disasters. The saddest thing is, the people of this planet have no escape and no place to go from the devastation of this world." The courtroom at this time was so silent, you could hear a pin drop.

Prosecutor: "What makes you think the world will be destroyed, and who are you really?"

Commander Siro: "My people have traveled and analyzed the whole planet of your wars, diseases, extinction of life in many forms, and the cracking up of the planet. Too many natural disasters, you could almost feel the tremor under your feet. The planet will probably destroy itself before this trial is over."

The spectators were still in a hush and in a trance. Then in a sophisticated voice the commander said, "I am Commander Siro of Spaceship Ventara from planet Thrae, in another solar system."

Prosecutor: Kind of stuttering, "What proof do you have that you are telling the truth of being a commander of a spaceship?"

Commander Siro: "My ship has been damaged on the trip to Earth, it has taken a year to repair. Now it is ready, and we will be here tomorrow morning, hovering over this building. We have already picked a few honest people to go back with us to our planet. There is also another spaceship that arrived for our safety, and boarded more souls for the venture back. One other note, do not have your military try to attack the spaceship. We are too advanced and will destroy anything that comes at us. We do not want to fight. My planet went through the same end your planet is going through now. But we were warned and got prepared for the end, and then started all over again. After twenty years, the people and animals living together on Spacecity Orant got prepared to repopulate planet Thrae. This time under a more civilized law and order, and a better religion."

Judge: "It is getting late. We will adjourn until ten o'clock A.M. tomorrow."

All the club members, including Commander Siro, were clawing their way through the reporters and a mob of spectators that the police could hardly control. They were calling them liars and crackpots. And they should be thrown in prison and throw the key away. Finally, getting away from them, they went back to their hotel and discussed the day's events; and what was in store for tomorrow's continuation of the trial. They talked late into the night for preparation of what would happen after the trial, before they all retired. It was pretty hard for them to fall asleep. In the middle of the night, Choa Mio got out of bed and went down the hall to Al's and George's room, knocking on their door. Al answered, "What is wrong?"

Choa with concern said, "I cannot sleep, and I can feel the tremors, I am frightened." Al held her for awhile and told her things would be all right after the trial. They talked the rest of the night and before you knew it, it was time for breakfast and to head back to the courthouse.

Everyone rose when the judge came in. Then they were seated. The judge started to talk, and gave a brief account of the trial on the whole. Ending with a specific remark in saying, "It is hard to actually believe in aliens from another world to tell the people of this Earth that we are at an end. Yes, we have wars and terrorists and the like, but we are still here."

Commander Siro and the club members looked at each other, whispering among themselves, "They do not believe us."

Judge: "And as sure as I am sitting here, I do not believe there is or ever was any such spaceship mentioned."

The audience started to get a little noisy.

Judge: "Furthermore, all the members of the Thorme

306

Club are now under arrest for conspiracy in trying to overthrow the government of the United States, and putting the public at risk."

Before the judge was finished, everything started to get dark with a whining noise. Everyone headed outside and watched with astonishment. It was the biggest ship ever witnessed. It looked as big as a football field. All doubts left their minds, including that of the judge and all the authorities. The United States Airforce was flying around the ship, but they kept their distance.

The commander communicated with the second in command in the Thrae language, but in code, telling them to leave within the hour. The public got a good look at this strange ship for an hour. The ship left slowly with the airforce right behind it for a few miles. Before the airforce pilots could blink another eye, the ship vanished so fast they were stunned.

Everybody filed back into the courtroom. They still could not believe it.

Judge: "I still cannot believe my eyes, but I will retract my last statement and the arrest of the club members."

As the commander said this world is finished, you could feel large tremors. A report just came in that atomic warfare had started in the Asian countries, which is making the whole Earth faulter.

Judge: "This trial is adjourned until further notice."

The commander and club members hurried along to a remote area to be picked up by one of the probes. They flew back to Ohio, gathering all their families with some belongings. They met at the club station where the spaceship landed, with everyone aboard. The spaceship took off and hovered far above, watching the destruction of Earth by fire, explosions, volcanic eruptions with upheaval of mountains, and the like. Cities with tall buildings tumbling and crumbling to the ground with a sickening devastation. The other spaceship was also hovering nearby watching the destruction. It looked like a repeat of what happened on planet Thrae a few years back. Commander Siro said, "This is happening sooner than I expected. May God have mercy on their souls. I think we have seen enough." Then the two spaceships circled the Earth a couple more times and headed home to planet Thrae.

For the first time, Commander Siro seemed to be all worn out. The spaceship physician gave Siro some kind of pleasant drink. He fell asleep almost instantly. He slept a long, long time. When he finally awoke, he asked the second in command if they were ready to take off from Spacecity Orant to their unknown destination of this planet called Earth.

Commander Siro told us about this stupid dream he just had. "We had this hectic space journey passing planets, getting caught in a vortex, with a star war, landing on the planet, finding out it was doomed to destruction. We could not leave because our ship was damaged when we got in gooey matter out in space. The strange matter was deteriorating the ship and we had to make repairs before we could leave, which took a year. We even had a trial on this planet because we were accused of a conspiracy to take over the planet. We left because the planet was being destroyed."

"Okay Commander Siro, it is time for the journey's takeoff to planet Earth."

Twenty-one
Surprise

Murry Hill Road in Little Italy, Cleveland, Ohio

I awakened one morning on the floor next to my bed with a big lump on the side of my head. It felt like I had been drugged, having this dizziness. Everything was spinning around in slow motion. Then suddenly I started to get my senses back and realized something did not seem right. It did not feel like me. I looked around the room and I did not recognize anything, until I saw the calendar on the wall, and to my horror and surprise, it said 1956. I know I must have hit my head when I fell out of bed, but this is ridiculous. Where am I anyway? Walking toward the door, I opened it and did not recognize anything, as I walked to the kitchen.

My mother said, "Good morning," and asked how I slept.

I said, "Mom, what the hell is going on? How did I get here? I thought I was in the army, in Korea."

My mother just stared at me in the darndest amazement. She said, "Say that again Albert?"

I repeated, "I thought I was in the army in Korea and what happened to the last three years? The last time I looked at the calendar in my barracks it was June 1953, and now it is 1956."

Mother was thrilled, "Thank God, you finally came

out of it. You were wounded overseas and were in a coma for awhile in a VA Hospital. When you came out of the coma you got up, walked around but you did not remember anything or anyone. After you left the hospital and got discharged and came home, it took the longest time for you to get used to your family because you were like a stranger to everyone. I guess they called it amnesia. Oh I am glad you are back with us. I am calling everyone to tell them you are well again."

Mom said, "Al, hurry and have some breakfast, you are wanted down at the bookstore."

Al said, "Hurry for what, and what bookstore?"

Mom looked at him and said, "You do not remember? You are supposed to autograph the book you wrote for the readers. It took you over two years to write it."

"I do not remember writing any book."

"You sure did, here is a copy of it."

Al picked up the book with a quizzical look and his eyes became big as saucers, as he read the title:

The Other Side of Destiny
A Science Fiction Novel
By
Albert A. Di Fiore